Praise for THE AFTERM

"In *The Aftermath,* Dr. Guillory continues the tale of our plight here on Earth. Cleverly using the genre of fiction, he weaves a spellbinding story that includes otherworldly entities, androids, professors, people of power, and people just like you and me to tell of a plausible outcome to the journey we are all on, going from a survival-driven world to one where we treat others with dignity and respect.

The story reveals how this will require more than change. It demands transformation. So, are you ready to transform from simply being human to a human being?"

— Dr. Heather Renee Sülitas

"*The Aftermath* is a science fiction story that dissects the process developed by missionary alien immigrants to assist the transformation of Earth's consciousness from survival to compatibility. Dr. Guillory introduces many eye-opening concepts and cleverly integrates science and parapsychology, giving mind, body, and soul a more prominent place in our human world. We are shown just how things are connected and how we must redesign our realities to accept and accommodate new input into our broken worlds.

Dr. Guillory brilliantly parallels the challenges in this story with those we face in our everyday lives. There are days when I find it difficult to maintain faith in humanity and our ability to win even basic battles. However, after reading *The Aftermath,* my belief became stronger that we can create a global world, live peacefully together, and win the battle of ending human suffering."

— Dr. Melody A. Cofield, author and founder of Divar, Inc.

"*The Aftermath* fast-forwards us into the short-term future to consider the impact of technology, artificial intelligence, inner exploration, higher levels of consciousness, extrasensory phenomena, and the next generation humanoid—inorganic (android) or organic (cyborg)? These decisions are presently being designed in laboratories everywhere on Earth. *The*

Aftermath gives us a peek into the future of humans on Earth in the coming decades. I strongly recommend that you immerse yourself into this 'fictional' story and see if you can come away the same as when you began."

— Ulla Knoll, Executor of IVR, Frankfurt, Germany

"*The Aftermath*, Dr William Guillory's wrap up of his Pleiadian trilogy, begins with the population of the world having been reduced by over 50% as a result of two pandemics. It is refreshing to see that strong, smart women are included in the team that is put together to save the world from the rogue Pleiadian. The infiltration into Consortium and the secret project create tension and make it hard to put the book down. You now have an urgency to find out how this exciting tale can come to a positive conclusion. The grand climax leaves you wondering, 'how close is our technology to letting a situation like this actually happen?!' Dr. Guillory weaves quite a fascinating story."

— Cindy Thomas, Wealth Manager

THE
AFTERMATH

THE
AFTERMATH

2ND EDITION

WILLIAM A. GUILLORY, PhD

SEQUEL TO THE PLEIADIAN TRILOGY

The Aftermath, Second Edition

Copyright © 2021 William A. Guillory, PhD

Published by The Center for Creativity and Inquiry
1416 East Farm Meadow Lane
Salt Lake City, UT 84117

This is a work of fiction. Names, characters, places, and incidents are the product of the author's imagination or fictitious, and any resemblance to actual persons living or dead, organizations, groups, events, or locales is purely coincidental. There is no northern town of Neustadt in Lichtenstein.

Cover design by Christy Collins, Constellation Book Services,
        www.constellationbookservices.com
Edited by Jessica Vineyard, Red Letter Editing, redletterediting.com

ISBN (paperback): 978-0-933241-31-2
ISBN (ebook): 978-0-933241-32-9

Printed in the United States of America

To Ulla, for her tireless efforts in creating a planet of human compatibility that embraces the welfare of Earth's human family.

CONTENTS

Wisdom

"Wisdom is not associated with any planetary belief system—religious, political, economic, social, or ideological."

"Then what is wisdom?"

"Wisdom is captured by the following expression: an in-depth understanding, empathy, and compassion for the human experience."

"Is that it?"

"Yes, but these words depend on how you express them in practice, not how you define them intellectually. Ultimately, wisdom is a way of being that cannot be defined by words."

—John, **The Consortium**

The crisis is not in the outer world but in consciousness itself.
—Jiddu Krishnamurti

FOREWORD

The *Aftermath* is a story of fiction—or is it? The deeper I got into this book, the more I knew there was much more involved—as usual for *The Pleiadian Trilogy*. Although the story is described as fiction, page after page reveals references to real-life situations presently occurring, sometimes in advance. In essence, this book awakens our awareness and connection to everything that is happening.

The message that impacted me most was the fact that in spite of all of our technological advances, we still have not exhibited the capacity to live compatibly with each other. In fact, we seem destined to a course of threatening confrontation in spite of all the heroic efforts of those who apparently oppose such a fate.

For those of us familiar with Dr. Guillory's books, it's no surprise that even when we finish reading one of his books, our minds continue to run with senarios he describes. *The Aftermath* fast-forwards us into the short-term future to consider the impact of technology, artificial intelligence, inner exploration, higher levels of consciousness, extrasensory phenomena, and the next generation humanoid—inorganic (android) or organic (cyborg)? These decisions are presently being designed in laboratories everywhere on Earth.

The Aftermath gives us a peek into the future of humans on Earth in the coming decades. I strongly recommend that you immerse yourself into this "fictional" story and see if you can come away the same as when you began.

Ulla Knoll, Executor of IVR
Frankfurt, Germany

PROLOGUE

||||||||||||||||||||||||||||||||||||||||||||||||||||||||||||||||||||||||||||||||||||||||||||||||||||||||||||||||||||||||||||||||||||||

THE TWENTY-FIRST CENTURY

In the wake of two pandemics in the first part of the twenty-first century, the Earth's population had been reduced to less than 50 percent of the original 8 billion. The dramatic events leading to the mysterious population reduction were unknown to the masses. As a result, there was still fear that it could happen again, without warning or obvious cause. Neither science nor religion nor divine revelation had been able to explain the mysterious illness and deaths of such massive proportions. Uncertainty dominated the consciousness of those remaining, along with a deep feeling of survivor's guilt for their selective preservation.

At one end of the distribution of survivors were those who desperately clung to the past and continually mourned those who had passed. They believed their security was vested in how they had always lived, in spite of its shortcomings. At least they were dealing with a known. At the other end were those who had begun to let go of the past and viewed the future as a blank canvas, as though a less-explored dimension of human potential were being aroused from a deep sleep. In the middle of these two extremes was the majority. They desperately wished for a better world and had secretly prayed for a miracle to stave off the inevitable crises that had occurred, in spite of the dramatic change occurring everywhere.

- - - | | | | | - - -

The Pleiadian Council had actually granted the peoples of planet Earth a reprieve. They had allowed a substantial fraction of the original 8 billion to survive; about 3.56 billion inhabitants remained after the two Great Tragedies. The council concluded a global nuclear holocaust was inevitable on Earth, most likely provoked by a massive act of cyber terrorism. It was simply a matter time, event, and the leaders in power before another perfect storm happened, as had occurred on two recent occasions. The resulting nuclear fallout from such an explosion, projected into space, would be directed by the solar winds and funneled into the vortex that connected the Pleiades Star Cluster and Earth. The exposure of the transparent energy-body inhabitants of the seven-star system to radioactive fallout would cause instant annihilation of their total population.

In order to protect themselves, the Pleiadians had to be preemptive in their survival strategies and their understanding of the human dilemma on Earth.

After the first pandemic, a second nuclear event occurred in the Middle East, again forcing the Pleiadians to act decisively on behalf of their own survival. However, through an agreement with the two leading members of the Pleiadian team on Earth, the council had agreed to further reduce the life-force instead of completely severing the connection and giving up hope for the peoples of the planet.

The most powerful group in opposition to Earth's transformation—the Consortium—actively worked to neutralize the efforts of those leading planetary transformation. The Consortium was secretly headed by a renegade Pleiadian who had lost hope in humankind's capability and intention to create a more humane planet. As a result, he had organized an ultra-secret governing board of fifteen members, and a much larger public organization, about 150 members, of the most wealthy and influential to oversee and guide the activities of Earth by the power of influence.

Their main interest was to maintain the status quo, since they believed earthlings needed to be guided by invisible leadership in order to guarantee their continued existence. Invisible leadership referred to a process of directing the actions of others by subconsciously influencing their thinking, giving them the impression that they were controlling their own destiny.

The Pleiadian reprieve, on the other hand, was based on the possibility that humans could transform their dominant consciousness from survival to compatibility. The Pleiadian Council assumed that a human population with a high degree of wisdom would transform their aggressive thinking and behaviors to a mutual understanding and supportive way of living.

However, to help ensure this result, the reprieve also involved an unprecedented condition for which the inhabitants of Earth had no choice. The purpose of the condition was to significantly influence ordinary earthlings into taking responsibility for becoming more caring and humane people instead of solely hoping for a great leader to do so for them. Meanwhile, the Pleiadian Council would continue to monitor events on Earth that involved the potential of a nuclear exchange, along with a determination of how they would respond on behalf of their own survival.

PART ONE

GLOBAL TRANSFORMATION

I

||||||||||||||||||||||||||||||||||||||||||||||||||||||||||||||||||||||||||||||||||||||||||||||||||||||||||||||||||||||||||||

GLOBAL TRANSFORMATION— POST PANDEMICS

The depth of grief experienced by those who survived the Great Tragedies was unimaginable. The only comparison that could be made was to the Black Death plague during the mid-fourteenth century. The pandemics affected every human on Earth, particularly those remaining, who experienced survivor's guilt. Most confusing was the lack of causation or explanation for those who passed. No answers were forthcoming by the respected sources of prediction or prophesy. Some cited Nostradamus and other prophets as well as the Old and New Testaments, including Revelation. But these explanations made little sense to the majority who experienced loss; they experienced a feeling bordering on numbed hopelessness.

There were those who felt victimized by forces beyond their control, which paralyzed their ability to act on behalf of their own well-being. Some felt that, in some mysterious way, they were reaping what they had sown: a form of punishment for how dissociated they had been living as a result of the ethics espoused by their weekly religious practices. In a mysterious twist of thinking, they believed that they deserved the form of punishment that they were experiencing.

There was a smaller but spiritually influenced segment who felt that, as earthlings, everyone was responsible for the events that occurred on the planet, plain and simple. They espoused that humans were insepa-rable from the planet, since it was probably the source of their origin.

This segment of the population proposed the following premise: If we somehow caused the situation we are experiencing in ways we cannot understand, then we also have the power to prevent its future occurrence by accepting responsibility for it. The source of prevention in the future will not be our leaders or our clergy, and certainly not the use of our great scientific and technological knowledge, but our willingness to manage the health of the planet that supports our existence and all other existent life forms. Then we might take the initial baby step in understanding events far beyond our comprehension.

These people believed that the acceptance of this premise would represent a major transformation in human consciousness. This was the underlying premise of the Renaissance Communities in their worldwide expansion.

- - - | | | | | - - -

For the masses, to be forced to deal with the basic necessities of survival—food, shelter, and clothing—so that existential issues could be set aside for the time being was a blessing. Most of the traditional systems of food and water distribution were of greatest concern. Every available person became a vital contributor to maintaining the health and well-being of their community. For the present, the normal human frailties of selfishness and looting were set aside in most places around the world—with the exception of places where the wealth disparities had been extremely severe over millennia.

In the former communities, a true sense of caring for and supporting each other was a priority. What began to emerge in those parts of the world were naturally constituted community families, which had existed in group-oriented cultures for centuries. These were underscored by a greater concentration of people who found satisfaction in helping others, most of whom expected nothing in return. Community families were defined more by natural relationships of caring and support than by bloodlines.

These were the seeds of human transformation. For humans with the Pleiadian code—a genetic Pleiadian lineage—this transformation was challenging at times, but it was like regaining a long-forgotten part of themselves. However, the groups who were experiencing the greatest sorrow and sadness had the most difficulty in simply functioning constructively.

The vast majority were still dealing with the vital questions of human existence: meaning, purpose, life, death, and whatever comes afterward. They continued to look for answers outside of themselves rather than turn their focus inward. The more they immersed themselves in external explanations, the greater confusion and frustration they experienced—not recognizing that confusion was a key element in redirecting their attention to the inner world of wisdom. Fortunately, most communities had members who would facilitate community gatherings several times a week or provide private consultation. The purpose of the gatherings was to allow a safe place for the expression of the loss of family members as well as to facilitate the smooth transition to a more compatible way of living. The focus was on ensuring that everyone in the community had the basics for healthy living, both physically and mentally.

In time, their attention would turn to healthcare, education, and a community format for spiritual fulfillment. The word *spiritual* was used to provide a context in which everyone's principles were included for discussion and democratic adoption based on the physical, mental, and spiritual well-being of the individual. They decided to initially avoid conscripted beliefs, practices, and behaviors, and focus on principles of human compatibility as a guideline for living.

The first principle they discussed was learning how to live compatibly with differences in ideas, cultures, languages, styles, and so on as a basis for mutual understanding. They all agreed that, at some level of human understanding, they knew how to treat each other with dignity and respect. The challenge was to do so naturally—regardless of how much wealth they possessed—instead of how they had previously lived in a survival-driven world.

In this way, the various communities began to slowly evolve a pattern of living based on principles and with the least necessity for written rules and regulations. They were learning the process of transformation from humans to human beings.

2

|||||||||||||||||||||||||||||||||||||||||||||||||||||||||||||||||||||||||||||||||||||||||||||||||||||||||||||||||||||||||||||

OPERATION ISOLATION

K arl Gustav Christen led a double life, one public and the other private. In his public life, he was a brilliant microbiologist who had founded and now headed the Institute for Cancer Research, a private corporation in partnership with the private university in the principality of Liechtenstein. The highly acclaimed research work that Karl and his team of brilliant scientists from around the world had done was published and offered in the public domain for anyone's use in a research capacity. As a result, Karl was privately suggested for the Nobel Prize in Medicine—which he just as privately refused to accept. On the strong urging and recommendation by Prince Frederick of Liechtenstein, Karl was literally conscripted as spokesperson for the recovery of Europe after the Great Tragedies.

At six foot four, 185 pounds, and with a Mediterranean skin tone, Karl was an impressive figure. When he spoke in person, he was charismatic and appeared to connect heart to heart with his audience. Their problems were his problems. Their joys were his joys. Their pain was his pain. His empathic connection with them elicited compassion, trust, and openness to his messages of inspiration.

In his private life, he was the Chairman of the Consortium, the ultra-secret organization that guided the major events on the planet. After his failed attempt to create an ally of the president of the United States to his philosophy for the recovery of Europe—based on strong leadership by the historical ruling classes—he concluded that a change in America's presidency would be necessary if global influence were to be successful in the new world order.

Karl believed that Europe needed a successful and respected businessman with no political ties to fill the vacuum caused by the two pandemics. The US president espoused a strong faith in ordinary people to create a self-organizing mentality with the least amount of governmental oversight—and certainly not leadership relegated solely to the wealthy.

In an unplanned flash of anger during his visit to the White House, Dr. Christen attempted to poison the president with an undetectable powdery substance that would have rendered him in a continuously confused state that would ultimately result in suicide. The president was saved by his chief of staff, who had knocked over the poisoned cup of tea that the president was about to drink. Karl still fumed over his spontaneous loss of self-control and failed attempt to eliminate the president, even though any harmful attempt on the president's life would not have been proved.

- - - | | | | | - - -

In a highly secluded villa on the outskirts of Neustadt, Liechtenstein, Karl Christen presided over his recently reconstituted governing board of the Consortium. The present board consisted of ten members; three of the original thirteen had succumbed to the second reduction of the life-force.

He began the meeting by saying, "I would like to congratulate each of you who made the cut." Most of those present smiled an obligatory smile. Two of them did not think his greeting was at all amusing. Karl made a mental note of these two individuals. He noticed everything about human behavior, which was much more revealing than a person's verbal statements. He had concluded that most humans had little or no awareness of their motivations at a subliminal level, and generally, few had any interest in knowing. However, those blind spots were obvious to those who, like himself, had a Pleiadian heritage.

After the first pandemic, Karl and his deputy, Lenhard Rieser, had spent considerable time selecting new board members who represented the future global power structure. This meant the inclusion of representatives from India and China, who had not been part of the original governing board. Given the large middle-class populations of both rapidly advancing countries—about 120 million each at present—their influence would be vital to the Consortium's global influence. They had concluded that in spite of the youth of the new board members, they were not mindless followers. They were highly skilled in terms of their ability to influence the thinking of their people. They were part of the new global leadership in business, banking, science and technology, medicine, and politics, which exerted power based primarily on lineage, class, and wealth.

Karl said that the sole purpose of the meeting was filling the leadership vacuum in Europe and then extending their influence globally. After establishing eye contact with each of the ten members, he said, "As you are aware, I have been selected by the European Union to lead the recovery of Europe—excluding the UK, of course. This is a responsibility I did not seek; however, because of increased public exposure, this appointment does measurably serve our purpose. What is the expression in English? Letting the fox guard the hen house?" He smiled.

The members found his little saying amusing. One even added, "And in disguise!", to which they laughed even louder.

"I recently visited the president of the United States. It's clear that our philosophies are at opposite ends of the leadership spectrum. He actually believes that ordinary people have the intelligence to play a major role in their own governance." Karl paused and reflected on his disappointment in attempting to convince average people of their responsibility for creating change during the earlier stage of his emissary role. He continued, "Ignoring the fact that their Constitution and Declaration of Independence were written by aristocrats and that all of their presidents, with very few exceptions, have been from the wealthy, privileged class."

One of the young aspiring and outspoken members of the Consortium from the Indian Brahmin class, Sanjay Krishnamurti, asked, "Is he serious, or is he clueless about how most of the world operates?" Again there was light laughter.

"More idealistic, I would say," replied Karl. "Perhaps the revolutionary spirit of Americans is more ingrained in their culture than I suspected. However, in the final analysis, people want strong leaders to take care of them." He paused to gather his thoughts about the point he wanted to make. "The point is, I believe our differences are too insurmountable to create an alliance with him."

"Can he be removed?" another member asked. The others went silent, as they wanted to be sure of what he meant.

"I don't think that strategy will work for the present," Karl said in the silence that followed. "It has been tried. Besides, I have another idea of how we might achieve our objective with respect to the president."

At this point he had everyone's undivided attention, even his deputy's. They all knew that Karl had a reputation of being insightful and brilliant, but most recently selected members had little knowledge of how cunning he could be.

"As things are at the present, the United States is still the most powerful nation on the planet economically and militarily, although not necessarily politically, in spite of how they try to bully those with differing views."

"What does that mean?" asked another member, who had not spoken throughout the meeting until now.

"It means we use their greatest weakness as a country, which they believe is one of their greatest strengths, for their own demise."

"And that is?" asked the member, skeptically.

"Their arrogance toward the rest of the world. That's why they are despised by most countries, including those they consider to be strong allies."

"What do you propose?" the member asked.

"*Isolierung*," said Karl, "the German word for isolation. I suggest we begin an exclusive series of economic agreements among Europe, Asia, and Africa. Without these major resources for fabrication and distribution of their goods and services, the United States will eventually become a second-class economic power."

The group was slowly becoming aware of how the arrogance of the United States could be used as the basis for its downfall.

"We now have an economic fulcrum with our present board to begin isolating America from the mainstream economic and business activity—particularly with the addition of our new members from India and China."

Given the brainpower of the Consortium Board, ideas about isolating America began to germinate and flow. Karl had again demonstrated his brilliance in influencing the thinking of others to create reality. Little did they know that this was only the first step he had planned of a sequential process to ultimately bring the president to his knees.

The Chairman thanked the board members for their ideas. He indicated that he planned to use them for strategically important functions consistent with their positions so as to keep them out of the limelight.

3

BIRTH OF A PARADIGM

The president wanted to use the National Medal of Science ceremony to assure the scientific community of generous research support in America's recovery. He realized the importance of science and technology in the new reality of the 140 million Americans who survived the second pandemic. He reflected on the fact that Americans consisted of an unusual concentration of explorers and risk-takers. Many academics and entrepreneurs worked in the areas of science and technology. He believed that in the present era of a reduced labor pool, highly advanced competency in science and technology would significantly influence the planet's balance of power.

As the president mingled among the awardees and the country's most prestigious and ingenious scientists to get their views of how to best use the US advantage in science and technology, he often found himself lost in their explanations. Scientists loved to talk about their work, especially those at this particular event. However, many of them had difficulty in not only effectively communicating to a layman what they were doing but also explaining the practical usefulness of their work. He repeatedly heard robotics as the answer to the shortage of workers and for performing routine household chores. Both in academia and industry, the popularity of the marriage between man and machine, incorporating artificial intelligence, had begun to create the next industrial paradigm in business design, processes, and innovation.

An unusually high number of the attendees older than fifty had survived the pandemics. The president, in consultation with Kenneth Clarke, his chief of staff, and Dana Hartman, his advisor from State, assumed that many were explorers by nature and were often faced with transformation in their thinking—particularly those who trained exceptional and outspoken young graduate students and postdoctoral fellows. Among them tonight was the awardee in brain research, Dr. David Carrington, who had also won the Nobel Prize in Medicine the previous year for his pioneering work in the interface of neurobiology, neuroscience, and psychology. David was looking forward to meeting the president to share his ideas relating to the recovery process.

David was a member of the core staff of ten at the UCLA Brain Research Institute. He had completed his undergraduate work at Cal Tech and his graduate work at Stanford, and then joined the faculty at UCLA. Early in his career, he had become associated with the UCLA Brain Research Institute because of the myriad of research dimensions it brought to his work. The more he interacted with the diverse perspectives within the Institute, the more he began to realize there was something missing in his interpretations and models.

David's association with his colleagues in psychology had already validated phenomena such as intuition, telepathy, and clairvoyance— none of which were adequately explained by the physical models he used. In fact, their work was often challenged by his colleagues when it was subjected to Newtonian-Cartesian considerations.

The occurrence of the two pandemics had turned his world upside down. There were no identified viruses or explanations for the illnesses associated with the tragedies. In addition, there was no exponential increase in the death rate that was typical for a virus spread by human contact—and therefore, no substantive leads for solutions. These events had led him to his present state of thinking and his excitement about meeting with the president. Most of all, he didn't want his comments with the president to be overheard by his colleagues.

The president made cursory eye contact with Dr. Carrington several times as he circulated among the gathering. Finally, the president approached him, glanced at his official White House lanyard, and extended his hand.

"Dr. Carrington, I'm delighted to meet you," he said with his infectious smile.

"It's an honor, Mr. President. I admire and respect your leadership during these very difficult times," David replied.

"Thank you, Dr. Carrington. I would be thrilled if most Americans thought as you do. Congratulations on being awarded the Nobel Prize. I am also pleased that you have been selected for the President's Award," he said, tongue-in-cheek. The belated President's Award had given David some idea of the politics involved in being acknowledged by his peers for exceptional scientific research that challenged existing conventions.

"Please, call me David. It feels more comfortable, especially with you. Truth is, we've both earned the respect of our colleagues, whether they like us or not. I have learned over the years that liking someone is not necessarily an expression of respect."

The president noted the maverick in David and was impressed with his insightful comment. However, keeping in mind the time and the others he had to greet before dinner, the president said, "I've been asking everyone their opinion of our future direction concerning science and technology. The consistent message I've received so far is increased funding"—*as usual*, the president thought—"with a focus on robotics to address our shortages of the labor pool. I'd like to know your thoughts on this question."

"Interesting you should ask that question, Mr. President. I've given quite a bit of thought to the direction we need to take and how we got to where we are in the first place."

For the first time in their conversation, David Carrington perceived that he had the president's full attention. The president nodded for David to continue.

"I'm afraid that what I have to say may require more than a quick one-liner."

On instinct, the president said, "Can we meet briefly at the end of this affair for a few minutes, Dr. Carrington?"

"I would appreciate that very much, sir. And I promise I won't take up too much of your time."

- - - | | | | | - - -

After dinner and the president's farewell to the distinguished group, Dana Hartman, deputy secretary of state and presidential advisor, secured Dr. Carrington and whisked him away from the group. After several twists and turns past a series of serious-looking Secret Service agents at various posts along the corridors, Dana stopped in front of an impressive-looking door. In spite of all of his scientific awards and recognitions, David was overwhelmed when she ushered him into the Oval Office.

"Please take a seat, Dr. Carrington," Dana instructed. "The president will be right with you."

"Thank you," David replied, sitting in the high-back chair to which Dana directed him.

Almost immediately a White House staff member entered, set out a tray of coffee, tea, and cakes, and just as quickly retreated, without a word or glance at anyone in the room.

"Please," Dana said, pointing to the tray, "help yourself. This is an informal meeting."

While dousing a tea bag into one of the bone china cups filled with steaming water, the president entered with General Kenneth Clarke in his wake. David stood. General Clarke extended his hand, congratulated

David on his award, and seated himself on a two-seat sofa across from the scientist. The president sat in a high-back chair, flanking them both. Dana positioned herself outside of the circle of three in the event that she needed to exit.

"Okay, Dr. Carrington, the floor is yours," the president said with a smile. "Tell us your thoughts on the way forward."

David put his cup down on the centered small table and spoke in a calm, steady voice. "Mr. President, I've been doing research with a diverse team of scientists on the interface of neurobiology, neuroscience, and psychology for more than thirty years. Our psychologist, Dr. Catherine Wang, is brilliant. She has often pointed out to us our lack of convincing evidence that most scientists don't pick up and that often defies an explanation solely involving the brain. Her observations commonly lead us in directions we would never think of exploring."

The president uncrossed one leg and crossed the other, a sign that David assumed meant get to the point.

"The lack of a reasonable explanation for the pandemics pushed me over an edge I had been avoiding for some time. In fact, the source of the symptoms and the infected population distributions are nowhere close to how we define a pandemic—except for the massive loss of life. Contagion seems to play no role. Most of all, there is no identified virus. The only conclusion I can come to is that something nonphysical is going on that causes the physical conditions we observe."

He paused to sense the reaction of the president, and noted that he was more interested than impatient now.

"Go on," the president said, sounding engaged with where David might be going.

"If this line of thinking has validity, particularly in the absence of anything else, then we are moving into the psychosomatic world of causation: the nonphysical world of the mind. Catherine refers to this realm in a more esoteric way with the concept of consciousness." David paused again to be sure the president understood the implications of what he was saying. "So, you can see why I wanted to speak briefly with you in private."

"I think I have a general idea of what you are saying," the president replied, staying on point. "My question to you is the same one we began with during the reception: What direction should we take in light of the two Great Tragedies we have experienced? More specifically, for you, David, what is it you want to do in going forward?"

David had not expected the conversation to move as rapidly as the president had taken it. After a long silence, he said, "I want to establish a research program that bridges the physical and nonphysical aspects of human behavior, illness, and wellness, hopefully in conjunction with the UCLA Brain Research Institute. I'm still trying to get my arms around the whole idea." He paused to see if the president would react with a paternal smile and a polite dismissal. Instead, he interpreted the president's smile as conveying acceptance.

"What can we do to help you, David?" the president replied. He was thinking, *Finally, a mainstream respected scientist with a Nobel Prize is exactly what we need. I wonder what his reaction will be when he learns of the true explanation for the pandemics. Even Nobel Prize winners deserve a little humility now and then. After all, he isn't God.*

David was astounded by the president's response, and for a moment he was speechless. However, he knew how to ask for what he needed when sparked by a new idea.

"Two resources immediately come to mind," David replied. "People and money."

"I think we can help you with both."

General Clarke had been impassive throughout the conversation, but at this point he broke into a broad smile, which David interpreted as the general being impressed with his proposal.

4

||||||||||||||||||||||||||||||||||||||||||||||||||||||||||||||||||||||||||||||||||||||||||||||||||||||||||||||||||||||||||||||||||

INSTITUTE FOR THE STUDY OF CONSCIOUSNESS

Having won the Nobel Prize at the relatively young age of fifty-four, David Carrington immediately began to turn his attention to more challenging frontiers. He sought an endeavor that would leave a legacy of his life, and not just as a member of a distinguished list that significantly moved the needle of science in understanding how the human brain functioned. The most obvious choice was to determine the source of the recent pandemics and how they might be prevented in the future. No one seemed to know the cause, so how could one proceed to formulate a cure, or more optimistically, some form of prevention for the future?

David was one of the first scientists to openly discuss the possibility of a selection criterion for those infected by the illness. By nature, he did not believe in random events where human illness was concerned. Oddly enough, he never felt personally threatened during the two Great Tragedies. He wondered why but had not come up with a logical answer. Among his colleagues and friends who survived, he noted certain interpersonal characteristics they all possessed in addition to generally good health: they got along well with others, were less judgmental, and were more open and thoughtful about out-of-context ideas.

The problem was that these characteristics were not real science—psychology, at best. His colleague from the Institute of Brain Research, Dr. Catherine Wang, a psychologist whom he had worked with for most of his professional career, would probably bristle at his thoughts. In truth, her ideas during their team projects over the years had redirected his thinking on many occasions. For sure, his thinking was now headed into uncharted waters.

He admitted to himself that the issue was not about science or non-science, it was about something Catherine had said repeatedly: it was about the science of the nonphysical world. It was where hard scientists felt not only out of their element but also untrained to explore, primarily because of their collective resistance to experiencing a world beyond Newtonian-Cartesian science, a world that could permanently alter their perceptions of reality. The easy reaction was to simply ignore what that world comprised, or at worst, invalidate it as nonsense, since no instrumentation existed to measure its cause and effect—at least, measurements based on a well-developed theory. Little consideration was given to the fact that this was exactly the way the currently accepted scientific paradigm began, when an ancient Greek philosopher, Democritus, was walking on a beach, picked up a handful of sand, and declared that all matter comprised spherical, solid particles he called atoms.

In truth, David had begun to feel a sense of ennui about the continuing theories associated with the brain. He thought about the mysterious illness associated with the pandemics: no new virus had been discovered, the symptoms that were contracted were not contagious, and everyone affected experienced flu-like symptoms and ultimately passed within a few weeks of each other.

This sequence of events did not at all fit the traditional definition of a pandemic; therefore, attempts to understand what was going on were equally frustrating. He reluctantly concluded that they were dealing with a phenomenon for which a validated science did not exist, nor was there any overwhelming movement to validate the study of the nonphysical world. The present course was to research the material world at infinitesimally smaller and smaller quantities until there was nothing left.

This was where David's internal reasoning had led him. The question was, was he willing to seriously explore that mysterious yet fascinating world? He had already won the Nobel Prize in Medicine, the holy grail of his scientific career. They couldn't take it back, so he concluded that he had nothing to lose, similar to Linus Pauling's fascination with aspirin as a prevention for the common cold after he won the Nobel Prizes in Chemistry in 1954 and Peace in 1962. However, David also knew that the exploration he was considering involved not only the questionable world of parapsychology but also the transcendent world of metaphysics, commonly referred to as the study of consciousness.

- - - | | | | | - - -

Based on the president's suggestion, David Carrington and Catherine Wang arranged a meeting with Dr. Frances Wilkerson, an internationally known behavioral scientist from Howard University; Dr. Gail Erickson, executive director of Garret College Foundation, whose work involved bridging extrasensory skills with the corresponding five traditional human senses; and Patricia Christensen, research associate in parapsychology at the University of Arizona, who was naturally skilled in multiple extrasensory competencies. Pat had been the leading subject for the federal government's Star Gate program for remote viewing, which had been discontinued in the early 1990s. All three researchers had been involved with unraveling the mystery source of the pandemics.

David began the meeting by introducing himself and Catherine, and gave a quick synopsis of their work in brain research at the UCLA Brain Institute. Each of the three invited women introduced themselves and gave similar descriptions of their work with respect to psychology and metaphysics. There had been a more in-depth exchange of this information prior to the present meeting, so the exchanges were more like an introductory icebreaker.

In spite of the polite exchanges, the tenor of the meeting was somewhat tense, with each side not knowing where the others stood with respect to their worlds of science, or how attached they were to their own scientific views. David assumed a formal demeanor, as he would with scientists he was meeting for the first time and having little or cursory knowledge of their work. He also had a fleeting thought about the fact that he was working with all women, which he immediately attempted to set aside. However, he did want to establish the fact, as diplomatically as possible, that any joint effort would be led by him and Catherine. On the other hand, Catherine appeared to be more comfortable and at ease with the other scientists with respect to hierarchy as they chatted about their work—more comfortable than David.

After introductions, David proceeded by giving a synopsis of his conversation with the president about the absence of a virus and the lack of contagion. He then shared his intention to immerse himself in exploring the nonphysical causation of the pandemic illness. "Based on Catherine's suggestion, I think we need to seriously consider some kind of scientific interface between consciousness and human illness."

He was about to continue when Dr. Erickson interrupted him and said, "We already know the source of the illness. Didn't the president tell you?"

David was taken aback and did not know how to respond, since the president had not informed him. He gathered his bearings—after all, he was a Nobel Laureate—and proceeded. "Based on my analysis thus far, I am strongly considering psychosomatic causation. This is, of course, a significant departure from my previous work involving the brain."

Dr. Erickson interrupted him again. "You're in the right ballpark. It's somatoform. But that wasn't the answer to my question. We know the source of the illness," she repeated emphatically.

David realized that he wasn't on firm ground and experienced a profound sense of embarrassment, followed by humility. He also realized
that he was at a critical point of gaining the respect of being in a true
leadership role. "No, the president did not reveal the source." He paused.
"Maybe that's why he suggested we meet. What is it?"

"Somatoform is technically a mental disorder that results in physical
illness from no identified medical condition. We've discovered that
the source of the pandemic illness is a lack of the life-force necessary
for the survival of those with insufficient wisdom. It's a long story, but
that's it in a nutshell."

David tried to process Dr. Erickson's answer but realized she was
using terminology he only had a fleeting knowledge of or even interest
in, involving his prior work on brain research. Since he still looked
confused, Pat Christensen joined in.

"The life-force is an expression of consciousness that sustains the
vitality of human functioning," she explained. "Individuals who have
more or less mastered the human plane require less life-force as an
external source because they have integrated spirituality as a natural way
they live their lives. Deeply religious Christians refer to the life-force as
the 'grace of God,' the Chinese as 'ch'i,' and Hindus as 'prana.'"

"Have you ever experienced people who appear to be in the world but
not of the world?" Dr. Frances Wilkerson asked, looking toward David
and Catherine. "People who are perfectly satisfied with what they have and
are not seeking to accumulate more than what's necessary to be happy?"

"Yes, I have," David replied. "I always thought they were a little off,
quite frankly. I thought they were faking the true reality of what was
going on within and around themselves."

"Have you ever thought that you were the one who might be faking
reality? And that you might be dissatisfied with how your life was in
that moment?"

David felt confronted and dumbfounded by the question. He had
not experienced such a feeling since the oral defense for his PhD in

graduate school. Both Frances and Pat smiled at his look of confusion. Catherine, who understood most of what was being said, was secretly enjoying his experience of humility. But she also felt a sense of loyalty to her colleague and decided to come to his aid.

"We have discussed these terms on occasion but primarily when we had no recourse to other evidence-based explanations. We assume that you bring background knowledge and experience of such metaphysical phenomena. Why don't you explain to us more of what you have learned so far about the tragedies?" David breathed a huge sigh of relief at Catherine's intervention and smiled to himself.

The three women explained their unique roles in identifying the cause of the pandemics and their work in attempting to ensure the prevention of another occurrence—excluding, of course, any mention of the Pleiadian team members or the Pleiadian Council. That was up to the president and Dr. Bill Bradley, who had also been involved in resolving the source of the two tragic occurrences.

After their explanations, David smiled and said, "Why don't we take a break and reconvene in fifteen minutes? That will give Catherine and me a chance to process the information you've shared with us."

During the break, David huddled privately with Catherine for a quick conversation. "I'm excited about the possibilities that could occur if we could find a way to work together," Catherine said. "I am equally impressed with their comprehension, knowledge, and experience with the world of consciousness. If we seamlessly interface our knowledge of brain research with their consciousness research, we could create an in-depth understanding of the inseparability of the integrated person—body, mind, and spirit. The possibilities I'm speaking of go far beyond the pandemic crisis to the psychic redesign of the human species my colleagues often speak of—not only mechanically but also in terms of human mental technology."

When the meeting resumed, David was more comfortable and light-hearted in demeanor as a result of his debrief with Catherine during the break. He began by inviting any thoughts, ideas, or concerns about creating a working relationship, focused initially on the pandemics. Everyone responded positively. Gail reminded everyone that they were in the initial stages of learning how to work together. "The work that we're about to take on is far too important to let personalities get in the way, including my own." They all smiled.

"What should we call our joint effort that would be future-oriented?" Frances asked.

"The Study of Consciousness," Pat proposed without hesitation. She felt that her work at Arizona's parapsychology department was at the forefront of what they were discussing.

"My original idea was something associated with the UCLA Brain Institute," David said. "However, where we are now, I am not so sure it would fit. Perhaps we ought to consider an entirely separate research facility."

"That's it!" Catherine shouted. "A separate laboratory that could establish its own rules of operation and direction for research studies: The Institute for the Study of Consciousness." An eerie silence followed her declaration, as if there were nothing more to be said. That was it. It was kind of scary—even spiritual.

David broke the silence and said, "I plan to donate my entire Nobel monetary award to the establishment of the Institute." Everyone was astounded by his commitment, which was several hundred thousand dollars, tax free. "Also, the president gave me a few names for financial support that should put us in great shape."

As they shared their ideas about the proposed institute, naturally participating roles began to formulate in their minds. "I'll contact a lawyer tomorrow for legally establishing the institute and begin seeking laboratory space and facilities for conducting our research," David said excitedly.

5

||||||||||||||||||||||||||||||||||||||||||||||||||||||||||||||||||||||||||||||||||||||||||||||||||||||||||||||||||||||

ECONOMIC CHAOS

Sowing the seeds of economic chaos was not that difficult, particularly since there was such a large wealth disparity between the top 10 percent of the US population and the other 90 percent. Karl surmised that one didn't need a degree in economics to conclude that accelerating this disparity would be the beginning of the breaking point. At the very least, there would be a severe global recession similar to 2008–2009, and shortly thereafter, probably the predicted global depression, exceeding the one following the US stock market crash of 1929. Such a sequence of events would be an ideal first phase of the grand plan the Chairman had in mind for the planet—followed, of course, by a global domino effect.

He didn't view this situation from an ethical standpoint of fair or unfair but simply from a perspective of the most expedient way to achieve his objectives. In fact, a major part of his disappointment with earthlings was that this way of operating appeared to dominate human transactions, with minor exceptions. The impending crisis of scarcity among the masses would be blamed primarily on those who held political office—in the case of the United States in particular, the president. When coupled with economic isolation, it would be the beginning of the end of the fearless leader of the greatest nation in the history of the world. At this point, the stage would be set for intervention by the Consortium as savior of the world. The key would be to replace the current president with someone committed to free, unregulated capitalism in order to ensure the continued increase in the wealth disparity.

Although Karl had not mentioned it at the most recent board meeting, selected members of the Consortium would play a major role in bringing about the increased disparity in global wealth. His plan was to begin with India and China, the two most populous countries on the planet.

In the case of India, the idea and acceptance of a hierarchical privileged class was the result of the centuries-old caste system and was hardwired into the consciousness of the people. In spite of its spiritual reputation, human equality by virtue of birth was mostly a foreign concept in practice. Therefore, it followed naturally that the Brahmin class was not only superior as a human species but also deserved to be in positions of power to own and control practically all of the nation's wealth.

The same was true of China in its own unique way. Because of its recent economic success, China had measurably increased the number and net wealth of its ultrarich as compared to the general population. China's continually evolving middle class, similar in size to India's, was strongly influenced by the creative comforts of the Western world. Based on its strong economy of Western technology labor providers and the emergence of its own economic power in the world, class distinctions had become more prominent, in spite of its historical communist influence. In essence, financial wealth had become synonymous with class distinctions, as in the West.

Such distinctions were the foundation for the increasing disparity between the haves and have-nots, not only in India and China but globally. They served as the justified basis for the gradual depletion of sufficient resources for all classes, excepting the rich, to reasonably prosper.

Karl had clearly established his two personas for ensuring the new world order. As Chairman, he would mastermind the chaotic economic breakdown of most of the world, particularly the United States. As Dr. Karl Christen, head of the Cancer Institute, he would be the leading figure for the recovery of Europe initially, and eventually, most of the world. He would be magical in both roles: destroyer on one hand and savior on the other. With a smile, he reflected on the fact that the role of savior had been handed to him on a royal platter by Prince Frederick of Liechtenstein.

Karl had decided many years ago that managing the prevailing survival mentality was the best alternative. After working for several years as a Pleiadian emissary to influence the transformation of the Earth's consciousness, he had concluded that such an effort was hopeless. At this point, his first thought was to return to Pleiades, but he had exceeded his timeframe for that decision. After a year on Earth, every Pleiadian had to choose within a month to return to Pleiades or remain permanently as an earthling.

When he had first arrived, he had been very optimistic that conversion was possible. When peace treaties had been signed to begin destroying nuclear weapons, he decided the leaders of the planet had reached a critical turning point. However, when it was revealed that secret plans were underway to simultaneously replace them with more sophisticated nuclear weaponry and expand the Earth Nuclear Club, he had reached the end of his crusade.

What Karl could never understand about humans was why ordinary people felt so powerless to create a desirable way of living, why they were so easily manipulated to believe that others among them who were different were the source of their problems—even as the overall disparity between the haves and have-nots increased. He couldn't understand why they resisted individual and collective responsibility for creating not only change but also transformation among themselves when the solution was so clearly obvious. Instead, they assumed an attitude of entitlement. Their solution was to look to a great leader to address their demise, coupled with the illusion that such a leader had the power to magically create human transformation with little or no effort on their part.

However, he did understand why the greatest subtlety of all was not understood, even among many of those who survived the two Great Tragedies. Transformation from a survival consciousness to one of compatibility could only come from within each individual. The ultimate solution to one's demise was internal, not external—which was the last place most humans were willing to look for resolution and greater wisdom.

He found himself in no-man's-land. He couldn't return to Pleiades, and he no longer felt any desire for his role of missionary to influence the achievement of a planet dominated by human compatibility. After experiencing a state of depression for several months, he concluded that it was not possible for the people of Earth to progress to a higher level of consciousness and live in harmony—but it might be possible to contain their aggression toward each other and preserve the continued existence of the inhabitants of Pleiades. He considered this conclusion to be a noble compromise.

In his time on Earth, Karl had noted that the various nation-states were easily influenced by their sacred documents, culture, and most of all, by repeated messaging, particularly when the messaging involved their core values, for which they were willing to die. In the West, these included freedom, democracy, Christianity, and capitalism.

Whether the messaging involved a valid threat to their survival was irrelevant. Through repetitive messaging, they had learned to accept almost anything communicated by their trusted leaders, so Karl set out to perfect the process of subliminal messaging. To drive his point home, he used such messaging at the most subtle level of human perception, in terms of hidden images and statements throughout the communications media and in products and services.

That was when he decided to organize the modern-day Consortium. To his way of thinking, he was implementing the famous quote by French philosopher Victor Hugo: "There is one thing stronger than all the armies of the world, and that is an idea whose time has come." As long as the idea was one that appealed to the survival of a group and wrapped in their collective core values, people could be subtlety influenced to organize and behave in predictable ways. No money, weapons, or coercive power over others were necessary, only the power of influence. These messages were easily disseminated globally using the influential resources of the greater Consortium membership, past and present—which numbered in the thousands.

The essential key to the Consortium's success in regaining control of planetary events through influence was economic isolation and breakdown of the United States. As long as the acquisition of greater personal wealth was firmly hardwired into the most influential, ultrarich Americans no matter how wise they might be, the Consortium would prevail.

PART TWO

THE IMMIGRANTS

6

|||||||||||||||||||||||||||||||||||||||||||||||||||||||||||||||||||||||||||||||||||||||||||||||||||||||||||||||||||||||||||||||

ORIENTATION

The non-negotiable condition for the reprieve by the Pleiadian Council was that one hundred Pleiadians would immigrate to Earth and take on human bodies. Their purpose was to assist earthlings in bringing about a more compatible global society. I, Dr. Bill Bradley, would handle the assigned placements. I made this agreement with Tony and John, two Pleiadians assigned to Earth who had chosen permanent residence. Tony was protector and advisor to the incumbent president, and John, my mentor and protector. The agreement was their best effort to avoid severing the life-force after the second nuclear threat.

All of the immigrants were avid volunteers who were excited about sharing their way of living. Most felt a sense of duty borne out of the value of serving others, which they had practiced on their home constellation of stars. They were also keenly aware of the crucial strategic importance of their objective in terms of protecting their own civilization. There were no illusions about the consequences of failure as communicated by the Pleiadian Council during their briefings. How the Earth functioned was a true potential threat to their survival. Most of all, they were informed about the challenge they were undertaking and the level of resistance to fundamental change they might encounter from humans.

I was charged with overseeing the quiet integration of the Pleiadians into selected regions of the planet. The seven regions, which were originally selected for conversion because of their dire need to avert a catastrophic nuclear confrontation or because of their strong spiritual persuasion, were chosen as the initial placements. These regions included the Middle East, France, South America, China, India, Japan, and the United States, as well as the Renaissance Communities throughout the world.

The emphasis of my welcoming remarks was on the phrase "quiet integration" and the subtle influence on those with whom the immigrants would live and work. I emphasized the fact that earthlings were somewhat comfortable with change but were, in general, highly resistant to transformation. They were instructed by the Pleiadian Council, and I emphasized that they were not to seek leadership roles of any significance. Their major objective was to influence others by being examples of how they lived in support of each other on Pleiades. The first step was to think of themselves as earthlings, not as saviors from another star constellation imposing their way of living on the people of Earth. I charged them to focus on establishing quality interpersonal relationships characterized by understanding, compassion, and acceptance of others.

I also reminded each of the immigrant groups that the spirit of the integration plan was to focus most of their efforts on the average person and that we were attempting to create a revolution in consciousness spearheaded by ordinary people, from which natural leaders would emerge. Hopefully, these would be leaders who had the best interest of all humanity at heart based on their personal experience. The ultimate aim was that the new emerging leadership would work to bring about a constructive balance between humanity and technology. More specifically, their work would aim to eventually rid the planet of all weapons of mass destruction—particularly those involving radioactive fallout. Such an ultimate outcome could only come about through a transformation in the consciousness of earthlings to a higher level of human sensitivity, compassion, and wisdom.

The more I spoke to the group, the more they understood the reality of their undertaking. Although I agreed with the spirit of the Quest in general, I was equally conflicted and dissatisfied by the fact that the Pleiadian Council had not given earthlings the right to choose immigration—which at this point was irrelevant. I'm not sure what difference it would have made, since prior to the pandemics we had proven that we were either incapable or unwilling to create a planetary society that was not a threat to our own continued existence or to other planetary systems in the galaxy.

After I completed my briefing, I opened the conversation to questions from the group. A flurry of hands immediately went up. I pointed to a young male assigned to the United States who had taken on a body of an African American.

"If we don't like the assignment we've chosen, can we change to another identity?"

"No," I said emphatically. "Your commitment to the identity you have chosen, and the consequences that come with it, is for one year. After one year, you will have one month to decide to permanently remain on Earth with that identity or return to Pleiades." I paused for someone else to raise their hand. "Next question?"

A woman asked, "To what extent are we allowed to use our extra-sensory abilities?"

"Not at all," I replied emphatically. "The reason you are here is to be an influential example of supporting the success and well-being of others, not to draw attention to yourself by displaying paranormal and psychic abilities or creating possibly life-threatening situations." I paused again, waiting for another hand to be raised. Someone did.

"To what extent are we allowed to form close relationships?"

"Friendships only. Nothing beyond." I was definitive with my response, but I knew it was not enforceable. Feelings and emotions that came with the immigrants' human identities would be their greatest challenge to master. Fortunately, with their inherent level of wisdom, the probability of harm occurring to the cause was close to zero—at least I hoped so. After responding to other logistical questions, I decided to talk briefly about feelings and emotions, and to not avoid what I knew would be their greatest challenge.

"I remind you again: you will be challenged most, in the initial stages, by your inability to manage your feelings and emotions. Unfortunately, there was no way you could have prepared for this challenge without the experience of being human. You must practice working on this skill immediately. However, you should be comfortable with your level of mastery in about a month. In the meantime, limit any involved contact with other humans until you have mastered this ability."

There were no further questions. I think it became clear that most of their individual processes of adaptation would occur through the personal experiences of their chosen identities.

Besides giving my welcoming speech, I was also in charge of addressing and assigning a smaller group of highly select Pleiadians. These were individuals who had achieved advanced learning in specific areas that included science, wellness, technology, socialization, competitive games and activities, education, and leadership, as well as having attained a high level of personal mastery in the area of wisdom. They would have a less structured role in global influence. Each would be assigned to one of the four remaining original Pleiadian team members: Tony, the leader of the team and now assigned to Eastern and Western Europe; John, now assigned to the United States and South America; Ravi, assigned to India; and Bin, assigned to the Middle East and Africa. The expanded assignments of these Pleiadian team members were planned to compensate for the three original members who had returned to

Pleiades. I was also in charge of personally tracking the progress of the advanced Pleiadians and handling whatever practical difficulties they encountered.

--- | | | | | ---

As is true of any undertaking of this magnitude, word had begun to leak of alien sightings and even abductions, particularly through social networking and media. Although the news media made light of such rumors through mild humor, the major militaries throughout the world took them quite seriously. Fortunately, most of the exchanges among the Pleiadian immigrants involved psychic communication, which was undetectable by human technology—mainly because security agencies did not believe in the validity of such abilities.

The president had not been informed of the immigration plan, nor had the Pleiadian Council asked for his permission. They correctly believed that he would reject outright any plan for mass immigration from Pleiades. However, as far as the Council was concerned, this was an agreement between them and the four remaining Pleiadian team members—and not negotiable. Tony and John had even suggested to the Council my taking on the role of immigrant coordinator without my knowledge. This suggestion was the key element in convincing the Council to simply reduce the life-force a second time during the Middle East crisis instead of severing it altogether, thus avoiding the extinction of all of humanity.

As the immigration process proceeded and rumors intensified, it became obvious that we would have to inform the president at the earliest opportunity so that he would not be blindsided. More importantly, he needed to be informed so that he could continue to play a crucial role in Earth's transformation—after he accepted the immigration plan as a *fait accompli.*

7

LARA HEADLEY—AN IMMIGRANT'S QUEST

In my role of assigning Pleiadian immigrants throughout the world, it was my responsibility to personally place those with exceptional potential for facilitating human transformation. I remember the first time I met Lara Headley. She was a volunteer with one of the initial immigrant groups to arrive from Pleiades. She was from Alcyone, the largest star of the open cluster system. On Pleiades, she was an advanced associate of the ancient history of our Sun's solar system. This title was akin to a PhD in Earth's educational system. Her favorite subject was the study of the ancient world, as she referred to Earth, because they had undergone a similar stage of evolution on Pleiades centuries before.

The body she had taken on was a middle-aged woman of European descent. It was difficult not to stare when I first saw her, although I tried, unsuccessfully, to not be too obvious. She smiled in return, knowing exactly the impression she had on me. Her gaze was direct, unfettered by any disguise of the emotions she felt. She had either not yet learned or had chosen not to temper the experience of her communications. But something beyond the communication of human biology also occurred:

a mutual, unspoken exchange that we knew each other, possibly from a prior experience. It happened in an *instance*, outside of time, that I wondered if I was simply hallucinating.

"I'm Lara Headley," she said, looking amused as she reached out her hand to me. At first I was reluctant to grasp it, recalling the Chinese duality of danger and opportunity. I'm not sure why. After breaking the spell she seemed to have cast on me, I replied, "I'm Bill Bradley," and reached out to shake her hand firmly. "I will be helping you with your assignment here on Earth."

"I already know my assignment, Dr. Bradley, and my historical heritage. I requested it." She paused briefly to allow me to find her prearranged dossier, and then she continued. "The first record of my family's existence is in France in the Middle Ages, about the year 1225; during the Hundred Years' War; Estienne and Catheline Beaulieu, or Stephen and Katherine in modern translation. It's all there, to the present." She smiled as I quickly sifted through her family's genealogy. "You can see things become a bit fuzzy once my ancestors relocated to southern England and took on their new identity as the Headley family. I think it had something to do with an English officer and a captured French female aristocrat." She smiled. "After many generations, here I am, alive and well."

I waited for her to continue. It was obvious that she was ahead of most of those who volunteered to help save humankind. I had grown accustomed to a spectrum of personalities—some who I knew would not remain, some with a heroic mentality, and a few with an evangelical disposition. Lara was none of these; she was more of a mystery.

She was a statuesque five foot nine, with no obvious country of origin or accent when she spoke. Her English was perfect, as were all other languages she spoke, I later learned. I noted during our handshake that her piercing green eyes shaded to blue-green when an emotion was aroused. Dark auburn hair framed her eyes and her decidedly European facial features. She radiated an outdoorsy look that appeared to be ready for action. Most amusing to me was the perpetual knowing smile she wore, which gave me the impression that she was two or three steps—or perhaps light years—ahead of my next statement or question. I later learned that she was doing a clairvoyant scan of events involving the two of us that had a high probability of occurring.

She finally said that she was assigned to Tony, the French-based leader of the original Pleiadian team. His territory now included Western and Eastern Europe. More importantly, he was the mentor and protector of the president of the United States. Again the feeling of connectivity between us entered my thinking as a result of an intuitive scene that popped into my mind. During my initial channeling sessions with John, he had introduced me to a guide named Lea. The sessions I did with her were designed to help me resolve issues I had with highly competent women in leadership roles. The sessions were humbling, to say the least.

Lara said, "I am sure we will run across each other again, perhaps sooner than you think. You may need my help with a situation in the near future."

I didn't dare ask what situation she was referring to. Besides, those in line behind her had noted the special attention I was devoting to her. I stood, took her hand again, and was lost in her eyes. I managed to blurt out, "I look forward to our working together in the future, Lara Headley."

"And vice versa," she said, again smiling as if she knew something I didn't. She turned and walked away without looking back. The next guy in line was amused by my reaction to Lara. "Can you help me now?" he asked.

- - - | | | | | - - -

Laurenia, aka Lara Headley, evolved within a family community associated with the Alcyone Star of the seven-star Pleiades system. The community consisted of twenty adults and thirty children. These numbers and compositions were considered to be ideal for the learning and care of the Pleiadian children.

The twenty adults composed the Community Guidance team, whose purpose was to cooperatively facilitate the socialization, learning, and well-being of the children. Although all of the children were reproductive offspring of unique, paired cohabiting adults of the community, none of them were considered to be owned by the reproductive pair; neither were any of the adult cohabitants owned by each other according to a legal bond. Rather, they operated out of a code of understanding consistent with their level of consciousness. Various adults were particularly skilled in certain aspects of child-rearing, and these and other skills—which included propensities for discipline, science and technology, wellness and healthcare, competitive games, mentoring and coaching, universal exploration, spirituality, governance, and serving others—were used for any and all of the children, as appropriate.

Socialization involved learning the cognitive and behavioral skills for accepting and constructively adapting to differences within each family as well as those between other communities and the Pleiadian star system. These skills had been mastered by the Pleiadians as they historically evolved through the mental (transformational) and causal (emotional) planes of consciousness. Learning involved the discovery of one's passion and the accelerated development of the competencies to fully express it on behalf of others, as well as to experience the value of contribution and service. Well-being involved the mental, ethereal, and spiritual integration of each child to achieve health, happiness, and success. Ethereal wellness was essential for Pleiadians since they existed in transparent energy bodies.

Within this framework, the greatest societal value was continual learning—instructional, experiential, and facilitative—to achieve expanded degrees of enlightened wisdom, as contrasted with Earth, where technology development and wealth were the most valued societal accomplishments. The various degrees of wisdom achieved by most

Pleiadians required little or no instructional behaviors to live a principle of operation, such as supporting the success and well-being between and among the various inhabitants of the seven-star civilization. This natural way of living was the reason for decreasing the life-force surrounding Earth and the resulting increased number of humans with a high level of wisdom as the key to establishing a dominantly humane civilization—a civilization, it was hoped, that would pose no nuclear threat to the inhabitants of the Pleiades and beyond.

Even as a child, Laurenia was fascinated by the stars, especially the planets associated with the nearby solar system that included Earth. With their advanced technology and extrasensory skills, the Pleiadians had been observing events on Earth for centuries. They had also surmised the dominant consciousness of the planet and knew from their personal experience that earthlings could eventually become a nuclear threat to the inhabitants of Pleiades—at least, as long as the Pleiadian Council allowed the vortex between the two systems to exist. Laurenia had also studied the first expeditions to Earth, circa 1000 BC, and the subsequent numerous emissaries sent to influence the transformation of earthlings from survival to compatibility.

When Laurenia and her senior avatar and mentor began mentoring sessions for Advanced Studies in the History of Earth Civilizations, they began by discussing the failed transformations of both Lemuria and Atlantis, based on the civilizations' fascination with energy and crystals, respectively, as power sources. In both cases, the uncontrolled utilization of the power sources for commercialization resulted in the deterioration of the environment, air and water, as well as the introduction of intractable toxins into their food chain. The result was gradual, but total, extinction. The time between Lemuria and Atlantis, and between Atlantis and the present civilization, was necessary to replenish Earth for subsequent human habitation.

Avatars were Pleiadians who facilitated the acquisition of wisdom. As such, their primary purpose was not only to share information and assist a student's experiential learning but also to facilitate the creation of agents of transformation through the acquisition of wisdom. In preparation for Laurenia's adventure to Earth, her senior avatar began with a discussion of the present human consciousness.

"Laurenia, I am sure you are aware of the prevailing Earth consciousness of domination, control, and power, driven by greed," she said without judgment, simply stating a detached description of what existed.

"Yes, I am."

"You are also aware that this consciousness has existed for more than ten centuries, in spite of the numerous emissaries for transformation we have sent throughout this period."

"Yes, I am," she replied again.

"Many members of the Council consider earthlings to be a lost cause, in spite of our evolutionary connection to them."

Laurenia replied, "I know."

"Then why do you have such an intense interest in sacrificing yourself to what appears to be a hopeless undertaking when you could begin the exploration of more advanced and civilized planes of consciousness?"

"My interest is simple. There are presently earthlings who are part of my spiritual family: the Guardians."

A spiritual family was a group of nonphysical entities with virtually identical spheres of wisdom (as measured by energy of vibration) bound by a common purpose. The purpose of the Guardians was to assist civilizations that were struggling to transform to a more advanced reality, which was required for their continued existence. The Guardians did so by taking on a bodily form of the struggling reality and assisting their process of transformation.

"Earth is at a critical transition point. It will probably go the way of Lemuria and Atlantis, unless we are able to balance the earthlings' fascination with technology with sensible management. At present, their priority is to convert their new technological advancements into weapons for security, destruction, and AI robotics rather than the more efficient management and functioning of their societies."

Laurenia's senior avatar sighed deeply. She was aware that once Laurenia had made a decision, there was no changing her mind. "Remember, the earthlings must learn, most of all, that they reap what they sow as well as what they do not sow, and that the acceptance of 100 percent responsibility and accountability are concepts necessary for bringing about the resolution of their dilemma."

"Thank you," Laurenia said. "I am clear about my objective. Fortunately, they don't fully view their situation as hopeless, as yet. I am confident we will not fail."

8

||||||||||||||||||||||||||||||||||||||||||||||||||||||||||||||||||||||||||||||||||||||||||||||||||||||||||||||||||||||||||||

THE BRIEFING

Tony sent a short communique to the president informing him that they should meet at his earliest opportunity. The president surmised that such a communique was unusual since most of their meetings were initiated at his request, not Tony's. The president hoped that the meeting wouldn't involve psychic inscription—one's psychic epitaph, such as a naturally existing state of goodness—since he and his staff were consumed with promoting the Seven Principles of Social Equality. In fact, they had brought in Frances Wilkerson and Gail Erickson, two of the Rebels, to assist them.

The Rebels was the top secret team chosen by the president to assist him in worldwide implementation of the Renaissance Revolution, a global plan for creating a new world order dominated by compatible existence. The Seven Principles were the framework for implementing that project. Frances and Gail were the team experts at implementing practical cognitive and metaphysical strategies for planetary transformation.

The nearer their agreed-upon time approached, the more apprehensive the president became. He suspected that he was becoming more paranoid with each passing day, ever since the whole Quest thing had begun several years ago. He just hoped he could make it through the end of his second term with some degree of sanity before he passed the baton to the next individual crazy enough to want to become president of the United States. In fact, what he feared most, given the Pleiadian situation, was someone who had no capacity to relate to one of Earth's nearest star neighbors. Just then, Tony teleported into the Lincoln Room at the White House, where the president was awaiting his arrival.

Tony's arrival startled the president, who had been thinking about an emergency meeting with a national high-tech group. The group had implied that the country was facing a serious economic crisis, which was their usual position when their financial interests were at stake. On the other hand, the president had learned long ago that requested meetings with him were rarely a harbinger of good news. Most of his executives typically chose not to make decisions about such meetings, for fear of a major faux pas or news that no one wanted to deliver to the president in person.

"Good evening, Ted," Tony said, upbeat. "I see you are in a reflective mood again, and I've only just arrived."

"Hi, Tony. Yeah, I was just thinking that most requested meetings rarely bring tidings of great joy. They usually bring new problems, often more difficult than the ones I already have to deal with."

"Well, I do have something new. I don't consider it to be a problem, but I guess it's all in how you look at it. However, it's definitely not something you have to resolve, if that makes you feel any better."

The president laughed. "Come on, Tony. That sounds like a riddle." Tony began laughing too, although he guessed that the president would not be amused by the news he was about to deliver.

"Okay," the president said, "I give up. What is it?"

Tony figured the direct approach was best; no use working up to it. "Mr. President, the Pleiadian Council agreed to a Pleiadian plan for immigration to Earth."

"A *what?!*" the president shouted. He wasn't sure if what he had heard was correct, let alone grasped its reality. "An immigration plan? To Earth?" he stammered.

"Yes, that's what I said." Tony's first inclination was to smile at the president's reaction, but he knew that such a response could have a permanent negative influence on their relationship. He continued more seriously, as an emissary instead of a personal friend, teacher, or protector. "Actually, the first phase is complete."

"How do you immigrate from one system to another?" the president asked, still in a state of denial. "It's not like simply sailing around the world."

Tony wanted to say no, it's actually faster, but he again withheld his comments to allow the president to continue his struggle with the acceptance of an unbelievable event. "Using the vortex between Pleiades and Earth is actually faster than sailing around the world. It is how we have been traveling back and forth for some centuries now."

The reality of what Tony was saying began to sink in as the president slowly accepted it as having already occurred. "You mean to tell me that your people from Pleiades have already arrived here on Earth—and are placed around the world?"

"Yes," Tony replied. "The other part of the agreement was to use Dr. Bill Bradley for placement."

"How many?" asked the president, still in shock—and ignoring Bradley's involvement for the time being.

"One hundred."

The president was not sure what question he wanted to ask next, so he paused for a moment to process what he had been told. Finally he asked, "Who was this agreement made with?" He immediately suspected the Russians of such a conspiracy. Without waiting for Tony's response, he continued with another question. "Why didn't your people ask my permission, as leader of the free world?"

"Because they believe you would have refused."

"You're damn right I would have refused!" said the president angrily. "What right do they have invading our planet?"

"After centuries of observation and dispatching emissaries to Earth, the Council concluded that earthlings are collectively either incapable or unwilling to create a planet that is not a direct threat to their civilization," Tony replied.

The president was stopped momentarily, not knowing how to reply with an explanation that countered Tony's statement.

"However," Tony continued, detached, "the Pleiadian immigrants have no intention of taking over Earth. They are here as emissaries to help achieve the Quest and the Renaissance Revolution, both of which you support."

"Then what happens?"

"Then the Council will observe the progress made and increase the flow of the life-force." Tony wanted to sound as encouraging as possible with respect to achieving the Quest and having the life-force increased again.

The president regained his composure and said, "This is our fight, not yours. We didn't ask for your emissaries to become pretend earthlings."

Tony was struck by the fact that most humans viewed transformation as a fight involving combat and conquering oneself rather than selectively giving up one's survival mentality and experiencing humility. He patiently and compassionately responded, "The Council felt that humans have come very close to a nuclear exchange on several occasions. Once such an event occurs, as you know, it will annihilate the total Pleiadian civilization without warning. They have no escape plan. Would you expect them to take your word that a nuclear holocaust is not going to happen on Earth, or would you expect them to be preemptive in their own defense?"

The president was stopped momentarily. Then he asked, "Who was this so-called agreement made with? The Russians, I presume."

"No, not the Russians. Me and John," Tony said.

"You and John!" exploded the president. "Are you and John taking over the decisions involving this planet?"

"No, Mr. President, we are just trying our best to stave off the total annihilation of human life, including our own. That was the alternative of the Pleiadian Council. There was no negotiation involved," Tony explained levelly, leaving out Dr. Bradley's participation as the clincher to the deal.

The president was breathing heavily. Everything Tony said made perfect sense at the mental level, but it was total nonsense at the emotional level. He knew he would have handled any ultimatum as a threat, and probably created a dire situation that would have jeopardized the entire planet, not just the United States.

The president did not reply. He was still struggling with immigration as an invasion of the planet. Now he understood the rumors of aliens among the population in the news. After a long silence, he said, "I have to think about this," although he was clearly still absorbing the fact that the Pleiadian immigrants were already dispersed globally and were probably impossible to identify or capture. There was also the perplexing question of how he would send them back.

He was slowly coming around to the reality of the situation. To him, the most important questions were how he could preserve the continued existence of those remaining, and what was going to be required of humans in terms of change—or more likely, transformation. He recalled a cartoon he once saw in a newspaper titled *International Conference*. In the cartoon, two seminar descriptions were on side-by-side easels. One read, "Happiness through Self-Actualization—FREE." The other read, "Happiness through Greater Wealth—$500." The Self-Actualization seminar had no one in line, while the Wealth seminar had a meandering line into the lobby. That pretty much summed up the challenge the president believed he faced with achieving the Quest, at least in America.

Tony waited as he silently observed the president's progression through Elisabeth Kübler-Ross's five stages of grief: denial, anger, bargaining, depression, and acceptance. Then the president said, almost in a whisper, "Thank you, Tony. Let's meet again tomorrow, after I've had a chance to absorb this; same time."

In the next instant, Tony was gone.

--- | | | | | ---

The president still felt angry and depressed as he recounted the events of his meeting with Tony. He was angry with Tony for assuming that he and John had the authority to make decisions for Earth—not that he could have done any better, even as president. As he reflected deeper inside himself, he was really angry at his loss of control of the entire situation when it appeared to matter most. As hard as he had worked over the past three years to create the change necessary for human survival, it just kept slipping away.

In his state of depression, he decided he needed someone to simply be with him, someone with whom he could share his frustrations as well as his debilitating emotional state. There was only one person he could reach out to for such support. He called her on her private line.

After several rings she answered, noting the identity of the caller. "Hello, Ted. What's up?"

"I need you."

She immediately sensed that he was in a dire state of anguish. Instead of asking him what was wrong, she replied, "I will be there within the hour."

"Thanks, Dana."

9

||||||||||||||||||||||||||||||||||||||||||||||||||||||||||||||||||||||||||||||||||||||||||||||||||||||||||||||||||||||||||||||||

THE CHAIRMAN

As the sun set lazily in the western sky, casting streaks of black, red, and deep orange shadows beneath the low-hanging clouds, Karl sat contentedly at his French Provincial desk. He sipped delightedly from the snifter containing Hennessy Beauté du Siècle Cognac. This was his favorite time of day, when he could reflect on the present state of affairs and decide on his future direction.

The recently arrived immigrants were beginning to have a small but significant influence on the people where they were assigned throughout the world. He had to admit that it was a stroke of genius to integrate them into the most spiritually inclined countries on the planet, because those were the locations that most likely consisted of survivors who were receptive to the message of personal transformation.

He was least concerned about those assigned to places of extreme conflict, such as the Middle East. He surmised, in keeping with the conclusions of prior Pleiadian emissaries, that such regions were hope-less. He had often wondered where he would be if he had not given in to his frustrations and prevailed, as Tony had. But it was too late now; his directives as Chairman of the Consortium, quite outside of moral and legal boundaries, had sealed his fate.

After refilling his snifter, he reflected on the initial years after secretly leaving the Pleiadian emissary program and taking on the new identity of Dr. Karl Gustav Christen, with a PhD in microbiology. Soon thereafter, he faded into the fabric and established his research studies involving a cure for cancer, which eventually led to the partnership with the private university in the principality of Liechtenstein. The Pleiadian Council had launched an extensive search to locate Karl, using his unique vibrational frequency, and return him to Pleiades. These searches were conducted around Earth at night to avoid hysteria about UFO sightings. However, detection required direct line of sight, and Karl was never located. The search was eventually abandoned.

What Karl hadn't expected was that the hundredth-monkey effect would come into play, in which nearby locales began to adopt ways of thinking and operating similar to the areas where the new immigrants were assigned, without the necessity of physical contact. In other words, when a group consciousness reached a certain critical mass, ideas and practices were spontaneously adopted by similar neighboring groups, as predicted by the work of Rupert Sheldrake involving morphogenetic fields. Although most scientists on Earth struggled with the credibility of this phenomenon, it was part of the general study of consciousness taught in elementary learning on Pleiades. Fortunately, the changes occurring in the advanced communities were still in the initial stages and had not become permanently embedded into the consciousness of a majority of those on Earth. And Karl believed they never would.

He remembered his early learning classes on Pleiades, where it was emphasized that behavior modification, if committed to and mentally intensified in confronting and challenging situations, was a practical means of achieving personal transformation. But such transformation also required a sustained and dedicated effort. So far, people in the immigrant areas were in the initial stages, which could probably be reversed if they were confronted with their well-known practiced values relating to human equality. The key to arresting and reversing any progress involving second-level thinking was to play on the fears that they would predictably experience, which appeared to threaten the safety and security of level-one thinking, even if such thinking was an illusion. The point was, as long as a level-one consciousness prevailed, the inhabitants of Earth needed to be overseen on behalf of their own continued existence. This was the work of the Consortium.

Karl possessed the major qualities of a charismatic personality and the ability to connect with people on an emotional level, particularly when communicating with the masses. Humans were most receptive to one-liners that appealed to their sense of entitlement and security, such as "let's rebuild together," "let's reestablish our place in the world," and "let's recapture our greatness as a people." He incorrectly assumed that most humans lacked the basic nature of resilience to proactively respond to tragedy, regardless of their level of awareness.

Karl had noted that, in truth, most humans responded in exceptionally humane and supportive ways to major crises, as though a completely different personality were revealed. However, once a crisis was addressed or the status quo was reestablished, they tended to revert to the comfort of level-one ways of functioning. The return to level-one operation was clear evidence that a transformation in consciousness had not occurred; rather, they reverted to a general lack of responsibility for the state of their lives and a corresponding lack of commitment to establish a more inclusive way of living. They principally sought to blame their leaders for their demise during difficult times—if not before the fact, then certainly after. As such, the two pandemics were decidedly difficult to deal with on all levels of human consciousness: physical, mental, emotional, and spiritual.

This was the state of affairs prior to the two Great Tragedies, and the reason the Chairman had established the Consortium in the first place—to have people put their trust in the hands of those who would solve their problems and provide the guidance for their overall well-being.

Karl surmised that the deeply ingrained, leader-led syndrome that was genetically passed from generation to generation was so firmly embedded in the human psyche that they would be lost and chaotic if their fate were left to themselves. It was the major reason he believed that any system that depended on people becoming sufficiently responsible and empowered was ultimately doomed to fail. Being led was simply the nature of the majority of humans. It was foolish and naïve to believe that the dominant majority could achieve a higher level of evolution like the Pleiadians had. They would continually seek an external source for their liberation. At present, the most viable candidate for that source was a new miracle drug coupled with surgically precise invasive technology. The strategy was to communicate this message to the remaining survivors of the two pandemics, a task that he had assigned to the Neustadt Consortium Communications Center.

The reports he had received from various countries around the world indicated varying degrees of success in terms of food distribution and spontaneous neighborhood group meetings. He would allow the most progressive countries a measure of success and then unleash his plan, which would have a devastating effect on the progress made thus far. The blow would be too great for them to recover.

In his role as leader of the European Recovery, Karl would continue to extend his message of strong leadership to Eastern Europe, starting with the NATO countries, including those bordering the Russian Federation. He believed that Russia would be difficult to bring into the fold, but not as difficult as orchestrating the downfall of the United States, which was still his number one objective.

10

CONNECTING

Adapting to the Earth plane was initially traumatic for most of the Pleiadian immigrants. They experienced varying degrees of difficulty adapting to human existence, depending on the locales of their chosen assignments and their levels of preparation. The Renaissance Communities were by far the most hospitable and progressive assignments. Many of their practices and systems of operation were similar to those of Pleiades, and many of the inhabitants were presumed to be descendants of those having the Pleiadian code. The immigrants described residing in these communities as living with kindred souls.

Prior to the two Great Tragedies, they had unanimously experienced living in the broader society as lonely, separate, and threatening. They had lived in constant fear because of their strong connection to the second-level compatible plane of human evolution, and were often mistakenly considered as gay, lesbian, or some other gender orientation because of their peaceful demeanor.

Arturo Alvarado was one of the "advanced associate" immigrants, in the cadre with Lara Headley. He was assigned to a small upstate Minnesota town technically overseen by John, who was in charge of the North and South Americas transformation. Arturo traced his

Earth-based family lineage back to the original Pleiadian explorers of the Greek Isles, and ultimately to a Spanish family who had migrated to the United States from Badajoz Province, Spain.

Arturo's Pleiadian name was Arcturus, the name assigned to him on Pleiades because it was the civilization of his origin. His Arcturian name was Aeschyleus. His assignment on Pleiades had been similar to the present one on Earth: to assist the transformation of the Pleiadians to the highest spiritual level in the Milky Way Galaxy. The Arcturians were the most advanced civilization in the galaxy in terms of technology and spiritual development. They had long ago transcended spaceships for galactic exploration but still used them for warp drive or superluminal travel—travel beyond the speed of light.

The Milky Way life-force, an expression of absolute pure consciousness that originated from the Arcturian blue planet (as yet undiscovered by humans) orbiting Arcturus—red giant sun in the constellation of Boötes—and was fed to Pleiades and numerous other civilizations throughout the galaxy. As a result, the Arcturians were also vulnerable, via the intergalactic network, to the radioactive fallout that would be projected into space by an Earth holocaust. The Arcturians possessed extremely high-frequency energy bodies similar to the Pleiadians but had never been human in their evolution.

On Pleiades, Arturo mastered the area of socialization with a specialization in group integration—the seamless connecting and functioning of groups with disparate ways of thinking, organizing, and living. During his short time in Minnesota, he had taken on a temporary appointment as director of human capital for a township. He had personally chosen this title because of his intense interest in people development and collective performance. It was a catch-all title for a variety of duties that brought him in constant contact with influential people throughout the community.

After learning about the presence of the nearby North American Renaissance Community, which consisted principally of Americans, he decided to initiate a plan for the integration of the township and the community residents. Similar processes had been occurring globally with widely varying degrees of success. From Arturo's perspective, at some point the American Renaissance Community would have to become part of the broader American society, and the broader US society could learn more humanistic, self-governing ways of functioning.

When he first floated the idea among the township leaders, the opposition had ranged from mild to strong; those in opposition viewed the communities as updated hippie colonies. On the other hand, the Renaissance Community was enthusiastic about the idea. In truth, they missed being part of the country of their origin but not the dominantly survival-driven ways it operated. Arturo wasn't at all sure he could bring the two groups together so as to begin functioning as an integrated community, but he was certainly determined to try.

In spite of opposition, the group agreed to meet and explore the idea of connecting.

- - - | | | | | - - -

The first meeting between the Renaissance and township groups included five leaders from each community. Arturo introduced himself, although he had previously met separately with both groups to set up the meeting. Then he began his formal statements.

"I want to personally thank each of you for your willingness to attend this meeting. It has the potential to be a milestone for how we move forward into the future in an uncertain world." The environment was tense as both groups began to size up each other. Some stared, some smiled, and some were disinterested. This was the first point at which the attendees were aware that the township group consisted of all males and the Renaissance group consisted of three females and two males.

"I sincerely hope we've come here to find common ground for what we all hold dear, and to simultaneously create what is necessary to accommodate the changes brought on by the pandemics." Arturo paused, smiling in an attempt to have each of the team members relax to whatever extent possible.

"Why don't we have everyone introduce themselves, share their greatest anxiety about this meeting, and suggest a positive outcome we might achieve together?"

The team members took turns responding to the questions Arturo posed. The responses ran the full gamut of considerations, from negatives—such as distrust and a waste of time—to positives, such as leaving the meeting as friends, and understanding and accepting each other's point of view.

Arturo noted a significant reduction of tension as a result of their mutual sharing. He smiled in an attempt to further reduce the remaining tension between the two groups. "I have titled this first meeting 'Differences' as a description to learn about difficulties we may have and opportunities to resolve them together. I specifically chose this title because I feel the word may help us move beyond the underlying reason we struggle with achieving permanent solutions. That is, we are not trying to solve problems per se but to resolve differences in the way we view our lives that will allow us to serve the best interests of everyone involved, not just the majority. In addition, this will put less emphasis on a right or wrong perspective." Arturo paused so that everyone could understand his explanations. "Any questions about this point?" he asked. The room was silent.

"We will devote the first hour to discovering the significant differences that exist in the ways we operate and function. Then we will take a ten-minute break, and conclude with a one-hour discussion and summary. I'll try to ensure that everyone gets an opportunity to contribute their ideas during our conversation. Okay, let's get started."

In the silence that followed, the township team looked at Will Favor, their mayor. Will, in turn, looked slightly embarrassed that his team so obviously deferred to him. "We've heard of ways you operate that are quite different from what's traditionally worked for us," Will said to the Renaissance group.

A Renaissance member asked, "Can you be more specific?"

"Yeah, we operate the same as we did before the Great Tragedies, using the model of the US Constitution and the Bill of Rights. That's why I'm the legally elected mayor. We've heard rumors that you operate in a less structured way."

Ling Miller, an adopted Chinese immigrant to the United States, asked politely, "Do you make most of the decisions about how the township operates and functions?"

"I seek the advice and guidance of others. But for the most part, yes."

"We tend to take the opposite approach," she said. "We've found that when people have a cooperative attitude, most of their differences can be resolved between them."

Before they could further pursue that point, another Renaissance team member asked, "Do you believe people have to primarily be led or be called upon to create shared leadership among them?"

"I'm not sure I understand what you mean," Will said levelly.

The Renaissance team member didn't respond but instead allowed the uncomfortable empty space of silence to fill with building tension. When the silence became deafening, another township member asked, "Do you mean decision-making should be left primarily to the people involved?"

"What's your opinion?" asked the Renaissance team member.

"A question with a question," the townsman noted, and then replied, "For the most part, yes. Especially in a small town like ours."

Ling smiled almost imperceptibly. "But what happens when a decision involves all of us, like education, local taxes, and community services? Or even gun control? Then what?"

Another Renaissance member asked, "Do you think a solution starts with people, information, facts, and serving the best interests of everyone affected by a decision? What form of decision-making do you propose be used?"

Then a community member, who had been listening intently up to this point, responded, "Majority or consensus? One is simply a number count. The other integrates both majority and minority points of view. Much has changed since the pandemics and the population reductions. In fact, without the pandemics, we probably wouldn't be having this meeting. We are beginning to realize that we must also change. At this point, we're not sure how." He and Ling exchanged almost imperceptible signs of agreement that were like a bridge across the Grand Canyon.

The groups engaged one another on a number of different issues with respect to a structure of governing, without attempting to find solutions or create agreement. Before they realized it, the hour was up. Arturo interrupted and said, "Let's take a ten-minute break and return for the second hour."

When they reconvened, Arturo said, "I'd like to share a few observations before we begin our conversation again. I am encouraged by the exchange we've had so far. I think our emphasis on viewpoints, instead of right or wrong, or even precedent, has allowed us to understand each other—not to imply that we've agreed on anything we've discussed." Everyone smiled to varying degrees. "In this sense, much of our exchange has involved questions rather than answers. Although we've discussed several critical issues and a few suggested solutions, we have not discussed the underlying common beliefs—sometimes called the dominant group consciousness—that a group has in common. More precisely, the ways we are consciously and unconsciously programmed to think." After this statement, the faces of a few townsmen clearly showed discomfort. They were beginning to wonder where this line of conversation was headed.

Arturo continued. "For example, if a group dominantly believes healthcare is a right instead of a privilege, the challenge will involve how to provide adequate healthcare for everyone within the community. If there is strong representative opposition to this fundamental belief, then it will be very difficult to achieve adequate healthcare for everyone.

Typically, arguments go on forever, particularly if there are special interests groups involved in the final outcome. Somehow, the health of the community is lost in the discussion. The point I would like to make is that the source of reaching representative consensus—ensuring majority and minority viewpoints are included in the adopted system—is the underlying consciousness of the group. Either chaotic opposition or cooperative resolution will follow naturally."

The group responded to Arturo's statement with silence. Arturo understood that most groups rarely had discussions at the depth of differing underlying assumptions. Most resolutions of differences were dealt with at a level of compromised action that involved give and take, where few were pleased with the outcome but chose to live with it without commitment.

In order to make his point more relevant and get the group involved, Arturo said, "Let's take food, shelter, and clothing, for example. Assuming these are the basic necessities for survival, are they fundamental rights that all members of a group should be provided?"

"That depends on a lot of factors," replied one of the townsmen. "Does the person work? Does the person contribute to society? Does the person pay any taxes? It's almost impossible to answer a question like that without much more information."

One of the women from the Renaissance team raised her hand, and Arturo recognized her. She began, "In our Renaissance Community, an overwhelming majority believe that adequate food, shelter, and clothing are necessities that all members should have, as a given principle of human existence. Therefore, most of our attention is devoted to how we ensure that everyone's needs are met. We also discuss how everyone can and should contribute. As a result, we have found little need for copious laws, rules, and regulations. This way of being feels more natural than any other way we've lived before."

"That's unrealistic!" one of the townsmen shouted, clearly agitated. "That way of operating only breeds laziness, dependency, and entitlement, not to mention that it sounds like socialism at best, and bordering on communism at worst."

Intense tension suddenly gripped the room. Arturo didn't know what direction to take. The silence persisted for more than thirty seconds. Then Ling Miller smiled at the townsman who had just spoken, and directed her comments to him. "In the initial stages of our community, we had intense discussions, as you have just expressed. After everyone commented, we had a decision to make: whether we were going to be imprisoned by the past or take a leap of faith into a whole new way of thinking and operating—without all the answers in advance. One thing we were all sure of: no homeless people, no starvation, and few, if any, of the innumerable problems they cause." Again an uncomfortable silence gripped the room.

"What happened? I am very interested in knowing. You seem to have weathered that storm," Will Favor said.

"Yes, we did," Ling replied. "We decided that meeting everyone's basic needs was the essence of what it meant to be human, of becoming a human being instead of just being a human who is driven by a scarcity way of thinking."

"What about those who chose not to work?" he asked.

"With respect to food, shelter, and clothing for everyone, a smaller percentage of people were unwilling to work than the percentage who were on welfare systems in the way we had previously operated. Eventually, even they were strongly influenced by the group to contribute, which we could never have predicted."

Again silence followed while everyone processed Ling's statements.

"Then what?" Will persisted.

Ling smiled again and replied, "We had to determine the overarching rules that would guide how human beings would live and work together. The context we adopted was, 'We care about each other's health, happiness, and well-being.' If we behaved consistent with that statement, then everything would take care of itself. At the beginning, that was pretty much it. We are still far from a Utopia, but we believe we are on the best track to compatibly take care of everyone."

Will Favor looked confused, his face a mix of both doubt and hope.

Ling added, "Compatibility, for us, means we resolve our differences without needing to resort to polarization and violence."

"What kind of people would be willing to live that way?" a townsman asked.

"The kind who survived the two pandemics and learned from them," she replied.

I I

RECEPTION

"**W**ell, it's been six months!" I shouted to the gathering of a hundred immigrants, even though I had a lavaliere microphone. We had decided to debrief the immigrants as one large group. "I congratulate you all for making it this far. Only six more months to decide whether you will remain with us or return home."

Someone shouted from the audience, "Dr. Bradley, how do you know some of us have not already decided?" A ground swell of hooting and clapping followed his question. The group appeared to be in great spirits in spite of their experiences of living in an ancient civilization that operated with a consciousness significantly different from their own. The environment reminded me of a Silicon Valley town hall meeting.

"The major objectives of our meeting are to get a sense of your collective experiences, hear your recommendations for going forward into the final six months, and evaluate how likely we are to achieve our goal of establishing the Renaissance Revolution."

"Is that all?" someone shouted.

"I thought that an advanced civilization of immigrants from Pleiades could easily accomplish that," I replied with a smile.

"It would, if we were allowed to use all or even some of our advanced abilities," someone shouted.

"That's a good point," I replied. "We'll have to discuss that further. Our original intent was for each of you to be like other humans in terms of their present level of cognitive evolution."

"Why is that?" someone else asked.

"So that we humans wouldn't think you have come to save us and, as a result, take no responsibility for the dominant way we live among one another. From the beginning, your role has been to assist us in transforming our dominant consciousness; otherwise, nothing will change about us. Does that make sense?" I asked.

There were mostly nods of agreement but with significant uncertainty. I finally said, "Let's put the issue about using your advanced abilities on hold and come back to it later." After a pause, I continued. "Let's turn our attention to the first question. Your experiences? Why don't we take turns? State your selected name and locale before sharing your comments."

"Jamie Shannon, Ireland. Family is everything to this locale. However, if you move beyond the boundaries of family, life-threatening conflicts occur easily, not to mention the polarization and possible hostility between Ireland and England."

"What did you personally experience, Jamie, when trying to be a positive influence for compatibility?" I asked.

"I experienced an intense emotional assault like nothing I have before. Of course, you know we are still trying to master the emotional thing. An Irish girl wanted to marry an English soldier who was posted in my locale. I thought love was the best thing that could happen to overcome fear. I was wrong. I was almost killed when I tried to intervene for love."

A profusion of hands went up with Jamie's last statement. I didn't have to choose anyone. There was a kind of psychic agreement about who would speak next.

A dark-skinned guy with ruddy features stood and said, "Walt Riesman, the Middle East. I don't know if anything could have prepared me for how women are treated in the locale I was assigned to; I saw everything from exaltation to total suppression and acts of death. I thought of our home, of how women are source. Women are the wisdom holders. Women provide the spiritual connection to that which keeps us centered as one. Perhaps I'm missing something, but in my locale, it was the opposite of how we view the role of women. How can we possibly expect to create a consciousness of compatibility? I am honestly confused. Unless, of course, that's what women in these locales want."

Another hand went up. "I am Anna Winstrom. Sweden. I worked for a high-spirited public official who is well respected throughout Europe. She often sought my opinion about the equality of women in society."

"And what did you tell her?" I asked.

"I told her that my experience was that equality, for anyone, began with a sense of equality from within oneself, and that once this realization was firmly accepted and nonverbally communicated, no one else had a choice about accepting that reality—regardless of how he or she chose to behave or react."

"And how did she respond?"

"Confused at first, but then a knowing smile spread across her face, as if she had been practicing this way of being all along. I thought, if she could do with others what we had just done together, compatibility was definitely a possible reality." There was silence afterward, as though no one wanted to follow Anna's remarks.

A strong voice came from the back of the room. "Hannah Strong, the US. I was very moved by Anna's comments. Then a thought popped into my mind. Perhaps women are the key elements in our quest for compatibility. I don't know how this might be accomplished, but someone like Anna's boss could be a significant advocate for transformation of both women and men." Hannah suddenly realized that her comment was spontaneous. If she had thought in advance about all she had just shared, it probably would have gone unsaid. But when she got to the heart of the matter, she felt that women had a significant role to play in bringing about human transformation.

Then a quiet-spoken but confident young woman raised her hand. I acknowledged her by a slight nod of my head.

"Germaine Wellesley, Australia. If women are to play such an important role as we have proposed, then I have a question to ask."

"And what is the question, Germaine?" I asked.

"Why are women more vulnerable to character assassination than men? From my short experience here, almost anything a woman is accused of is taken as truth until she can prove otherwise, whereas accusations about men have to be proven by the accuser when a woman is involved." Germaine paused briefly and then continued. "My point is this: if women are to play a crucial role in bringing about global change, how can we be successful if our credibility can be so easily compromised?"

Germaine's question was followed by an eerie silence, as the men in the group began to examine their experiences of the underlying perceptions about equality or, God forbid, the superiority of men over women.

Several more individuals shared their experience, but my interpretation, in general, of what they said was that progress was slow but positive. At this point, I suggested they engage in informal conversations among themselves.

- - - | | | | | - - -

When we resumed, it was clear to everyone in the group that we had embarked on a journey more difficult than we had imagined. Perhaps the idea that the average person would respond to this call to action was an unrealistic pipe dream. Even when revolutions occurred, what evolved from the underlying dominant consciousness was different in form but only temporarily better than what had previously existed. Change without a transformation in consciousness would lead us into the endless cycle we humans had been repeating for centuries. And whatever character flaws we possessed would continue to persist.

I continued the session by suggesting that we needed to push the envelope, with an emphasis on actions that could result in irreversible change, something that would create the anxiety and urgency within the group that the average human experienced.

A tall, imposing figure who had not been present during the first part of the debrief stood at the back of the meeting room. He exuded a commanding energy that captured everyone's undivided attention, even before he spoke. Arturo began almost in a whisper so that those of us at the front had to strain to hear him. Then he gradually increased the volume of his words.

"I don't think we fully understand the gravity of the question you are posing," he said reverently.

"What do you mean?" I asked.

Arturo's eyes blazed. His body emanated a soft glow as he replied. "We are discussing the future evolution of humankind, human or machine—in essence, either the conscious evolution of both or simply defaulting into task-oriented automaton. A unilateral, survival-driven tract will eventually evolve a machine with a consciousness that dominantly exists today."

"And the alternative?" I asked, even though I could guess his response.

"A human-driven tract, with an emphasis on personal transformation, will eventually evolve a human with extraordinary physical and mental abilities, similar to advanced civilizations we refer to as spiritual. It's that simple. What's important to understand is that we are establishing the blueprint for the next-generation advanced species that will control the destiny of Earth—whether human/cyborg or android."

Stunned silence filled the room as the gathering began to get a glimpse of what Arturo was saying. He continued. "The rate at which technology is evolving is more staggering than most of us realize, beyond personal smart devices. The inhabitants of Earth are mostly, but not completely, unaware that the development and applications of advanced AI devices involve decisions that are being made for them—and I am sure most of you are aware of where that is headed. I suggest we advise humans to think twice about those who sell them the idea of the wonder of robots. In some arenas, robotic technology is being developed as the forerunner of machines void of humanity."

I stood there, stunned, and wondered how could I have been so naïve about what was going on let alone the short- and long-term implications. The signs were plainly displayed in movies, television, video games, and most of all, by those who reported the news and the edited interpretations of events.

Arturo broke the silence and concluded, "This is the real reason we have been sent to Earth: to help save the humanity of their species—if they so choose—and ensure that it endures, even as the inevitable development of technology continues to exponentially explode. The preservation of humanity is synonymous with its true evolution to higher levels of consciousness."

PART THREE

THE CONSORTIUM

12

||||||||||||||||||||||||||||||||||||||||||||||||||||||||||||||||||||||||||||||||||||||||||||||||||||||||||||||||||||||||||

ISOLIERUNG

The Chairman of the Consortium smiled to himself as he sat in his villa in northern Liechtenstein, overlooking the valley below. It was going to be easier than he had planned. He was reading the international edition of *The New York Times* after scanning an article on the internet. The mood of the United States was strongly veering toward nationalism, particularly in light of the fear associated with southern hemisphere immigration, as many of the Western European countries were experiencing. The plight of most of the poorer nations south of the equator had worsened as a result of the two pandemics. The United States was enfolding on itself in terms of its own self-interest, particularly in maintaining a viable middle class.

As the middle class continued to erode into greater survival mode, a significant percentage of the population had begun looking to the federal government for relief. Most of the population wanted jobs, as promised by the congressional leadership, not handouts. After all, the mantra used by the successful party to sweep the congressional election was "Jobs for the Middle Class." Meanwhile, the laws that were passed, almost without public notice and described as conservative, still failed to produce more jobs for the majority of middle-class workers, particularly those with minimal IT skills. No one had bothered to tell the middle class that they had to reinvent themselves in terms of evolving technology and progressive management systems fostered by the Millennial and the 2020 generations.

The Chairman chuckled to himself about the state of affairs in the United States. He reminded himself that great nations were rarely, if ever, defeated by an outside force if they remained united. He seriously wondered if the United States had ever truly been united, except in war. Its population of people of color, including recent immigrants, exceeded 45 percent of its total population, and was growing at an accelerated rate compared to the historical majority population. He wondered when, if ever, the United States would truly transform to racial and cultural inclusion—not merely through greater access and participation but in the fundamental acceptance of human equality for all people. He doubted it. After all, no other civilization in history had ever done so. He concluded that maybe it was just a genetic factor of the human psyche— not only the desire to be superior to someone else in some way but also the life-confirming necessity to do so.

Implementing "Project Isolation" within the present American state of turmoil would not only achieve business, economic, and political isolation of the United States from the rest of the world, it might also accelerate the decline of the president's popularity, and hence, appease his revenge.

- - - | | | | | - - -

Shortly after the last Consortium Board meeting several months earlier, Sanjay Krishnamurti returned to India to begin establishing Project Isolation by increased partnering with Western Europe. Since the British had colonized India throughout the nineteenth and the first half of the twentieth centuries, underlying hostility still remained about the suppression and the measures that had triggered the independence of India in 1947, shortly after the end of World War II.

Sanjay began establishing economic relationships with France and Germany, as suggested by the Chairman. Both Western European countries were beginning to establish widespread competition with America for the partnership Sanjay had in mind. His plan was to provide Indian graduates for European employ in high-tech industries and an expanding Indian customer base for their new high-tech products. This approach to economic and business partnerships encountered little or no resistance as America continued to withdraw into itself in terms of selected global political partnerships.

The obvious result was a deceleration in the exceptional engineering and computer graduate pipeline from India, as well as the reciprocal decrease in customer base with the second-largest country on the planet. Even the recent East Indian graduates employed in the United States had begun moving back to India because of greater opportunities for accelerated advancement. Western Europeans also proposed investing, through European funding, in engineering and high-tech operations owned and operated by East Indians.

The ultimate objective was to create a seamless business and economic system, and an integration of cultures and cultural exchange. This business transformation in mindset had begun with the large influx of refugees into Western Europe in the early twenty-first century. The Western Europeans decided that many southern hemisphere populations had suffered the ravages of poverty long enough. It was time to include them as a valuable human resource, particularly after the population reduction created by the two Great Tragedies.

Sanjay reasoned that such a progressive approach was simply a reconfirmation of a future in which everyone prospered sufficiently to warrant optimism regarding having adequate resources for most of the surviving population. One of the primary objectives was to stem the tide of mass immigration. This approach was the opposite of that taken by America, who had always been a world leader and influencer. They had apparently decided to become more isolationist in an expanding, globally interdependent world.

The new Chinese board member, Li Yong Wang, was the nephew of Zhang Wei Wang. Zhang Wei had been a member of the Billionaire Club during the early part of the twenty-first century. The club had attempted—and failed—to have the president of the United States assassinated. Although Zhang Wei had voted to oppose the assassination of the president, he was considered an accomplice by association. When the president activated his Special Projects Team and approved the assignment of a "deep black operative"—who was officially dead and buried in Arlington National Cemetery—to exact revenge, Zhang Wei's fate, and that of the other members of the Billionaire Club, was sealed.

Zhang Wei officially died of a heart attack while on a Chinese mission to expand business and economic relationships in Ghana. The president's deep operative and personal friend, Colonel Gerald Washburn, was the actual source of Zhang Wei's heart attack, which had involved a surge of potassium chloride into his blood stream and subsequent heart failure. Zhang Wei's nephew, Li Yong Wang, neither accepted nor believed the finding by the Chinese investigators of natural heart failure, in spite of the fact that no foul play was detected after an in-depth autopsy was conducted. He was well aware of the ways of the West, especially those involving the sudden death of prominent businessmen.

Li Yong had attended UCLA for his undergraduate degree in computer science, and Pennsylvania's highly regarded Wharton School of Business for his MBA. With his family connections, he had moved rapidly into a highly influential government position for strategic business development.

The Chinese approach, coached by the Chairman and led by Li Yong, was to partner with select progressive African countries. Their goal was to bring these countries progressively through the stages the Chinese had experienced in their own economic development, beginning with comprehensive education and the fabrication of uncomplicated technical devices and modern tools to support agricultural production.

The world was changing dramatically in terms of partnerships and cooperation, and a sense of collaboration was steadily creeping into the picture. Against this backdrop, Li Yong Wang sent an encrypted message to Sanjay Krishnamurti in India to meet secretly, within the coming month, to design a plan to ensure the demise of the United States.

13

TRADING PLACES

The president strode confidently into the Cabinet Room in the West Wing of the White House. Alerted by the most respected member of the high-tech group a few months earlier, he convened a top secret meeting of the heads of the twelve most influential high-tech corporations in America. Everyone stood as he walked into the room, according to protocol, which he personally found amusing.

"Please be seated," he said. He felt very comfortable with the group, who were mostly friends and supporters, especially those with a Silicon Valley or otherwise Western base of operation. "Ladies and gentlemen, I apologize for putting this meeting off for so long, after your request to discuss several matters of great concern to the high-tech industry. Specifically, the delay was related to the two Great Tragedies we have experienced. As most of you are aware, we've been unable to separate politics from people's welfare. Personally, I am confident that your sector will play a crucial role in the direction we are headed and our adaptation to the incredible loss of human resources we have suffered."

The president turned to Harry Simmons, of Grooves Corporation, the respected member of the group who had requested the meeting. Harry's organization wasn't the richest, but it was one of the most crucial to advances in computer processing. Harry was fifty-five years old, and had an inviting demeanor that made others feel comfortable no matter the seriousness of the situation. Harry began.

"Thank you, Mr. President, for meeting with us. As you are probably aware, we are noticing two serious trends in our industry. Both appear to be of a global nature."

The president's silence was an indication for Harry to continue.

"The first is our assumed pipeline of talented graduate-level students from two major countries who are studying in our most prestigious universities. We have become accustomed to their easy movement into our high-tech industry because of a lack of interested American talent."

The president was thinking more along the lines of the American dream. He made a short note in response to Harry's statement, then asked, "And the second?"

"The second is a slowing of requests for our mainline products to expanding economies, specifically India and China, which you know are still the most populous countries on the planet, each with middle classes the size of the total US population."

"What do you attribute these two trends to?" the president asked the group, with a look that indicated he knew more about the trends than his question implied.

One of the more outspoken CEOs, Carey Anderson, who was based in northern California, immediately raised his hand and said, "I think it's basically political, Mr. President. Something is going on within their governments that has begun to change policy with respect to the US." He had a sense of having gone to the core of the issue.

The president made imperceptible eye contact with Myra Westbrook, head of Global Business Industries, one of the oldest and most prestigious high-tech corporations on the East Coast. She raised her mocha-colored hand, and the president nodded.

"Mr. President, regardless of the cause of the slowing of the pipeline from which we have traditionally benefitted, our industry has done an abysmal job of fully developing and utilizing our existing US talent. It's been far too convenient to simply skim the exceptional students from other cultures and then stereotype them as the norm. I guess water takes the easiest route down the mountain." Myra knew she had made several points in her two statements. She glanced at the president. He simply smiled and again imperceptibly nodded his head.

After further discussion, the president said, "I think I have a clear idea of the situation. Why don't we begin discussing the initial steps we need to take to address these issues?"

The president not only had a clear idea of what was happening in Asia but also what the group expected of him from the meeting. Little happened anywhere, at any time in the world, that General George Maxwell over at NSA didn't know about and briefed the president on, on a daily basis. The Russians may have the upper hand on hacking, primarily because of defections from the United States' own security personnel, but he felt confident that they were still the best at intel surveillance and gathering. He felt confident that the United States would quickly resume its dominance at hacking, which they had been doing for some time now, even of their closest allies.

The president continued. "As Bob Dylan once warned us, the times they are a-changin', and we have to change with them—or, preferably, stay ahead of them. That's been the key to our continued success. Without it we decline, like all great civilizations of the past. It's as simple as that. The truth is, the kind of change we need now will come primarily from you, not from me or the federal government. With that said, I would like each of you to take a minute or so and let me know your most burning idea for significantly addressing these two issues. That should take no more than fifteen minutes."

It took fourteen minutes. The group was surprised by what they came up with when challenged to state their ideas in one minute. Each went right to their most personally committed action that would benefit their business most. The president's basic assumption was that leaders always had the best solutions to the problems they encountered if challenged to reveal them with no personal consequences. Now the hard part would begin: how to implement their most realistic ideas in a way that would cooperatively benefit both China and India, in the midst of an environment that was seeing the country withdrawing into itself when global cooperation was needed most.

When everyone completed their statements, the president said, "Thank you. I believe we got this!" The group laughed, which was an indication of how skillfully he handled groups who were at this level of leadership.

Then he turned thoughtful and said, "Ladies and gentlemen, I believe we are at a more serious crossroads than our people realize. I believe this is true globally. There are drastic changes occurring in Asia and on the European continent that we cannot reverse, but we can constructively respond to them in kind; just recall your comments of a few minutes ago. I can promise you, I will provide whatever resources you need to go forward with your passion for both change and organizational transformation, resources that cannot be blocked by Congress.

"With respect to the second issue, the global customer base, global realignments are occurring at a rapid pace, about which I cannot discuss at present. As Carey implied earlier, they are political in nature. However, I feel that when we seriously resolve the first issue, involving the development and retention of human capital, resolution of the second will follow naturally."

As if on cue, one of the president's aides whispered something in his ear, after which he stood and said, "Thank you, but another appointment calls. I promise you will see support for your suggestions in action very soon." He turned and walked through the passageway toward the Oval Office, with a convoy of Secret Service agents in front of and behind him.

14

A NEW REALITY

When Myra Westbrook's private plane touched down in upstate New York, she had her aide call each member of her board of directors for an emergency meeting for Saturday evening, the following day. Myra instructed her aide to refer any telephone requests to her if she met with any resistance. She also asked her aide to communicate to each of them that she believed they needed to discuss matters vital to the future success of Global Business Industries.

Myra continued to feel a sense of urgency as she reflected on the president's meeting. He appeared to convey a message greater than the two issues they were focused on. What was it he was trying to say? She felt it was just out of reach. But her board members, particularly Joshua Peake, had an uncanny ability to see the big picture with the fewest definitive facts. That was why they all referred to him as the Sage, and why he was wealthy and successful.

Myra's aide reported to her that eight members of her executive board could make it to the five o'clock meeting, with the exception of Joshua. He said that he was attending the birthday party of one of his numerous grandchildren. He went on to say that he had attended his share of emergency board meetings in his lifetime, and one week from now the emergency will have dissipated into little more than an annoyance. That was when her aide indicated that Myra would be calling him the following morning.

At eight o'clock sharp the following morning, Myra called Joshua. "Good morning, Myra. I guess I expected a call from you, given the persuasive conversation I had with your aide last evening."

"Apparently not persuasive enough."

"She may have forgotten my age, even though I am widowed."

"I called, in part, to tell you that your favorite granddaughter, Jennifer, would be receiving a small gift from the board for her birthday, since we know how special she is to you."

"Myra, I am shocked that you would stoop to such a level in order to have me miss part of her birthday party."

Their bantering was a special part of their professional relationship. Joshua had known Myra for more than twenty-five years. He had personally mentored her throughout her career with GBI. When the time was right, he had suggested to the full board that she take over as president and CEO, which the board had enthusiastically accepted. It didn't hurt that Joshua was the major stockholder in the corporation. He was an enormously wealthy investment banker from Maine and a good friend and supporter of the president. In addition, he was a member of the top secret team of presidential advisors called the Rebels. They were presently charged with advising the president about how to influence the establishment of the Renaissance Revolution in the United States.

Myra replied, "Keep in mind, you taught me everything I know." Then the tone of her voice changed dramatically. "Joshua," she said, sounding serious, "there is something going on at the highest levels of government. It involves the United States and probably others. I think the president was attempting to convey this message in our meeting with him yesterday."

Equally serious, he asked, "Do you have any idea of what it might be, Myra?"

"He handled our concerns about human capital and customer flow as though they were spin-offs of something much bigger. I'll share my thoughts with you when I see you tomorrow."

Wheels started to turn in Joshua's mind about some things he had heard in dealing with the European investment markets—but something was glaringly unspoken.

"Okay," he said. "I'll be there. Sounds like fun." Truth was, Joshua enjoyed crises more than he did smooth operations. They got his blood pumping and involved creativity and wisdom, both of which he possessed.

"Thank you, Joshua. I really need you for this one. I'll send a car to pick you up."

"Thanks, but I think I can find my way."

Myra smiled and disconnected.

- - - | | | | | - - -

The board of directors meeting convened at four thirty the following afternoon at the global headquarters of GBI in upstate New York. Small dishes of healthy food and the usual array of non-alcoholic beverages were served while the board members engaged in both serious and light conversation.

At precisely 4:55 a light chime rang, and each of the members assembled around the modern, high-tech boardroom table. Since Myra had become president and CEO, the seating was less formal, except that she sat at the head of the table with the descending sun at her back in order to capture the "glory effect." It was understood that Joshua Peake would be seated to her immediate right. The mood was cautiously light, but with the seriousness that this was an emergency executive board meeting.

The executive board consisted of four women and five men. The odd number was intended to avoid tie votes, which Myra's vote would then resolve. In extremely rare cases, she would cast a deciding vote when a measure she opposed was favored by one vote. In such cases, it was understood that her vote was not only intended to create a tie, but also break it, since the chairperson would decide a tie vote. In essence, her vote counted for two in such situations. This was a practice with a long tradition at GBI, and so predated Myra.

Myra began the meeting by sincerely thanking the board members for their personal sacrifice by coming in on a weekend. Then she quickly got to the point.

"Yesterday morning, I attended a White House meeting with the president of the United States and eleven heads of the major companies in the American high-tech industry. As you are aware, the purpose of the meeting was to discuss the dramatic slowing of foreign human capital into our organizations, particularly from our graduate education programs, and the slowing market demand of our high-tech products, particularly from China and India. Well, that was a mouthful," she smiled.

"And what did our fearless leader have to say?" asked one of the board members.

"He threw the ball back to us and asked what we thought should be done about both situations."

"And?" another board member asked.

"Well, as usual, Carey Anderson suggested that both situations reflected a change in political policy, and that change was probably happening with respect to policy as it involved the United States."

Dr. Peter Ferguson, one of the board members who demanded the same respect as Joshua Peake, said, "In spite of Carey's impulsiveness, let's follow that train of thought. A government policy change would mean that what we are observing is not only going to prevail for the time being but perhaps intensify."

Another member quickly intervened and said, "Now they are truly tampering with our lifeblood, some of our brightest employees."

Another board member said, "They're not ours. It's a privilege that we have had access to them as a resource."

Joshua smiled as the spirited conversation took on a life of its own, as Myra had hoped. He suddenly realized where Myra was leading them and why she had insisted on his attendance. Finally someone said, "If we lose our foreign sources, where do we go to replace them?"

The question hung in the air. They had obviously led themselves to an impasse that required going beyond a temporary band-aid solution, a solution that required serious discussion and decision-making. Myra turned to Joshua and said with a smile, "Joshua, what are your thoughts about that?"

He smiled; *the master being led by the student*, he thought. "It really comes down to two choices: we breed them, or we import them from somewhere else. At present, we use importation to meet our needs, to compensate for the lack of local breeding." He noticed some of the board members smiling. "What did I say that's funny?" he asked.

"Joshua, you breed animals, not people."

"We *develop* people," another chimed in, chuckling.

"Okay." He paused and threw his hands up in surrender. He knew, of course, that his breeding comment would lighten the mood for what he was about to suggest. "Then it comes down to either developing an untapped source or importing them from a new source." At this point Joshua began to recognize what the president had been saying to the group of high-tech executives—using Myra, of course, and by extension, him.

Silence followed his last statement. Everyone knew what his reference was to the untapped source.

15

||||||||||||||||||||||||||||||||||||||||||||||||||||||||||||||||||||||||||||||||||||||||||||||||||||||||||||||||||||||||||||||||||

MYRA'S LEGACY

The silence that fell over the GBI board meeting was a direct result of the choices Joshua Peake had stated: develop or import sustaining talent. Since development implied a serious effort in addressing America's major untapped STEM human capital—women, recent immigrants, and non-Asian people of color—no one wanted to be the first to venture a comment. The board had been at this juncture on several occasions previously. The result had always been a different directive to the GBI Global Diversity team to implement yet another impressive-sounding but symptomatic program that would make no real difference. It was easier to throw money at the situation than to seriously deal with it. However, this time the executive board seemed ready to explore something radically different, since their literal long-term existence might be at stake. Perhaps it was the gauntlet Joshua had thrown down in a way he had never done before.

In spite of the source, Myra spontaneously decided to seize the moment. "It appears that, for the foreseeable future, the low-hanging fruit we've all had available is going to continue to dwindle. The first reaction will be to increase our competitive efforts for the majority base of American human capital. Importation won't be as easy as before because our usual sources are beginning to measurably improve their own teaching and research institutions and exchanging students between themselves. We're no longer the only game in town." She paused, then asked, "Have I sensibly reasoned through our challenge so far?"

A somber but realistic mood prevailed momentarily. Then the well-respected engineer, Peter Ferguson, whose inventions and patents had earned millions for GBI over the years, said evenly, "What you said makes perfect sense, Myra. The real question for us is, are we ready to seriously take on the task of developing our underutilized human talent?" He paused and scanned the faces of several board members. Some engaged his scan with an intuitive message of assent while a few dropped their eyes to stare at the boardroom table.

Joshua repositioned his seat to indicate he wanted to speak again. The board members turned to him. He took his time, then began with a sense of quiet urgency. "We have been around for more than 120 years, unlike many of the high-tech, Western-based organizations. I was thinking on my way here today and during our meeting, what has been the key element in our continued existence and success? I ask because Myra's message for this meeting was to discuss matters vital to the future success of GBI."

He paused as if gathering his thoughts, then continued in the vacuum of silence and expectation. "We've been willing to take measured yet bold risks on our direction throughout our existence. But most of all, we've backed our decisions with commitment to create success, no matter what it took. Where our underutilized human capital is concerned, we've never had to make that commitment. I guarantee you that, in short order, one of our competitors will come to the same conclusion, particularly one of the progressive ones from the West Coast. And we will be playing catch-up." Each of the board members was in deep introspection, not about the reasoning, not about what needed to be done, but about their own personal commitment to creating the followship necessary for success.

One of the young fast-track board members tentatively raised her hand and said, "There are other factors for our consideration we have not mentioned." Myra nodded for her to continue. "As the US becomes a more difficult or even hostile environment for immigrants to live in, students from many countries, not only China and India, won't want to study here, either. Even those currently studying and working here are considering returning to their native countries; I know this through private, confidential conversations. Word spreads fast through social media but even faster through private conversations." There was silence again as each board member considered her comments.

Myra said, "Does anyone else have thoughts, ideas, or considerations we need to discuss?" Continued silence. "If not, I think we have a clear idea of where we are. Unless there are more questions or comments, I would like to entertain a motion that we move decisively and aggressively to identify, develop, and employ exceptional human capital from the underutilized American population."

"So moved," an Asian female member immediately responded.

In order to avoid any peer pressure to adopt the resolution, Myra added, "I also recommend that we use a secret vote for this motion. The question of who, when, and how we decide whether to implement is not part of this vote. Anyone opposed to these stipulations?" There were no objections.

The result of the secret ballot was six in favor of the resolution and three against.

Myra thanked the board and indicated that it was time for a light buffet dinner. She also said that the remainder of the board meeting would take place at eight o'clock, when they would begin discussing implementation guidelines, with a hard stop at ten o'clock. She reminded the group of the importance of confidentiality and secrecy, although she didn't expect it.

Accommodations would be made for those who wanted to stay over, but most already had privately arranged transportation.

During the one-hour dinner break, Myra returned to her office to consider where the organization was headed, and what the consequences would be. Her aide brought her a small plate of food and a bottle of water. She resisted the urge to invite Joshua to join her to seek agreement with her decision. He had passed the baton back to her, and now she would discover what she was made of.

It was from moments like these that she would learn what the board expected and what it meant to be president and CEO of GBI: loneliness, along with whomever and whatever she turned to in moments like these. The next two hours would define her legacy as president and CEO of GBI. She knew deep down inside that the confidence and surety she exuded would be crucial to the followship she would require.

At precisely thirty seconds to eight o'clock, Myra Westbrook confidentially strode into the board meeting and lightly tapped on an empty glass. Her executive board responded by finding their seats a few seconds before the meeting was to begin.

Myra began. "I thank each of you again for spending this weekend day on behalf of GBI. I didn't know in advance where our discussions would take us, but I did know it was important that we address the president's comments as quickly as possible." She noticed how rapt they were, and she gained greater assurance as she spoke—as did they.

"For the remainder of the evening, I would like us to have a brainstorming conversation regarding how we might identify, develop, and employ a highly diverse group of high-potential young people." Everyone noted how Myra added the word *diverse* to the underutilized group description. It included an expansion of STEM-oriented individuals, regardless of race, ethnicity, or sex, and inclusive of bright young immigrants, often referred to as Dreamers. "Does anyone have a problem with recording our comments? More specifically, would a recording impede your open and honest comments for what we are trying to achieve, or a reluctance to state your opinion?"

No one objected. The board primarily consisted of individuals who wanted their opinions accurately recorded for such an important decision.

"I think the emphasis should be on technology-based learning, so as to not spread ourselves too thin and lose our focus," Peter Ferguson said.

"As well as people skills, particularly where differences are involved," someone added.

Another member shouted, "Well, that involves everybody, including us." They all laughed.

Myra had instructed her aide and an assistant to record the comments on flipcharts at the front of the room and to activate the recording device with microphones in front of each board member.

"We should also incorporate culturally integrated learning based on the GBI core values."

"That's a great idea," one of the members responded.

Myra smiled as she noted how alive and interactive the meeting had become. The group continued to generate multiple ideas around the initiative they had decided to take on.

Then someone suggested, "I think we need to balance our emphasis on technology with personal development and self-mastery as the basis for working constructively with differences. Personal development for our trainees, and self-mastery for our management. The approach should be based on the inclusive leadership model used by GBI executives and managers." Everyone unanimously approved of this suggestion.

Myra intervened again and said, "I think we can learn a great deal from diversity leaders who have made considerable progress in their organizations by using a variety of visionary approaches, including, most recently, artificial intelligence."

"That's the first time diversity has come up in this conversation, although it has been implied everywhere," someone said. "I think the word *diversity* can become a counterproductive trigger. We definitely need to explore another type of designation." Everyone agreed with that suggestion.

"That's true, and an excellent point," Myra replied. "Branding is important. We just have to make sure that the Global Diversity team is aligned and included, and assure them that their efforts have been an important part of the change process, that what we are doing is simply an expansion of their efforts."

"Perhaps the Diversity team could report to the individual who oversees this new initiative," someone suggested.

Joshua said, "In that case, that individual should report directly to Myra, and possibly become a member of this executive board." The group looked stunned. "And most of all, this individual should have my guidance, support, and mentorship and that of two or three members of this board. That's what I meant when I said 'commitment to success.'"

"Why don't we just make this individual a vice president or vice-CEO," someone said laughingly.

"In other words," Joshua added, ignoring the comment, "let's put this individual in a no-lose situation, whether diversity is involved or not. We need to send the strongest message possible that this initiative is crucial to GBI's future success. Remember, our message is that we are responding to our need for new, exceptional human capital, without which we would have a questionable future."

The group continued to creatively brainstorm the suggestions raised until fifteen minutes before the meeting was to end. Myra then said, "In order to aggressively move on this process, I'd like to suggest an impressive individual. Her name is Ms. Sandra Charles-Henley. I have been following her career for some years now, ever since I first met her at a women's leadership conference."

Myra distributed the woman's resume to each board member. "She is vice-president for human capital at one of the most prestigious and successful defense corporations in America, and has been with this organization for more than thirty years. So, even if we were interested in her, she would be very, very difficult to recruit. However, I believe she sets a standard for the type of person we want to consider. Take her resume with you, and send me back your thoughts on this and anything else you have in mind. I'll appoint a three-person team to move on your recommendations as soon as possible. Finally, please do not announce our decision to seriously address this way-overdue issue to anyone."

Everyone, including Myra, began laughing, since she knew their plan would be in *The New York Times* by the middle of the following week, if not sooner, and on the internet by Sunday.

16

REUNIFICATION

The president of the United States exited the meeting with the twelve high-tech executives and presumably headed for the Oval Office. The press was purposely led to believe that the meeting was highly confidential, thus drawing their attention to learn as much as possible about the decisions made to address the high-tech business sector.

In the meantime, the president was secretly led to the south lawn of the White House, where a helicopter was waiting for an immediate departure. After lifting off, the helicopter banked sharply south for the thirty-minute flight to Camp David. When the president arrived at the mountaintop presidential retreat, he was escorted to the elaborate conference room, where numerous historic decisions had been made during the twentieth and twenty-first centuries, none of which was going to be more historic than the upcoming conference.

Present around the conference room table were high-ranking representatives from Canada, New Zealand, Australia, Ireland, England, and two representatives from the Republic of South Africa, one Black and the other White. Each of these emissaries was there to discuss the present progress and plans for the future of a group called the Tawhid Confederation—a transcendent Arabic alliance whose name meant the inherent oneness of a group bordering on the divine. They were given specific instructions to act on behalf of their respective heads of state or, in South Africa's case, the overwhelming population of Blacks within a rapidly changing and dominantly White-owned business community.

The Tawhid Confederation had been conceived a few years earlier by a group of wealthy, aristocratic Englishmen. It had begun with the question they posed to themselves: How do we reestablish the British Empire? They had assumed to simply pass the baton to their crown colony, the United States, to take over during the twentieth century. By no means had this aristocratic group presumed to represent the British government in any way. However, they decided to float the idea as a trial balloon and see what happened.

As they predicted, the idea caught on in highly influential English governmental circles, and evolved, in form, to fit the economic and military realities of the twenty-first century. The central idea evolved into a reunification of England and its former economically viable global colonies. The reunification was centered on a military-economic banking bloc, with a common cultural core value system that was English in origin. Such a criterion would be an ideal way of establishing an economic-political-military alliance in which cultural disparities would be minimized.

The alliance would, of course, value a diversity of cultures in order to accommodate the various ethnic minorities in each locale but within an English-Eurocentric context, as currently existed in all of the represented countries by population—with the exception of South Africa. They all shared a common dominant language, English. This element was essential to the alliance since language and culture were inseparable. The major traditions would simply follow naturally.

The formation of the Tawhid Confederation would follow a three-phase process: communications, financial integration, and fluid integration of human capital across the seven sovereigns (much like the EU). The communications phase had been underway for some years now, primarily between England and the United States. It involved comprehensive integration of entertainment, television, sports, movies, news, and most of all, a political alliance that inseparably bound the two countries—and would eventually bond them all. Australia followed close behind.

The meeting was organized to begin making plans for phase two of the confederation. The most important action in anticipation of this meeting was to ensure that England could freely participate in financial and economic integration of the alliance. This process was well underway in terms of the financial and economic withdrawal of the UK from their European ties, a step that was crucial in setting the stage for the comprehensive business integration of the United States and the United Kingdom.

The major topics of the meeting were the future of a global free market and how various economic sectors outside of the Tawhid Confederation could work cooperatively with them and each other instead of in pitted competition. The cooperative statement was a direct request from the president of the United States, and a majority of the alliance countries agreed.

The president began the meeting by suggesting that the first hour be devoted to a conversation about the two related issues, with no agenda.

"Ladies and gentlemen, thank you for journeying here to the United States. Although rustic, I hope you find your accommodations comfortable here at Camp David. I think you will all agree that secrecy is our most important consideration, although I hope you will not want for anything in order to have our meeting be successful." He paused to allow for any questions and considerations. "I am open to your thoughts about these two issues."

The representative from Australia spoke up first. "I think we can serve as go-betweens in Southern Asia to distribute many of your high-tech products that would normally be handled directly from the US."

The representative from New Zealand chimed in, in agreement. "The same is true for us, since we have excellent relationships with the South Asia countries."

The president noted reluctance on the part of the New Zealander. "Is there more you would like to say?" he asked.

"Yes, Mr. President. Using us for distribution is merely a stop-gap measure. We'll have to come up with a long-term solution. I think it's fair to say that America is losing its global influence."

Although the president tried to appear open and receptive to the New Zealander's statement, he could feel a tightening in his chest.

The English representative said, "I think a real focus on communication of a global free market is vital. None of us can survive without access to a global audience. And let them decide what best fits their needs."

The president said, "That stance and statement from my office does not require Congress's agreement. We support, and have practiced until recently, a regulated free market that addresses everyone's economic success. Although a nationalistic stance weakens the United States' reputation and our global leadership, I think we can handle it for the short term as long as the EU and China do not establish exclusive long-term trade agreements with India and Africa, respectively. Obviously, I am confident our upcoming elections will help to reverse our go-alone trend."

The Canadian representative said, "In spite of our historical allegiance to the UK, our economy is inseparably tied to the United States; therefore, we strongly support a regulated free market, and we'll keep that message at the top of our agenda."

"What about Ireland, Jeremy?" the president asked Jeremy Kennedy, special emissary for the Irish president and secretly approved by the Irish cabinet.

"As you are aware, we have a significant stake in the American high-tech industries. We credibly support a global free market, with the proper checks and balances. We can offer support for whatever America needs until this nationalistic idea subsides. Clearly, such a policy has no future in the globally merging world of today. I think the strongest response we have, in spite of the emerging EU partnership with India, is the innovative entrepreneurship of our alliance. Creative entrepreneurship is programmed into our DNA and has been for centuries, which means that all of our constituent countries have maintained sustained quality and creativity. I believe the world will ultimately opt for the best global products, as long as we can get the commodities into a global flow stream."

The president was extremely pleased with the direction and agreements of the meeting, so on this high note, he suggested they break for dinner and wander around the compound.

- - - | | | | | - - -

The members of the confederation met again that evening after dinner. The president began the meeting on an informal note in order to have the group relax as much as possible for the matter he wanted to discuss. In fact, that was why he had purposely waited until after dinner to bring it up.

"I want to thank each of you again for getting into Dodge without being noticed, and hopefully getting out tomorrow will be equally successful." Despite the fact that the comment referenced the old American West, everyone understood the point he was making. They also laughed at the success of the diversion the president had used with the high-tech group. However, a few of the experienced diplomats detected a serious undertone in the president's voice and were immediately alert for what would follow.

The president smiled and took on his serious executive demeanor. "We had a great conversation today about the formation of the confederation and a business approach that may have limited success for what we are facing with respect India and China." Now he had everyone's heightened attention.

"I honestly don't think our business agreements alone are going to create a lasting alliance if we don't have an honest discussion about major differences that exist within and between us, differences that I think have intensified over the last fifty years. If we don't begin to get these issues handled constructively, then all of the elegant plans we make will be of little long-term value. I think we have naïvely assumed that we all share a common value system because we were all originally English colonies. Nothing could be further from reality, especially here in America. With that said, I'd like to get your thoughts about issues involving differences in values among and between our nations."

The representative from Australia immediately responded. "Why do you feel we are compelled to change our English core values in any significant way? My impression is that the indigenous populations and immigrants are clear that they have to assimilate into the existing system we've established. They have no choice," he said, annoyed. The others looked at him as though he had missed some significant aspect of recent history, which annoyed him even more.

The president smiled and responded levelly, "There are three major factors we will have to deal with: First is the existing and rapidly changing country demographics. The ethnic minority population in the United States is about 45 percent, not counting our recent immigrants. Britain is about 20 percent, Canada 25 percent, and even New Zealand is 33 percent. Second is the resistant attitude of these populations toward total cultural assimilation at the expense of their own cultural values. Third, and foremost, the total global population with our Eurocentric value system is less than 10 percent of the Earth's remaining population."

The Australian looked surprised but not astounded. He had assumed that everything would continue more or less as it had before the two Great Tragedies. The others had suspected that governance, economics, and some of the underlying principles of operation would be different. The real questions were how and to what extent change was necessary.

The president intervened. "Besides these issues, I would like each of you to take back to your governing bodies a document titled 'The Seven Principles of Social Equality.'"

A copy of the document was passed to each representative.

"I share this document with you because I believe this is the direction the world is headed if we are to survive—whether we like it or not. I believe we are at the same stage of evolution of those individuals who participated in establishing the blueprint for the founding of the United States out of their frustration with King George III. This document establishes a fundamental underlying theme for how we can progressively live together in the future: we care about each other. I also want to acknowledge that there have been many such examples of humanistic declarations of governance throughout history. Maybe the time is right to begin living up to these noble directives in reality."

Each member of the alliance was given a copy of the document by the presidential aides, and began reading it.

The Seven Principles of Social Equality

1. All humans are equal by virtue of their existence; no human should be exalted as superior to others.

2. All humans have an inherent right to be fed, clothed, and sheltered, with the support of others where necessary.

3. All humans have an inherent right to be educated to learn both physical survival and global adaptation.

4. All humans have an inherent right to freely explore and express their spiritual values through creativity, innovation, and any other form of human understanding, compassion, and love.

5. All humans have an inherent right to explore consciousness for the continual acquisition of wisdom.

6. All humans have an inherent right to religious expressions that provide spiritual growth in concert with the well-being of all humanity.

7. All humans have an inherent personal and collective responsibility to preserve a planetary social, physical, and spiritual environment for their continued existence.

As each of them scanned the document, their reactions ranged from shock to recognition—recognition from the British representative. If Canada was tied by the hip to the United States, then England and the US were similarly bound as the anchor republics.

"I suggest we spend some time in the morning discussing the meaning of the Seven Principles and their impact on how we proceed into the future. Obviously, we are not discussing agreement at this point, simply understanding the principles and their implications in practice. At least we can get some idea as to whether we are up to this level of human existence or not." The president paused and then asked, "Agreed?"

Everyone nodded their assent, and the group retired for the evening.

17

||||||||||||||||||||||||||||||||||||||||||||||||||||||||||||||||||||||||||||||||||||||||||||||||||||||||||||||||||||||||||||

THE CONSORTIUM—
POST PANDEMICS

As he reflected on their most recent meetings, the Chairman had concluded that both the composition and the dynamics of the Consortium Board had changed dramatically. The most recent additions based on wealth, societal position, and political philosophy, had resulted in the selection of much younger members who had risen to significant leadership positions of influence, in their own countries and globally. As a result, these members lacked experience and maturity and, most of all, a lack of proper respect for those who possessed such qualities. They tended to talk more than listen, without fully comprehending the issues the board was attempting to resolve, and, most of all, they lacked a big-picture perspective.

They also tended to lack recognition of the global implications of the true mission of the Consortium and the role it had played in maintaining the status quo through many turbulent decades. Seen through the Chairman's eyes, the never-ending sequence of wars had been the major safety valve for expending the energy buildup of continuing conflicts of a dominantly survival-based planet; so far, all of the conflicts had been contained without the necessity of nuclear weapons, with the exception of World War II. At least the two nuclear bombs dropped on Hiroshima and Nagasaki ending the war, and subsequent above-ground tests afterward, had not permeated the Earth-Pleiades vortex. It had been at this point that the Chairman and others were dispatched to Earth to ensure underground nuclear testing and continued efforts of planetary transformation.

The Chairman again attributed this accomplishment to the insight and wisdom of the Consortium, in spite of the continual development and production of more sophisticated weapons of mass destruction. From his perspective, the interventions by the Consortium were the stabilizing factors that had prevented Earth's self-destruction to the present. What the younger members didn't fully comprehend was that the board existed because humans did not collectively have the capacity to transform from a consciousness of survival to one of compatibility. Therefore, their continued existence required an overseer to initiate and control the events that would satisfy their inevitable survival instincts.

The Chairman's perception was that the younger board members viewed the Consortium as a means of prioritizing the acquisition of greater wealth and power, where power was viewed as resulting from the direct acquisition of wealth, similar to the Billionaire Club. It was like going backward in human evolution.

He further reflected on how much he missed Sir Charles Ethan Wellington's stabilizing influence as a member of the board. Sir Charles had been from an aristocratic British lineage and clearly understood the role of the Consortium. He had also been the Chairman's most important advisor, even though he wasn't Pleiadian in origin. Sir Charles had been killed as a result of a clandestine Black Ops staged by Colonel Darin Thomas and Monique Rashad—members of the president's Special Projects Team—because of his association with the Billionaire Club. The Chairman's closest confidant now, by default, was his deputy chairman, Lenhard Rieser, who had been with him for more than twenty-five years.

Lenhard had been his rock, the person on whom he could depend with unquestioned loyalty. As a result, he found himself deferring greater responsibility for the Consortium to Lenhard as he focused more of his efforts on his role as the unofficial voice of Europe on determining the new world order. In recent conversations with Lenhard, he had the feeling that the change he had doubted humans could achieve might slowly become a reality. His dominating interest in thwarting this possibility was his ultra-secret project. It involved the conception and creation of the new twenty-first century *Homo sapiens*.

- - - | | | | | - - -

The decline in sales volume of some of the more popular high-tech US brands began slowly, several months after the White House meeting. Most of the CEOs who had attended the meeting assumed the situation had been handled by the president, since there was no further drop in sales after the meeting. In fact, there was a temporary recovery. The cause for the initial decline gave no reason for alarm, since the reported reasons were mostly attributed to misplaced shipments, wrong products, and deliveries to wrong addresses—all resulting in a tolerable reduction of the demanded products.

Under the assumption that everything had returned to normal operation, Sanjay Krishnamurti and Li Yong Wang met secretly in the private condominium area in Singapore and proceeded to discuss a plan that would further impact the American high-tech companies. They were well aware of America's attempt to circumvent the initial reductions by their own governments through enrolling supply distributions from Australia, New Zealand, and other Southeast Asia outlets that were not targeted.

Li Yong began the conversation. "I don't know how you feel, but I'm not pleased with the slap on the wrist our governments have given to the Americans because of their most recent immigration policy. It was an insult!"

"I don't take it personally," replied Sanjay. "I know what they think of us. We both went to school there. All they want is to use us to stay ahead of the world in IT."

"I take it more personally than you. I'm sure the Americans had something to do with the death of my uncle ten years ago, although we could never prove it."

Sanjay smiled and asked, "You like your revenge served cold, don't you?"

Li Yong didn't immediately reply, but it was clear he didn't think the comment was funny. He said, "What I would like to do is to make them seriously feel it—and if we both squeezed them, it could really make them hurt."

"Is this something we should clear with the Chairman?" Sanjay asked.

"Most of those guys on the board should be in an old folks home. The Chairman is just a step behind them." Li Yong smiled knowingly. "We're the future of the Consortium."

Sanjay knew he was favored by the Chairman, and didn't want anything to happen to jeopardize his position. So, instead of agreeing with Li Jong, he replied, "Tell me what you have in mind."

Li Jong spent the next fifteen minutes describing in detail how they could "really hurt" the US economy. When he was finished, he sat back and asked, "What do you think?"

"I think we're playing with fire. The US is no banana republic. We can expect serious personal repercussions from our governments, the US, and possibly the Chairman if they find out that we are the source of what you have in mind."

"Okay, let's just scare them with my second choice so they don't think they can treat us like second-class countries," said Li Jong. "Just a month or so, until they get the message; then we cut off the process. Okay?"

Even though he felt uncomfortable about the agreement, Sanjay said, "Just a month or so, but that's it!"

They implemented their second-choice plan, which involved the sales and performance of several of the most successful American companies in both China and India. Once selected shipments arrived at the various ports of debarkation from the two down-under countries, Australia and New Zealand, they were planted with compromised products, particularly phones, tablets, and laptops. That was followed up with online chatting about the breakdown in quality of the imported products surfacing on the internet. The local salespeople in commercial outlets became more cautious about pushing and promoting the American products, and hence, the decline in sales began slowly and quickly built up momentum.

Both China and India were basically relationship-oriented cultures in which person-to-person contact was often the most persuasive factor in convincing a purchasing customer. The floor salespeople were aware of the difficulty by experience, particularly when it was demonstrated by senior personnel. Therefore, no conspiracy charges or undertones could even be suggested—or proven, if they were suggested. The sales personnel were also reminded of the recent laws passed by the American Congress that made it extremely difficult to remain in the United States in sabbatical-like employment, even if an individual wanted to remain. The unstated conclusion was that individuals from Asia were unwelcome, and possibly undesirable, in America. This conclusion was aided by the recent increase in violence directed at Asians in the U.S.

Given the Asian response to Li Yong's second-choice idea, Sanjay was delighted he hadn't agreed to Li Yong's original plan. In essence, it had involved convincing his government to corner the global technology market in areas critical to military and consumer materials and components, exclusively produced in China.

PART FOUR

TRANSFORMATION

18

||||||||||||||||||||||||||||||||||||||||||||||||||||||||||||||||||||||||||||||||||||||||||||||||||||||||||||||||

SPONTANEOUS TRANSFORMATION

Over time, something surprising began to happen after the two pandemics. People quietly, and unannounced, began to relate to each other with greater compassion and understanding. Apparently, something deep within the human psyche had ruptured—something that went beyond the tragic loss of friends and family—that had triggered a spontaneous realization of the value of others. It appeared that a line had been crossed from which there was no return. Most unsettling of all, there were no answers as to how to express this realization. A void had been created.

In essence, a majority of those who had survived experienced transformation from a well-structured, albeit dysfunctional, way of living to one that posed a question instead of an answer: "What is existence without relationship with others?" The transformation, triggered by the massive loss of close relationships, was the most profound event humans had ever collectively experienced, even greater than the Black Death pandemic in the fourteenth century, which reduced many European communities by more than fifty percent.

The sequence of the two recent pandemics and the resultant massive loss had literally *imposed* the experience of transformation on those remaining. They had, in essence, achieved the Quest. But they were now faced with the question of how to begin living in a way that was consistent with their new way of being. That question comprised the void.

One of the most progressive responses to addressing the void was the worldwide adoption of the practices of the Renaissance Communities. These communities had begun organizing some years prior to the recent global transformation. They comprised individuals possessing the Pleiadian code and those who had experienced transformation as a lifelong journey of personal exploration. The major objective of the Renaissance Communities was to introduce an inclusive way of living based on human compatibility.

--- | | | | | ---

The Renaissance Communities clearly recognized that if the dominant consciousness of a group was that all humans are of equal value simply by virtue of their existence, then true human equality would naturally follow. In practice, however, they discovered that a context of equality was a two-part proposition. One part involved authentic behaviors of respect, acceptance, and support by those assumed to be superior, and the other involved the corresponding assumption of full responsibility for behaviors involving empowered performance of those assumed to be inferior. They eventually learned that human equality was the fundamental basis for acceptance of the Seven Principles that eventually evolved.

Similarly, if the dominant group thinking was that each member deserved healthcare simply by virtue of their membership, they discovered that the best systems of delivery would naturally follow, without exclusions. They also discovered that the fundamental issues of implementation were easier to resolve if the dominant way of thinking was that healthcare is a human right, not simply a privilege. The point was, establishing the principle first was crucial to creating committed implementation strategies. In practice, the surprising result was that the overwhelming majority of individuals in such communities voluntarily began practicing preventive healthcare measures using all available forms, including various folk medicines and practices, Eastern medications and measures, spiritual healing, and of course, Western medicine based principally on Western science and technology.

In other words, where human equality was a fundamental given, healthcare naturally followed as a human right in addition to being a privilege. A similar consciousness existed for education, which was seen as a means not only for an individual to gainfully survive but also to prepare individuals to contribute to the betterment of society. Ultimately, the Renaissance Communities naturally adopted the Seven Principles of Social Equality—based on equality, healthcare, education, spirituality, wisdom, religion, and planetary preservation—and shared them throughout the world.

--- | | | | | ---

With increased wisdom, humans slowly began to redirect most technological advances in AI robotics to critically reduced workforces, addressing the needs of underdeveloped countries and the creative exploration of quality of life instead of primarily for security and armed conflict. In other words, the shift in consciousness from survival to compatibility spontaneously triggered a rebirth in the restoration of humanity.

These realizations were the result of the spontaneous global transformation that societies began to adopt, along with carefully written methodologies for behavioral change. They were the first real breakthroughs that the president and others had been trying to achieve through the Renaissance Revolution.

19

MAKING A DISTINCTION— OPENING TO CONSCIOUSNESS

The first official meeting of the core team of the Institute for the Study of Human Consciousness convened. The team consisted of director Dr. David Carrington, Dr. Frances Wilkerson, Dr. Gail Erickson, Dr. Catherine Wang, and Pat Christensen.

The sole item on the agenda involved consciousness and clarifying the distinction between the mind and the brain. These distinctions were essential if their research efforts were to proceed from a common ground of understanding. Dr. Carrington opened the meeting by welcoming everyone to the newly designed research center. The facility had been constructed and staffed in record time because of the efforts of Dr. Carrington and a few highly influential anonymous donors.

"I think we are about to embark on something truly groundbreaking," David began. The spark of his Nobel Prize-winning work appeared to come through by his enthusiasm. "Again, the overall mission of our work is to develop the technology for continuing human transformation and evolution."

In fact, everyone who was part of the Institute was equally excited. They also felt challenged by the magnitude of the project on which they were embarking; funding and research associates were not a problem, which meant that resources with respect to people and funding were not going to be a limitation to their success.

"I think our discussion for this meeting is exploring the distinction between the brain and the mind—and from an expanded perspective, consciousness—and ultimately, how they are all inseparably connected." Everyone nodded in agreement.

"Since I'm the brain guy," David said, smiling, "I think I'll begin. In neuroscience, and even some psychological circles, most, if not all, human behavior and responses are attributed to measurable activity in the brain. In essence, practically all of our respected research has been done using experiments that stimulate and examine electrical signals that emanate from within the brain."

Gail immediately responded, "So where does that leave the mind?"

"Some of my colleagues describe the mind as simply the dynamic action of the brain," David said, tongue-in-cheek. "Most of us tend to use the terms *mind* and *brain* interchangeably, although we all know, at some level, that they are not the same."

"Why do you suppose that's the case?" asked Dr. Erickson.

"At a conscious level, I think it is our attempt to avoid seriously dealing with a possible distinction between the two, particularly in terms of the mind being a nonphysical phenomenon. Acknowledgment of this possibility would also complicate the well-ordered theories we have developed by not having taken this distinction into account," David said, feeling like a Benedict Arnold to his neuroscience colleagues.

"Isn't there more, Dr. Carrington?" Pat asked.

David smiled. Pat was the type of colleague he enjoyed most. She asked, or implied, questions at a deeper level of examination. The questions she asked about the unconscious level of resistance were at the heart of his conversion after winning the Nobel Prize.

"Yes, Pat. There is more. I was about to say, opening the door to the validity of the nonphysical form of the mind would mean that we would have to deal with a phenomenon that is unmeasurable using our familiar scientific instrumentation. In truth, it never made sense to subject metaphysical phenomena to measurements designed for physical experiments. I suspect we commonly do it as a way to invalidate the phenomenon before an experiment is even conducted."

"In other words," inserted Gail, "it would be like Copernicus proposing the Earth circumvented the sun using visual observation rather than a telescope."

"Almost," replied David. "Except there is a significant number of researchers who are convinced of not only a nonphysical mind but also of a more expanded existence of consciousness, even beyond human perception."

Frances added, "So we've replaced the Catholic Church with the conservative scientific community."

David's colleague at UCLA, Dr. Catherine Wang, felt a need to come to David's support as well as her colleagues' work at the UCLA Brain Research Institute. "My experience is that *conservative* is the wrong word," she offered. "*Careful* and *questioning* are more accurate. We tend to be more accepting of research proof through evidence-based measurements than is the legal system, which accepts circumstantial evidence."

Everyone laughed, which dissolved the building tension. Then Pat asked David a question. "David, what is the effect called that was published in 1942 by Abraham Luchins?"

David smiled; he realized Pat was setting him up. Dr. Wang started to intervene again, but David raised his hand to stop her. Then, like he was reciting a class assignment, he said, "The Einstellung effect. It's the brain's or mind's tendency to stick with the most familiar solution to a problem and stubbornly ignore other alternatives."

"Probably the best example of this effect in science is discussed in the book *The Structure of Scientific Revolutions*, published in 1962. The author, physicist Dr. Thomas Kuhn, describes what he calls 'normal science.' Normal science is commonly practiced by a decided majority of scientists in a given discipline. Their major endeavor is to prove beyond a shadow of doubt what we presently believe. Experimental evidence to the contrary is often considered to be in error or, at best, an anomaly. This means that the same or similar experiments are repeated until either the anomaly goes away or is ultimately ignored. In extreme cases, like my Nobel-winning work, it is the basis of a whole new paradigm of study," David ended with a smile.

Since winning the Holy Grail, the Nobel Prize, David had become more detached to the sacred findings of his brain research. He smiled more when challenged, and actually enjoyed more totally different ways of interpreting experiments involving human behavior.

"Which confirms my earlier point," said Frances. "We've replaced the Catholic Church with the conservative scientific community."

Everyone laughed this time. In the silence that followed, David decided it was a good time to move on to another topic of discussion. He said, "I'm more excited every time we meet. First, I love to work with people who are counterculture, but most of all, those who are outliers." The latter term referred to individuals well removed from the normal distribution of people in terms of being driven by exploration for success. "We seem to be a team of such a composition, so that none of the really tough questions should be missed, not discussed, or prevented from finding their way into our research studies."

"What we've really done is establish the real purpose of the Institute," said Gail.

"And when we add to it the value of continued human existence," said Dr. Wang, "it's one of the strongest arguments for the unquestioned scientific acceptance of the nonphysical mind I can think of. After all, Sigmund Freud and other colleagues suggested the existence of the conscious, pre-conscious, and subconscious mind more than one hundred years ago."

"In addition," picked up David, "this is the crucial point I was going to make. We have all the money and resources we could possibly want."

"And finally," Pat added, "all we have to do is make the president look like a prophet."

"Now that we've got the objections about an independently operating mind out of the way, let's begin a discussion of what it is and how it works in *concert* with the brain," offered David. "If we can get a reasonable explanation for these questions, then maybe we can begin to conduct our individual research projects." He paused. "Does that sound like a sensible approach?" The team nodded their agreement.

Frances raised her hand and began. "I don't think we'd be sitting here today or be part of this Institute if each of us didn't believe that the mind exists separate and apart from the brain. As you said earlier, David, most of those involved in brain research probably know, at some level, that the mind exists as a nonphysical entity. But the level of denial is so great that few from that genre of research have dared to become outliers—until David."

"Why do you think that's so?" Gail asked.

Before Frances could answer, Pat said, "Because accepting the mind is the easy part as long as it's contained within a psychological or even a psychiatric context. The real threat is opening the legitimate existence of consciousness, the same as René Descartes did in 1637 for the separation of science from philosophy and religion during the scientific revolution."

"That's really what we're doing, isn't it?" asked Catherine. "The question of the mind is just the appetizer."

"Once that door opens, we are in for a roller coaster ride," said Pat. "Our first destinations beyond the astral plane are the mental and causal planes, which are already being used for psychic communication by the Star Network."

"What planes?" asked Catherine.

"The mental and causal planes. Mastery of these planes is one of the primary requirements for achieving Pleiadian wisdom."

David said, "If I understand you correctly, Pat, the Institute's studies involve a spectrum of states and planes of consciousness beginning with the brain—its emotional, feeling, and creative states—coupled with the nonphysical mind, which serves as the police to monitor and control constructive and destructive decisions that translate into human behavior."

"That's it perfectly so far, David," Pat replied.

Gail said, "And that's where I come in, seamlessly connecting the five human senses to the five metaphysical senses. The objective is to capture a holistic experience in order to better determine the nature of its intent—either a true threat or a non-threat to one's survival—so that an appropriate behavior naturally follows."

"And from there, Pat takes over," interjected David.

"Right again, David," Pat acknowledged. "The mastery of more evolved states of consciousness. The mental plane is essentially the ability to accurately interpret our experiences of others in terms of a threat or non-threat to our physical survival. A disagreement about different religious beliefs is not a threat to one's survival. For that matter, differences in political ideas, educational ideas, or family philosophy are not inherently physical threats to others. And yet, throughout the history of human existence we have interpreted them as such."

"And the causal plane?" asked Catherine.

"As you might guess, the causal plane is the mastery of emotional states corresponding to a given accurately interpreted experience. Such states include joy, enthusiasm, compassion, empathy, and passion, as well as grief from an appropriate experience of loss."

"Is that it, Pat?" David asked.

"Well, to top things off, something else happens when you begin to master these evolved states of consciousness."

"And what is that?"

"An ability to project your consciousness over great distances, experience what is occurring elsewhere, and intervene. These experiences are variously described as out-of-body, communication with guides, astral projection, remote viewing, empathic experiencing, and remote healing.

Probably the most famous American in this category was Edgar Cayce, the Christian mystic. In a trance state, he apparently answered questions about remote healing, reincarnation, wars, Atlantis, and future events. For many Americans, he's probably second only to Nostradamus. I think I'll stop there for the time being."

The team was transfixed by Pat's descriptions.

David concluded, "I think we've made exceptional progress in defining our vision, mission, and the roles that we each can play in both global transformation and the study of consciousness as it influences our everyday life."

It was clear to Catherine that David wanted to say something more, so she asked, "What is it, David?"

"During our conversations, something popped into my mind about the question we started with about distinguishing between the mind and the brain."

"And what is it?" Catherine asked.

"Well, using a computer model, the mind is simply the software of the brain."

20

‖‖

FILLING THE VOID WITH COMPATIBILITY

The work of Dr. Frances Wilkerson dealt with how to function compatibly as a human species—*a simple yet overwhelmingly challenging statement in practice*, she thought. *In spite of all the technological advances we have made, along with our self-declared crown of exceptional intelligence, we are still deathly afraid of each other. Fear is the underlying, mostly suppressed, emotion that dominates human existence.* She thought of the plethora of security and defense systems, not to mention surveillance, to which we devote excessive human and monetary resources. *The point*, she thought, *is that we seem to perceive that differences of almost any kind are a potential threat to our physical survival. We don't seem to understand and accept the reality that differences in physicality, ideology, religion, customs, and culture are not inherently threats.*

Her initial thinking in addressing the paranoia was that they first needed to undo their present mental programming, which was based on a survival paradigm. She assumed this programming in humans was historically and probably genetically necessary in their evolution. That is, it was probably hardwired into the psyche during the period of human evolution when survival was, in fact, a moment-to-moment, day-to-day reality. At some point in human history, survival from each other became as much of a threat as from other animal forms, so that, collectively, they never made the distinction of viewing others who were different as expressions of diversity but rather as something to fear—perhaps even more than the ferocious animals that lived among them.

Fortunately, the transformation to compatibility had unexpectedly been occurring in the aftermath of the two pandemics. Quite frankly, Frances was relieved, since she had no foolproof way of undoing the hardwired programming of the centuries-old survival paradigm. She had spent the majority of her career using the techniques of cognitive behavioral therapy with only limited success.

But with a substantial part of the first phase resulting in human transformation, a void had been created with respect to what would replace their survival-driven practices. Even though a traumatic transformation in consciousness had occurred, it was not immediately clear how the majority of those remaining would behave and organize their day-to-day living. The approach she decided to use in her research involved the practices of mindfulness, where mental programming was involved. These practices fell into two major categories: an awareness of one's inner self and personal motivations, and an awareness of the mental and emotional states of others and their responses to communications and behaviors of others.

An essential part of the new research conducted by Dr. Wilkerson was a holistic approach involving an inseparable bodymind model. Such an approach combined the advanced brain studies of Dr. David Carrington with nanotechnologies and mapping the mind's interpretation and responses to moment-by-moment experiences of the body. Dr. Carrington was responsible for setting up brain-oriented experiments requiring a mental interpretation of experiences involving understanding, empathy, compassion, and love.

Their research employed a computer model approach, in which it was assumed that the mind was simply the software of the brain, similar to the way computers work. They noted that the development of the present-day computer appeared to be a replica of their own mental and behavioral processing and experiencing, respectively. As such, the model was not surprising.

According to their initial computer model, the brain was similar to a highly advanced hard drive that could store, process, and retrieve information. It could also create new, more efficient ways of functioning from its continual learning capacity, far exceeding the capacity of computer hard drives.

In essence, the mind was the nonphysical software that continually monitored every event an individual experienced through the five human senses. Each event was interpreted as either harmful or supportive, and an appropriate behavioral response was programmed and stored for future reference. Making this distinction was a vital aspect of the mindfulness practices. They also assumed, for the present, that the nature of the mind was a high-frequency, transparent energy form not yet discernable by existing scientific instrumentation.

Thus, the mind's first response to perceived threats was its interpretation relative to fight-or-flight, followed by instructions to the brain of how the individual should react. Where non-threats were concerned, the instruction involved how to respond through choice-making based on previous experience, which was possible only with a mindset of compatibility.

These were the basic assumptions the team employed and that provided the context for the bodymind experiments. That is, body and mind were simultaneously distinct and one. In response to positive compatible characteristics, such as those previously stated, Dr. Carrington's measurements simultaneously mapped the neural pathways used by monitoring the brain's electrical activity using electroencephalography during emotional states of empathy, compassion, understanding, and love.

The Carrington-Wilkerson team's approach was to complement the neuroscience experiments to date. Their experiments were simply expanded to include the nonphysical mind as the interpreter and instructor, separate and apart from, and in concert with, the brain. The team expected that the results of their work would lead to a model of practical application to fill the void with respect to states of mind consistent with the Seven Principles of Social Equality.

- - - | | | | | - - -

After several weeks of experimentation, Frances suggested that the team discuss what they had learned so far. "As your previous work shows, David, we know the areas of the brain that appear to be affected by acts of kindness as well as hostility. However, these effects appear to be the *result* of the actions, not the stimulus. Do you agree?"

"I must admit, Frances, I agree with you. My guess is that something in the mind interprets and triggers the corresponding response," he suggested.

She sensed that David was introspective about his response, as if he had more to say, so she waited for him to get his thoughts together.

"As I think more about how we interpret our neuroscience measurements, such as stimulated blood flow and other measurable electrical activity in the brain, we have no real basis for the conclusions we draw about intelligence, traits, and other characteristics except those that are clearly visible by tangible results. Simultaneously, we are careful to ignore the possible role of the mind, sometimes at all costs."

She paused to allow him to process what he had said. There appeared to be something significant, though not intellectual, going on in David's thinking. She went with the flow.

"If we use the practices of the Renaissance Communities as the template for filling the void for what's been happening, it might serve as a good model for how we proceed," Frances said. "What do you think?"

"Quite frankly, I don't know very much about the practices of the Renaissance groups. My original ideas, before the two Great Tragedies, were pretty much formed from the televised news reports, which were, in essence, a bunch of nouveau hippies with Brave New World ideas about how to reorganize the world. The reporter concluded that the world had 'a few' problems here and there, but for the most part it was just fine in lieu of the alternative."

"What do you think now?" Frances asked.

"Just between you and me, Frances, I don't know where I am now. The more I work with you and the team, the faster my ideas are changing."

"How?"

"I think I'm beginning to see the world from an entirely different perspective. And quite frankly, it scares me."

"What scares you, David?" she asked.

"I am afraid that I am losing my identity as a mainstream scientist. Starting the Institute was an impulsive attempt to discover significant missing pieces in the way we interpret our work on brain activity and experiential processes."

"Where are you now?" she asked.

"Confused. And I've started something I can't seem to stop."

Frances smiled sympathetically and said, "It's the chute."

"The chute! What the hell does that mean?" asked David, chuckling. Truth was, he enjoyed working with Frances.

"It means you're in transit, in a smooth tube with nothing to grab on to."

David's fear increased as the process proceeded, in spite of the fact that Frances tried to distract him.

"Let's get back to the Renaissance idea," she suggested.

"The what?" exclaimed David, disinterested in her distraction.

"Okay. Why don't you tell me what you are experiencing now, David?"

"My anxiety is subsiding, as though I have arrived. I am experiencing a disconnect between my predesigned experiments and my interpretations. And I think I understand Heisenberg's quote for the first time."

"Whose quote?" she asked.

"Werner Heisenberg, one of the creators of quantum mechanics."

"Oh, I see," Frances replied, not having a clue what he was talking about. "And what did Heisenberg have to say?"

"He is reported to have said: 'What we observe is not nature itself but nature exposed to our method of questioning.' What I think he's implying is that science is not the study of reality but the study of mimicking reality, using a model that produces the results we observe as accurately as possible."

"What!" Frances exclaimed. She had never heard such a suggestion by a renowned scientist, let alone a Nobel Laureate.

David quickly interrupted her and said, "I think I am through the chute, and I've arrived at a destination. Do you want the good news or the bad news?" he asked with a maniacal laugh.

"Both," Frances said.

"The good news is that I made it through without invalidating the scientific observations of physical reality, in spite of how afraid I was of discovering the opposite."

"And the bad news?" she asked.

"Frances, I know that what I am about to tell you won't make much sense, but I need to say it anyway."

"Okay," she offered tentatively.

"I think what I realize is that we are not studying an experiment, we *are* the experiment!"

"What do you mean, 'we are the experiment'?" she asked, looking confused.

"Whenever I've conducted experiments that didn't work—code for those that didn't produce the results I expected, or the 'the point didn't fall on the line'—I used to discard them. Then, after one of those experiments. I was sitting there, frustrated, when a thought popped into my head: *follow the signs*. I interpreted that to mean that I should pay attention to the unexpected results as a sign of a new direction I should take, both in the experimental design and interpretation of the results. This nugget of wisdom is exactly what happened to me that led to my Nobel Prize-winning work. It opened the door to my realization of the necessity of including the mind in our interpretations. You know J. Krishnamurti is quoted as saying, 'The observed and observer are one.'"

Astounded, Frances looked at David with a satisfying grin that implied that, like Pauling, he was about to win his second Nobel Prize.

Smiling, he concluded, "In simple terms, the tail is wagging the dog."

21

CONNECTING THE DOTS

Catherine Wang was an accomplished and highly recognized psychologist in her own right. She was a full professor in the psychology department at UCLA as well as a collaborator with Dr. David Carrington on his Nobel-winning work in neuroscience. She had applied the theory of cognition to the brain research of Dr, Carrington. Although Dr. Wang was somewhat skeptical about Dr. Gail Erickson's parapsychology work of naturally connecting the physical and metaphysical senses, everyone else on the team felt the pairing of Catherine and Gail was ideally complementary. Gail viewed the separation between the physical and the metaphysical as being similar to the land bridge that once naturally existed between Asia and Alaska. Gail's vision was resurfacing this natural connection to produce a more perceptive and compassionate human being.

At their initial meeting, Gail explained to Catherine, "The objective of my work is to create conscious awareness of the natural connection between the physical and metaphysical dimensions of consciousness so that any experience of another person or a situation can be processed holistically by the mind and one's metaphysical consciousness. In that way, we are able to hear and see what an individual says and does while simultaneously perceiving his or her authenticity, or the person's true motivation and intent. Deception is possible only at the bodymind level. It can add a whole new dimension of authenticity to our relationships. Let me show you a diagram I use to map these experiences."

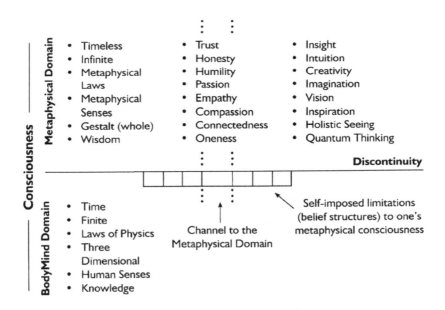

Domains of Consciousness

Gail walked Catherine over to a diagram titled "Domains of Consciousness" that hung on the wall of her office. "You can see, above and below the horizontal line, are domains, or states of consciousness, corresponding to the metaphysical and bodymind domains. Below the line is where we live most of the time, on a day-to-day basis. We navigate this domain using the five physical senses: sight, sound, touch, smell, and taste. Babies unconsciously use all five senses in their learning. We spend a lot of time teaching them not to taste everything." Gail smiled to break the trance Catherine was in. She asked, "What do you think so far?"

Catherine shyly responded, "In truth, I've been reading about this stuff for years. As you might guess, I'm very careful who I talk to about it. I always figured that if David and I had enough to drink, we could easily get into such a conversation."

"You were probably right. However, now that he's come over to the dark side in leading this whole project, it should be easier." Gail laughed.

Catherine replied, "Tell me more."

"Okay, the descriptors, top and bottom, speak for themselves. Notice that wisdom does not come from the mind but rather from a metaphysical transformation, probably as a result of a human experience. Common experiences that trigger metaphysical transformation include such events as separation, divorce, physical trauma, an accident, or a conflict with the same person, over and over again. In such conflict situations, one day something snaps, and out of nowhere you get a realization, followed by a nugget of wisdom, such as, 'That which I dislike in others is a mirror reflection of myself.' This probably happens because a spouse or someone else accuses you of having a quality that you dislike about them."

Catherine looked reflective for a moment as she recalled events leading to her divorce, which she had blamed on dedication to her work rather than an underlying issue in her relationship. Gail recognized Catherine's reaction as one she had seen many times before when her offhand remarks had provoked introspection in others. She paused and asked, "Would you like some water or coffee?"

"Water would be fine," Catherine responded.

Gail retrieved bottled water from her small fridge and gave it to Catherine. After a few sips, Catherine said, "Okay, let's continue."

"Notice in the center here is the channel to the metaphysical domain. It is the connection between the physical and metaphysical worlds. The first step in our work is to create a connection, or a naturally existing channel, between the two. The second step is to make that channel wider and wider over time, so that movement between the two domains occurs without effort. The wider the channel, the greater the amount of consciousness and wisdom from higher states that can be downloaded. In essence, the more conscious a person is, the more constructively they function in human relationships. That, in a nutshell, is what my work is all about—or should I say, what *our* work is about."

Catherine smiled. "What about the descriptive words above the line?" she asked.

"The objective in putting those words above the line is to indicate the domain they originate from, as a way of being. The corresponding actions are then expressed in the lower human domain. When the actions originate from above the line, they are authentic. When they originate below the line, they are more likely to be inauthentic and possibly manipulative. I sometimes call these behaviors 'practiced pretense.' That's why, in communication, listening at the upper level indicates a perception of the person's true intention. This is what commonly occurs."

When Gail and Catherine resumed their conversation after lunch, Gail suggested they do a quick debrief. Catherine said, "I do have a question or two about what I've learned so far. Why do you assume that most people need conflict or trauma to learn and grow?"

"That's a great question. First of all, I make the assumption that learning and growing are the result of personal transformation instead of stemming from elaborate coping mechanisms, which are often non-challenging and within a person's comfort zone. I refer to coping strategies as change in behavior, how things are done, or when things are done. These don't necessarily result in learning and growing unless the intervention creates a significant confrontation within a person's structured reality. It appears that, for most of us, firmly held beliefs about the way we are programmed must be challenged. Thus, the response is commonly reactive and emotional, similar to a trauma. That's what those boxes are that prevent the creation of a channel from one domain to the other. That's also why a discontinuity exists. Whatever the unique nature of the boxes is for an individual, the most critical ones preventing the connection must be resolved."

"Why can't people just use practical ways of changing that they can adapt to over time? Like the ones you see in magazines or on the internet?"

"Great question again. Just because someone learns to behave in a prescribed way doesn't mean the self-limiting belief is no longer there. Usually, the original intention is the same, and nothing has irreversibly changed about the nature of the person. Most of all, the conflict eventually reappears, often in a different form, so we fool ourselves into believing that we are experiencing a different problem."

"I see," replied Catherine reflectively.

"Those are the questions that I hope you can answer for us, in time. That's the psychology stuff we struggle with most. The main reason for the channel, however, is to continually funnel nuggets of wisdom from the top domain into the bodymind domain to solidify a mindset of compatibility in place of survival-driven ways of thinking. We believe the easiest way to accomplish this is through 'small acts of transformation,' those small acts of kindness we do for others and for which we have no expectation of anything in return. For transformation to occur, it's not about what we do on behalf of the other person as much as it is about what we learn about ourselves."

Catherine stopped to think about that last statement for a moment.

Gail said, "Now I have a question for you."

"Shoot," Catherine said, beginning to understand and even becoming excited about the work that Gail performed.

"Why do you think most people resist introspection to learn the true source of a problem, and instead continually search for band-aids or escape mechanisms, such as alcohol, drugs, and other behavioral addictions? Or even continue to suffer, assuming that they know what's truly going on and that it's not associated with *their* mental programming?"

Catherine smiled, almost laughed, and replied, "I'm not in

clinical,"—meaning clinical psychology—"but I guess that many of the patients and clients would not come back again after the first session."

Gail laughed at Catherine's comment and said, "I'm aware of that. But what I'm really curious about is, why do people generally resist exploring inner space, while they are perfectly willing to risk their lives experiencing outer limitations in mild or extreme activities—or just life in general?"

"I really don't know, Gail," Catherine said with sobering introspection.

"Well, if we are going to come up with a solution other than a pill or a new drug, part of your job is to find out why."

Gail continued. "I'd like to share with you the model I've come up with to use for the connection, then see if we might try it out. Okay?" Before Catherine could answer, Gail added casually, "I've done it numerous times in the past, so it shouldn't be a problem."

Catherine looked at her skeptically and wondered what she meant when she said she had "done it numerous times and it shouldn't be a problem." Gail simply proceeded.

"In both domains, we have five senses. Somehow, the sense of sight has to connect with the extrasensory sense of clairvoyance, then sound with clairaudience, and so on. Okay?"

"I understand perfectly," replied Catherine, although she wasn't quite sure about where this experiment was going.

"Great," said Gail. "My model involves two right or two left hands, whichever hand is natural for you, with five digits each. Each digit represents one of the five human and five corresponding extrasensory senses. Okay?" Catherine was getting a little annoyed with Gail's "okays" after each statement. In truth, as Gail proceeded, Catherine was beginning to get more than a little annoyed.

Gail asked, "Why do you think I've used hands for my model?"

Are you serious, Gail? Catherine thought. *I am a PhD researcher with more than two hundred publications to my name, and you're asking me a stupid question like that?*

With a neutral look on her face, Gail said, "Just humor me."

"You're obviously going to have the two hands shake and form a permanent clasp. With thumb to thumb, index finger to index finger, and so on to meld the physical and metaphysical senses," Catherine said.

"In the simulation we use, you are going to visualize the hands and the shake. Have you ever done a visualization exercise before?" Gail asked.

"I regularly use visualization for my meditation exercises. Is that the same thing?"

"It's very close, but we will be doing visualization beyond the senses you are familiar with. Just let your natural imagination take over. If at any time you become too uncomfortable, just give yourself gentle instructions to return to the laboratory." Gail was careful not to add "okay?"

"Okay," replied Catherine, smiling.

"I'm going to take you through a relaxation process first, similar to what you use for meditation. Then, I'll suggest your mental exploration of three experiences. Finally, I will bring you back to your fully conscious state. Okay?"

"Fine," replied Catherine. It was at this point she realized that Gail never asked her if she wanted do the visualization exercise, but it was too late to back out without looking scared.

"Just use the same relaxation process you use for meditation. Take three deep breaths through your nose, hold each one, and exhale through your mouth as you gradually move to the alpha state of relaxation. Just begin whenever you feel ready."

Three minutes passed as Catherine went into a state of deep relaxation.

Gail said, "Recall the diagram, and then visualize your hand moving through the blocks in an attempt to create a channel from the physical to the metaphysical domain."

As Catherine attempted to extend her hand through the blocks, the medium became dark, murky, and resistant. When she pushed harder, she experienced fear for reasons she couldn't figure out. Then she visualized her colleagues at the UCLA Brain Research Institute warning her not to go further. She sensed danger after their warning. In her confusion, she lost all concept of time.

Then she heard Gail's soft, mesmerizing voice saying, "If you experience resistance, just pause, take a deep breath, and continue to move through the resistance very, very slowly."

Catherine's hand continued to move slowly through the murky medium. She could hardly see in front of her. The medium got darker and heavier. Her fear increased. She was almost ready to quit and open her eyes when she heard a soft voice, not Gail's, encouraging her not to give up. Her fear started to lessen, and her hand moved forward, almost involuntarily.

Gail said softly, "Extend your hand further, and make contact with your extrasensory counterpart. Take a leap of faith, and it will be there."

Catherine did not see a hand, but she did sense that something was there, just beyond her reach. She experienced a feeling of safety, as if she were touching something she could not see. Slowly, a hand grasped her hand, and she experienced a euphoric jolt throughout her entire body. The medium around her suddenly became clearer and brighter than anything she had ever seen before. She felt whole, clear, and safe. Just as she was about to pose a question about the bodymind connection, she heard Gail's soft voice encouraging her to return.

When she retreated from the channel, there was no murkiness. No resistance. No fear. Gail instructed her to open her eyes, and she was suddenly back in the workspace. She knew something dramatic had happened to her and that there was no return to the safety of the "old" Catherine. When she turned to face Gail, they both smiled knowingly.

22

HUMAN NATURE

"What about you, Pat? What's your passion, and how does it fit into what we're trying accomplish?" David asked.

When David asked Pat that question at the board's weekly meeting, it made her think a little deeper about her connection to the Institute's purpose instead of what she had prepared to say. She knew she belonged there, but how? Certainly not like her Star Gate experience with the military, where she was, in essence, a CIA psychic spy. She was so naïve then, mixed with a heavy dose of egotism and patriotism about what she could do. She never did accomplish what she was capable of, what with the military's emphasis on accuracy and detailed intelligence in a field heavily criticized by the established scientific community.

Her appointment at the University of Arizona was a godsend. Being around the scientists in the parapsychology department had taught her a whole new perspective about the work they did. Most of all, Pat had become convinced that the institutionalized study of consciousness as a mainstream discipline was inevitable, and probably on the near horizon. The appointment had also made her aware of all the pioneers in the field who had performed this work in an academic environment for years. With these thoughts in mind, she began her response.

"I guess I am interested in exploring the source of humanistic consciousness and the behaviors it naturally stimulates in human beings. In simple terms, why do we care about each other, beyond those closest to us? Do we care primarily during emergencies and crises and then return to business as usual? Why do human beings exhibit authentic behaviors that we classify as understanding, empathy, compassion, patience, support, humility, and love?"

"You know the old saying in psychology," Catherine said.

"What is it?" asked Pat.

"You can't ask a question for which you don't already have an answer at some level of understanding. So, how would you reply to that question?"

Pat paused momentarily to gather her thoughts, and then she began. "My first response is that all of the characteristics that I just described as humanistic originate from a different way of being, one that results in a natural state of mind. And the behaviors, actions, and even inactions that follow can be described as humanistic. I call this predisposed way of being 'humanistic consciousness.' It's the source of a person's authentic response to the experience of another person. For example, when someone experiences a tragedy, an authentic humanistic response is sympathy. When someone excels in performance, a humanistic response is happiness. When someone struggles to find something deep within them and is encouraged to express it, a humanistic response is patience. When someone behaviorally expresses their passion, they simultaneously experience joy. The question is, where does this way of being, or predisposition, originate? What is its source?"

David asked, "Why is this question so important to you, Pat?"

"It's important to us all, because decisions are now being made about the conscious design of the so-called evolved human species of the twenty-first century. In other words, can artificial intelligence be programmed into a machine or a robot to produce authentic human characteristics, such as understanding, empathy, compassion, and love? Or do we require essential elements of a human being to retain authenticity?"

Frances said sarcastically, "Like artificial understanding, empathy, joy, happiness, and love. Those are all oxymorons."

Pat replied, "I have concluded, at least for the present, that the authentic expression of humanistic characteristics requires a human organic connection, namely, the brain; or perhaps equally important, the heart. I further assume that the brain interfaces with the mind as well as expanded states of consciousness from which humanistic consciousness is sourced." She continued as the team listened, fascinated with her explanation.

"The question being discussed is, do we transform the nature of the human species, or do we design an inorganic species with programmed behaviors to replace us?"

"What's the difference?" Gail asked.

"In the former case, we preserve humanity as we know it, and in the latter case, we abdicate it without knowing in advance the consequences to our humanness."

Gail asked, "Is it even possible to program something android that has an authentic way of being?"

"I doubt it," replied Pat. "A way of being is a result of or identical to one's personal consciousness. Artificial intelligence programming is based on the recognition of a *behavior* indicative of an emotional state, such as anger, joy, happiness, or depression, followed by a programmed behavioral response. The question is, is it necessary to have authenticity as the driving motivation for that response?"

Frances raised her hand and asked, "Is it even possible to program human attributes that we haven't mastered ourselves? Mastery would mean that we have humans involved in AI programming who have mastered the mental and causal planes of consciousness. What I suspect is that they would program the androids to be subtle replicas of themselves, overlaid with appropriate-looking behaviors that, in crisis or back-to-the-wall situations, would resort to our usual survival strategies, such as security measures, with more sophisticated technology. After all, we've already programmed the public with the Star Wars movies and Legos, about what to expect of our future. Recent articles in respected news media suggest our military is already planning a defense system for outer space—which is simply an extension of our present system of operation on earth."

Catherine added, "And the more sophisticated the technology, the more we delude ourselves about how evolved and advanced we are as a human species."

Gail said, "The concept that one cannot mentor in others what one has not mastered in oneself is as old as time, easily dating back to the Greek philosophers. We simply need to substitute the word *program* for the word *mentor*."

"Or rather," said Frances, "we program into androids what we have mastered about ourselves, both conscious and unconscious, and we all know what that is: the pre-pandemics state of the world."

Everyone was silent for a minute or so, then David filled the silence. "We are technology junkies. That's not going to stop in the short run, especially among the younger generations, where our hope really lies. In fact, it will probably accelerate in development. Perhaps the best approach is to learn how technology can aid human learning and wisdom, as well as physical and mental abilities, without sacrificing or compromising that which makes us human. It's about focusing on how technology is applied instead of focusing solely on its destructive potential."

Pat added, "I guess it comes down to whether we want to retain our humanness as the priority or want the drivers of society to ultimately be programmed androids. My basic premise is that we can only retain our humanness, no matter what the ultimate source is, by mastering advanced states of consciousness. And that, in a nutshell, is what my work is all about," she ended.

23

OUT OF CONTROL

Sanjay and Li Jong had no idea that their sting would take on the life of a wildfire, as if the Eastern global market had been waiting for some reason to rally against America. The isolation and dominant ethnocentric attitude of the United States had silently inflamed the Asian world. No longer were all things American considered to be the goal. A definite shift was beginning to occur in valuing Eastern innovations and styles, albeit much of it American and Western in origin. It was like the old saying, "If you take your hand out of a container of water, it refills with the surrounding water as if your hand had never been there," meaning that without America's participation and contribution, the Eastern world would be forced to learn its own creative and innovative potential, and the balance of power and influence would never be the same again.

The downswing started to impact other areas of science and technology businesses, and two of the major Eastern corporations based in China and South Korea began to take full advantage of the opening. Of the six major global confederations, Isolierung coupled with the S&J Sting, Tawhid, in part, anchored by America began to experience a decided decline in economic technology success.

Li Jong was so excited about the economic decline, which primarily stemmed from the impact on America, that he initiated a call to Sanjay on his secure line. "Well, my friend, how do you feel about what we've created?"

Sanjay was not as elated. He figured they had created a phenomenon that was clearly out of control—at least out of *their* control, with no end in sight as the unraveling continued unabated. After all, none of the defective IT devices they had planted had any widespread validity. He said, "I'm not sure I'm as comfortable about what we've created as you are, particularly since we have no control over how to stop it."

"Stop it?" Li Jong replied incredulously. "For what? This is what they deserve for using our cheap labor to make profits and using our most talented people to further their economic and technology dominance."

Sanjay knew that what Li Jong wanted most was revenge for his uncle's death. Justified or not, Sanjay believed that they were living in a new reality, still trying to understand themselves and define their direction.

"That was another world and another time, Li Jong. The rules have changed. Global stability is based on some kind of balance between the six confederations of the world."

Li Jong didn't reply at first. He felt betrayed by Sanjay's response, which he had at first interpreted as caution. Now he was beginning to feel alone in his effort to bring America to its knees. He replied to Sanjay, "You are probably right. I guess at some point it makes sense to let go of past sins and start over."

Sanjay was pleased with Li Jong's parting statement but doubted if he really meant it, so he concluded by saying, "Let's catch up next week. Think about what I've suggested. And let's get on the same page."

"Okay," replied Li Jong. "Next week."

More important to Sanjay were the future of India with respect to its business partnership with Western Europe and his respected position with the Chairman of the Consortium. The business partnership would eventually become a confederation called Eurodia.

- - - | | | | - - -

Nothing of global significance occurred without the knowledge of the Chairman, since anything of significance was usually initiated by the Consortium, at least prior to the two pandemics. As events involving the American high-tech corporations began unfolding in the Eastern world, the Chairman was somewhat surprised by how rapidly such events had begun to spread, primarily because neither India nor China had any representatives as part of the Consortium until after the two Great Tragedies.

The Chairman kept tabs on his board members using the Consortium's intelligence surveillance—the Consortium Communications Center—as well as the intel of major governments from around the world. The Consortium had members in all of the major intel countries and organizations, including Interpol, in spite of the loss of memberships due to the pandemics. The Chairman was also aware of the meeting between Sanjay and Li Jong because of his low-level contacts in the NSA, although there had been insufficient time to tap in to their conversation. Lenhard Rieser, the Chairman's deputy, had traced the source of the "American High-Tech Affair," as it had become known, to the two board members. The Chairman's fear was that the paranoia and economic decline in the United States would spread to other Western-oriented countries who were members of Tawhid and Eurodia. However, as long as total global breakdown was avoided, the Consortium would benefit.

In his role as de facto leader of West European recovery, Dr. Karl Gustav Christen initiated behind-the-scenes support for Eurodia as well as economic support for the European-Asian alliance—with little reference to the United States. He assumed that sooner or later, the president would come to his senses and realize that most of the world still viewed their countries as functioning through a hierarchical lens. The idea of a true people-involved society was folly, even among people with great wisdom.

The Chairman and Lenhard both agreed that Sanjay and Li Jong were the key players in their respective countries in ensuring the smooth transition to an elite-led democracy. After all, those remaining after the pandemics were more advanced in their thinking and personal awareness. Their highest priority was getting Eurodia off on the right foot. In order to do so, the Chairman wanted to do something dramatic, indicative of his progressive leadership. He had an excellent idea of what it might be. *Always one step ahead*, he thought.

24

THE MEETING

I was at home in Salt Lake City, reflecting on my first meeting with Lara and her statement to me: "Dr. Bradley—Bill—you may need my help with a situation in the near future." I was certainly fascinated by her calm demeanor, how everything she did was effortless. Her smile was unnerving and set off thoughts of something familiar just beyond my conscious perception. Over the time she had been here on Earth, I had come to the conclusion that she was not a stranger to me. We had history—a conclusion that made no sense, given her Pleiadian origin.

There was a knock on my door. I wondered who it could be, since I wasn't expecting anyone. Two serious-looking men in light-sensitive glasses—in spite of the fact that it was dusk—greeted me. The song "Nowhere to Run" ("got nowhere to hide") came to mind as they confronted me with stern looks. Then one said, "He wants to see you."

Since I was not assaulted, the only "he" I could think of was the president. My first question was, "Can this wait until morning? I've had a tough day."

Neither of them thought my comment was amusing, and didn't reply. The one who issued the request said, "We have twenty minutes before the flight to DC."

I attempted to gather a few things for the trip when the marine-like DI said, "We have everything covered. Would you please come with us? Now!"

The flight on the Gulfstream Citation X took about three hours to Andrews Air Force Base just outside of DC, and the helicopter ride from there deposited us on the White House lawn. It was dark by now, so our arrival went unnoticed by the press.

I was taken to the Lincoln Sitting Room on the second floor, and the president, Tony, John, and Lara were there. I couldn't have predicted a more unlikely cast if I were on a quiz show.

"Come in and have a seat, Bill. I am pleased you could make it," said the president, a stern look on his face.

As if I had a choice, I thought. I was certain I was not being invited to have drinks and shoot the breeze.

"Sorry we had to invite you on such short notice," he said as the two Secret Service agents exited with a nod from him, "but events move rather rapidly these days." My real question was what Lara was doing here. In truth, she was a mystery, more like a wild card. She obviously wasn't like most of the other immigrants, including the advanced ones. As she smiled invitingly toward me, I had a feeling I was about to find out why.

"I'll come straight to the point," the president said.

Shit. I hate that kind of opening statement, particularly if it involves me in some way, I thought.

"We have been discussing the stalemate we are experiencing in our efforts to firmly establish the Renaissance idea and eventually convince the rest of the world to join us. And we think we know the major source of the opposition—at least, in part."

I didn't say anything in response. I had learned to keep my mouth shut about anything that might involve me in response to a presidential invitation.

The president continued. "We believe the Consortium conceived and set into motion events in opposition not only to the Quest but to most of the major events on this planet."

My first inclination was to laugh, except everyone else was stone serious. So I asked, "What events are you referring to, Mr. President?"

"Well, after discussing that question with Tony, it depends on where you want to start."

"From the beginning," I replied without thinking.

"Tony has informed me that shortly after we exploded the two nukes over Japan in 1945, another emissary was sent from Pleiades after him who had similar developmental powers. After this individual's first year on Earth, he simply vanished and was never seen or heard from again. Tony believes that this individual, in human form, began orchestrating the activities of the Consortium. He believes he may have turned rogue. We know the Consortium has a Chairman, whom we have not been able to identify. We tried to get to him through Sir Charles Ethan Wellington. That effort, unfortunately, led to the elimination of Sir Wellington—and dead-ended our direct access to him.

"In any case, the Chairman of the Consortium appears to have been one step ahead of us at every turn, in terms of events in opposition to the Quest—and now the Renaissance Revolution. It also appears that the Quest has been accomplished in spite of his efforts in opposition."

"I don't quite understand," I said.

Tony responded, "I arrived here shortly after your first successful atomic explosions, when such activity became a direct threat to the inhabitants of Pleiades via the radioactive fallout projected into the Earth-Pleiades vortex. My guess is that another emissary was sent shortly after me and for some reason has become an influential part of the Consortium's operation. Why? I don't really know. But, as the president stated, he always appears to be one step ahead of us. I don't think any human—even a highly advanced one—could wield the resources and influence that we have dealt with in the recent past."

The president took the baton again. "The existence of the Consortium is public knowledge. We know there is a highly secretive board that advises the head of the group, probably the Chairman. General George

Maxwell, over at the NSA, has been working tirelessly with an elite team of cyber personnel to learn as much as possible about their secret operations. We've pieced together most of what we know from its broad membership and two young members whom we believe to have been recently chosen as members of the board. Fortunately, they are not as schooled in secure communications as their more experienced counterparts.

"We also know that the secret members of the board carry out the head's will, often using members of the broader organization, and have been dating back to the twentieth century after World War II—the Korean, Vietnam, Iraq, and Afghanistan wars. We believe all of these conflicts were orchestrated through the Consortium and have now evolved into global terrorism, including our conflicts with ISIS and the Taliban. We have predictably responded with military-type interventions by primarily using IT for intelligence. Only the form has changed, not the essential elements, as contained acts of war called terrorism. Since John's arrival, their actions appear to have been in opposition to the Quest; that's where our intel stops."

"I think I understand most of what the two of you have explained," I replied. "But why am I here? And more to the point, why is Lara here?" I had the distinct impression that the president was going to come to point again, and he did.

"We would like you and Lara to work as a team to identify the head of the Consortium, and neutralize him."

I smiled and replied, "Is that it?"

No one else smiled, so I extinguished my stupid grin. I still wondered why me. I asked again, "Why me?" I got a blank look from Tony and John. "For the most part, I think I understand the necessity for Lara—although I don't know why." *Instinct*, I thought.

"First of all," the president said with a calming smile, "we obviously don't need you for strong-arm stuff. However, we do need someone with the background and experience involving the Quest and with the knowledge to understand why someone would want to sabotage it. We also need this person to have the Pleiadian code to understand how to deal with a Pleiadian having a human identification. Hopefully, this will assist the process of identifying the human side of the head of the Consortium."

"And Lara?" I asked.

"Once he or she is identified and we move to the neutralization phase, Lara takes over," Tony replied. "She is on the same advanced level, or possibly beyond, as the head of the Consortium, at least when he was dispatched to Earth. Even in making a plan for neutralization, she needs your assistance and human perspective in her planning. It's not like you haven't done this before."

I wanted to say, *but never under your direction; just me, John, and Gala as free agents fighting to achieve the Quest.* Instead I said, "Now I have the most obvious question. Why hasn't the Pleiadian Council handled this individual?"

"Good question," Tony replied. "I'm convinced the Chairman was able to sever contact with the Council, particularly if he took on a new human body different from the original one—and even had plastic surgery, as I informed the president. Our only absolute source of identification would be the measurement of his vibrational frequency, just like a fingerprint for humans, which was probably unsuccessful after an exhaustive search."

"So, what we are apparently dealing with is a rogue Pleiadian who opposed the Quest and now opposes the Renaissance idea. Someone who has the same powers as Lara and Tony. Is that accurate?"

"Yes," replied Tony. "What we don't know is how he has created the resources for operations, since all support from a Pleiadian Resource Center was cut off by the Council when communication was severed. Our assumption is that he uses the unlimited human and monetary resources of the Consortium."

"So in essence, if we don't identify and neutralize this individual, the Renaissance idea and the Seven Principles ain't gonna happen. Right?" I said, using my best Southern colloquialism. I always tried to be funny when I was scared shitless.

"Yes," said the president evenly. "That appears to be the situation."

I looked at Lara, who hadn't said a word throughout the entire conversation. She just looked at me and smiled. That smile.

PART FIVE

PURSUIT

25

EMMA RUSHLAND

Emma Rushland was the second woman to be invited as a member of the Consortium. When she was invited, she made it clear to the selection committee chairman that she was not a token. Apparently, the first woman selected had been paraded in front of the public for maximum display and then faded into the busywork, along with most of the other one hundred-plus membership. Emma wanted the selection committee to know that she had no interest in becoming an invisible part of the fabric. This message was communicated discreetly and privately to the selection committee chairman.

Most of the members of the committee found her note amusing. It was extremely rare that anyone set conditions for becoming a member of the Consortium. It was informally known that after attaining membership, an individual's personal success and wealth skyrocketed—even if their visibility within the organization faded. After all, they were among equals, where very few, if any, advantages they normally benefitted from played a factor in their importance. It was also made clear by Lenhard Rieser that competence, creativity, and performance were the keys to recognition and responsibility, where here recognition and responsibility referred to those selected from the membership body to execute the directives of the Consortium's executive board. He had also made it known to the selection committee that Emma's approval was a foregone conclusion.

Emma was born in Amsterdam. Her mother died shortly after her birth. Her father, Matthias Streefkerk, became one of the most famous magistrates of the Dutch judicial system. Eventually, he was appointed to the Supreme Court of the Netherlands, which sits in The Hague, the official seat of government. Emma was raised by her father and their housekeeper. She was strongly influenced by her father in her demeanor and her sense of independence.

In growing up, she often played alone. She enjoyed many of the complex assignments her father gave her. As a result, she created several imaginary friends to assist her learning, as children often do. One particular friend appeared to be available most of the time to guide her through difficult decisions. Although there were no verbal responses from Emma's special friend, she referred to Emma as "Em." Emma kept their intuitive conversations to herself as she grew older, although her housekeeper had been fully aware of Emma's ongoing childhood dialogues.

Emma followed in her father's footsteps, becoming a renowned Dutch lawyer known throughout Scandinavia and Europe. Many of her cases involved reconciling cross-cultural differences between European nations rather than strictly legal matters. These differences, in many cases, appeared to be infinitely more difficult and intractable. It often baffled her how people evolving so near each other over centuries could retain such divergent beliefs and values without considerable integration occurring. In some cases, people were fanatic to hold on to the past, as a child does with a security blanket. During these times, she learned perseverance and patience.

Emma Streefkerk met an American lawyer, Mark Rushland, appointed by the International Tribunal for Crimes against Humanity, who was as equally ambitious and brilliant as she. After a short, intense dating period, they were married in Amsterdam and moved to Virginia, in the United States, to settle. For Emma, the arrangement was perfect at first because it allowed her to move from under the shadow of her father's fame. However, she soon learned that Mark wanted to start a family and settle into a typical American lifestyle—although he assured her that he would not interfere with her professional career and would share equally in their domestic responsibilities.

At an intuitive level, Emma had an innate desire to have an impact on the world. The mass populous was still recovering from the two pandemics and attempting to adapt to the design of the emerging new world order. Most agreed that the previous governing arrangement, both within and between countries, did not serve the basic needs of most inhabitants of the planet. Somewhere during the process of reformation, she sensed a need for a fundamental change in how people related to each other, and a corresponding desire to participate in it. This desire to help address the needs of those less fortunate was a fundamental difference between her and her father that was not passed on genetically nor encouraged by him.

Mark and Emma eventually concluded that the best arrangement was a mutually agreed-to trial separation. Emma moved back to Amsterdam, and Mark remained in their home in Virginia. Several months into their separation, Emma phoned Mark to discuss a proposal that might work for them both during their separation.

"Mark, how are you?" Emma asked compassionately. After all, she still loved him.

"Work is fine, but honestly speaking, it's hard for me to be separated from you, Emma." He paused to compose himself, then continued. "I do love you. And I probably always will. What about you?" The two of them could always speak honestly, without the usual drama in complicated career-based relationships.

"I feel the same way," she replied, "but my passion for life is here in Europe. I don't know what it is, but I feel we are on the verge of something great."

He continued to listen as he felt the simultaneous excitement and sadness in her voice. "Do you want a divorce?" he asked, his voice cracking.

"No. I want our arrangement to remain as it is for the time being—unless you find someone who fits your life's passion within a marital arrangement. Can that work for you?" she asked. They both knew the same applied to her, though it was left unsaid.

"I'm not sure. But I am willing to give it a try," he replied.

"I want to assure you this is definitely not an open marriage. I also think we should meet four times a year for a week or two to celebrate our marriage—unless or until something happens," she offered.

"You Europeans are so practical about intimate relationships. But okay, let's try it and see what happens," he agreed, trying not to get his hopes up for some kind of miracle reunion.

"You often forget, Mark, that I am part of the lower countries of BeNeLux [Belgium, the Netherlands, and Luxembourg] first, and European second. We are a culture that tends to balance practicality with affairs of the heart."

- - - | | | | | - - -

All new selections to the broader Consortium were vetted and approved by the Chairman, along with input from Lenhard Rieser, at their regular weekly meetings. Those who served as members of the Consortium were always available to take on special projects after leaving an official term in the broader organization. The rotation of membership served to constantly bring in new ideas and next-generation leadership of the world's political, economic, financial, science and technology, and business directions. Oftentimes, some were visionaries with the intention of molding the world's future. However, what they all shared in common was the necessity to create the future almost exclusively in concert with their views.

Emma Rushland was different from most members of the Consortium in her view of how people should be governed. She believed, somewhat idealistically, that people would find their way to a situation that benefitted them all, which was the reason she secretly admired the worldwide Renaissance Communities. She discovered that the most difficult challenge with respect to the idea of self-empowerment was most people's timeless belief that they needed to be led by someone more capable than themselves. Breaking the mold of that way of thinking was the greatest obstacle she faced when working with refugee groups and the European mass populous in the wake of the two Great Tragedies. She realized that she was dealing with centuries of programming and continual reinforcement that was probably genetically inherent at this point in time.

Unknown to Emma were the secret conversations her father had with influential members of the Consortium. He felt that if she could be exposed to visionaries as well as the movers and shakers of the world, she would find her place among them. So, he had prevailed among them to extend her an invitation to become part of their membership. His convincing point was that the benefit in the long run would be worth their investment in her skills and contributions. She was destined to be a force in European affairs, and even better, within the fold of the Consortium.

26

||||||||||||||||||||||||||||||||||||||||||||||||||||||||||||||||||||||||||||||||||||||||||||||||||||||||||||||||||||||||||||||||

THE EURODIA PROJECT

In his role as leader of the restoration of Western Europe, Karl Christen convened a meeting of the pivotal countries to move forward with their integration with India. In truth, the urgency of the meeting had been created by the progressive organization of the Tawhid Confederation and the departure of Britain from the European Union. In practice, the whole idea of a collaborative attitude between the confederations was still evolving. The old urges of pitted competition were still latent but clearly recognized as an undesirable knee-jerk reaction.

The representatives present at this initial meeting consisted of those who would play leading roles in establishing Eurodia from cultural, business, and economic standpoints. They included representatives from the foundation states of Germany and France, and representation from Scandinavia, Southern Europe, and selected Northern European countries, such as Poland and the Czech Republic. A special role was proposed for Switzerland as the financial center of the new confederation. In the spirit of transparency, the group had also approved the attendance of the Indian prime minister and his aide, Sanjay Krishnamurti, who had been charged to coordinate the Eurodia project on behalf of India.

Prince Frederick of Liechtenstein proposed the sole agenda item be the formation of Eurodia, as suggested to him by Karl Christen. After the prince introduced Karl and briefly described his role in Western Europe's recovery, Karl opened the conversation by proposing the questions for discussion in the morning and afternoon sessions.

"We have an unprecedented opportunity to create a new confederation for Earth unlike anything we have ever imagined before. Why don't we begin by openly sharing our thoughts about the greatest challenges we face in creating Eurodia and then move to prioritize them. That should consume the morning session." Everyone nodded in agreement.

"Then, in the afternoon, we can begin discussing our joint overall mode of operation. I'll stop here and invite short opening statements by the prime minister of India; Mr. Sanjay Krishnamurti, coordinator from India; and Mrs. Emma Rushland, coordinator representing the European Federation."

The prime minister of India expressed his thanks for the proposed confederation with Western Europe. "I believe India is on the threshold of a new era in terms of our participation in the post-pandemic world order. Our strength is based on the potential of our human resources, represented by a strong, highly educated middle class. We want to focus on business expansion and economic prosperity, with an emphasis on addressing the condition of the poor and infirm of our country. We look forward to your support and expertise in these pursuits."

Sanjay spoke next. "I echo the thanks of our prime minister. As coordinator for Eurodia-India, our focus will be on education, economic, and business expansion using an integrated approach with Western Europe. We will continue to build upon our traditional leadership class and the comprehensive integration of cultural differences throughout the confederation. I look forward to working with Mrs. Emma Rushland and the member European countries."

Finally, Emma rose to provide her remarks. "I believe we have an unprecedented opportunity to provide our know-how and technology to create a new world culture, one based on equality, equity, and opportunity for all members of the confederation. I envision the emergence of a new integrated human being from this process of cultural transformation."

In spite of Dr. Christen's invitation for the group's input for challenges and mode of operation, these topics had been identified and discussed some weeks prior to the gathering. The major challenge facing the confederation was prioritization. The contention was primarily between business and economic expansion and cultural integration. However, from Dr. Christen's perspective, both of these activities were irrelevant in priority as compared to the grand plan he had for the peoples of planet Earth.

The Chairman of the Consortium had known Matthias Streefkerk, Emma Rushland's father, for many years, although Streefkerk had no knowledge that Christen was Chairman of the secret Consortium Board. They shared similar philosophies regarding the governing of Europe. The Chairman had decided long ago that Matthias was best placed in the high tribunal of The Hague instead of having any association with the Consortium. This was particularly true in cases where such trials involved the judgment of war criminals who were the collateral damage of the various "safety-valve activities" of the Consortium Board on behalf of global stability. Streefkerk's complete independence was essential to retain his neutrality and credibility.

The Chairman had also been closely following the career of Matthias's daughter over the years. He concluded that his next progressive move would be to place her in charge of Eurodia-Europe, in spite of her lack of South Asian experience. This move would also avoid any issues of "face" between the Germans and the French: a neutral party from a neutral municipality they could both trust in lieu of a representative from their own country. In order to keep his finger on the pulse of the process, he also wanted her to be a member of the Consortium—but not the board. Their relationship would be Karl Christen, head of West European Recovery, and Emma Rushland, coordinator of the European

Federation. This would mean that her Indian counterpart, with whom she would be working, would be Sanjay Krishnamurti. The characters and scenarios the Chairman had orchestrated were perfectly falling into place, from his perspective.

However, there was a piece of the puzzle that no one knew: the Chairman's trump card.

- - - | | | | | - - -

Back at my Salt Lake City oasis, I began to give thought to how Lara and I would work together as a team in apprehending the head of the Consortium. There was no role for myself that I could conceive of playing. Sure, I had had fun being chased around the world with John and almost being killed on several occasions, even though we put Gala's life at risk too many times to count. But this was a big game, way out of my league. And that story about needing me for identifying the "human side of a Pleiadian" was total horseshit. Pleiadians didn't have a human side. They operated from a perspective of what was best for the preservation of spiritual human traits and absolute avoidance of a nuclear holocaust. That's it! I knew it, and they were aware that I knew it.

In my state of reflection, I heard a soft knock at my door, as though someone had been listening in on my private thoughts. I opened the door, and there stood Lara, all five foot nine of her statuesque body, smiling that smile.

"Hi, Bill. I knew you were still up, so I wondered if I could spend a few minutes with you explaining how we might work together as a team."

I was still having a hard time adjusting to the Pleiadian clairvoyant scanning ability, in spite of my years with John.

"Sure," I said. "An explanation for what I'm supposed to do, and why, would be very helpful to me." *Given that I didn't have a clue about either*, I thought, forgetting momentarily that she could perceive both clairvoyantly and telepathically.

"First of all, let me clarify our connection. We belong to the same spiritual family: the Guardians."

"What's a spiritual family?" I asked, looking confused.

"A group of entities, both human and nonhuman, having almost identical levels of spiritual wisdom and vibrational frequencies. Most of all, they have the same universal purpose."

"And what is their purpose?" I asked.

"To assist struggling civilizations within the Milky Way Galaxy through various stages of transformation to a more evolved state. That's it."

"Why can't civilizations decide what they want independent of our interference? Maybe they want to remain as they are," I challenged, just to play the devil's advocate.

"They don't have a choice, Bill. The universe is not static. It is always dynamically changing to maintain overall balance and harmony through transformation, both physical and spiritual. At certain points of progression, every entity or aspect of the universe reaches a point of transformation. At that point, the entity or aspect transforms, and survives and thrives—or it goes out of existence as a result of its own resistance. Put simply, it chooses to self-destruct rather than transform," Lara said. "Does that scenario sound familiar?"

"So, we were at a point of transformation before the two Great Tragedies?" I asked.

"That's right. The Pleiadian intervention, on behalf of their own survival, provided the inhabitants of Earth a means of transforming to your present state. I doubt whether you would have been able to accomplish such a transformation on your own." She paused. "As you know, both Lemuria and Atlantis were unsuccessful in transcending their unique points of progression—and chose to go out of existence. Fortunately, your transformation was metaphysical in nature. You should understand that there are literally millions of these events simultaneously occurring in our Milky Way Galaxy alone."

"Okay, I think I get it," I said, even though I had no comprehension of the dimension she was describing. "Now, back to how we work together as a team."

"At some point in the coming weeks, you will be invited to partner with someone on a very important project. Do not be shocked by the appearance of this individual. It's all part of the plan for capturing the Chairman. You will also be required to do something significantly outside of your zone of integrity."

"Sounds familiar. I didn't know I had any integrity left," I replied jokingly.

Lara smiled and continued. "Now let me tell you what I have in mind."

27

STORMING

Emma Rushland and Sanjay Krishnamurti met in Amsterdam to begin discussions for implementing the Eurodia Confederation. Emma had suggested a small initial meeting of four individuals—Sanjay, Emma, and their top aides—to get to know each other in their planning process. Sanjay introduced his top aide, a very wealthy prominent businessman from Delhi. They had been friends for most of their lives and were both from the Brahmin Indian class.

Emma introduced me as her top aide, and said, "I selected Dr. Bradley as a neutral party and because of his considerable experience in working with groups globally in the new era. I think he can be of considerable value in helping us find our way through the initial difficulties we might encounter." Emma paused and added, "And maybe even guide us to navigate the future."

"Welcome, Dr. Bradley," Sanjay said, using his perfectly accented British English. "Of course, I am aware of the years you have dedicated to global unity, as well as your work with the Renaissance Communities. We look forward to your insights." I was aware that Sanjay had taken his undergraduate studies at Oxford College and was an honors graduate from Stanford Business School.

I replied, "I'm only here to offer observations and suggestions for your consideration. I congratulate you both on launching such an ambitious effort; it is unlike anything being attempted by any of the other confederations, with perhaps the exception of the Tawhid Confederation. Theirs is presumably based on cultural similarities, in spite of a considerable variety in their ethnic composition. We'll see how that works out once implementation begins." I was particularly intent on establishing a close relationship with Sanjay.

Emma invited Sanjay, as the guest coordinator from India, to begin the opening remarks. "Our thinking is that we should prioritize business integration, the establishment of independent Indian business operations involving finance and selected business ventures that we mutually agree to," Sanjay said.

Emma replied, "Besides business ventures, we also have three other equally important areas in our integration process: education, economics, and culture. In fact, cultural integration will probably be part of everything we do. Does that make sense to you?"

Sanjay reacted with a decided but almost imperceptible shift in demeanor. First, he diplomatically questioned the idea that an outsider would presume to know what was best for the Indian economy, and second, because it came from a woman, a reaction he tried to suppress. In Sanjay's experience, women knew their place in the world of business, and were demure and almost apologetic in expressing their opinion.

I observed the evolving fireworks and decided to let them proceed until everything was out in the open. Emma looked at me for my input, and probably support, but I just sat there pretending that I wasn't aware of her expectation.

"That's one of the main reasons I selected my top aide," Sanjay said confidently. "He is on the front line of what is taking place in India in the post-pandemics era, especially as it relates to business. We have overtaken China in terms of the global GDP." Then he turned to his colleague and invited his comments.

Being a polished global businessman, Sanjay's top aide paused to allow elevated emotions to subside, and then he began.

"As we are all aware, India has been attempting to find its place in the global economic picture since long before the pandemics. The aftermath of those tragedies has provided the opportunity we have before us to create business alliances across cultures." He locked eyes with Emma and displayed a polished sense of sincerity. "Such alliances have the potential to rival the English—excuse me, the Tawhid Confederation. However, we can accomplish this goal only by establishing income-creating ventures that feed our economy and education expansion."

Silence descended upon the meeting. No one knew where to go next, so Sanjay said, "My colleague is representative of the type of visionary leadership that benefits our efforts most, and—" Emma interrupted him mid-sentence and asked Sanjay's aide, "What do you mean by 'business alliances across cultures'?"

Again the aide hesitated as if to gather his thoughts, and then looked at Emma as one would a child asking about the obvious. "I simply mean two different cultures, one Eurocentric and the other more people-centric, doing business in a cooperative manner," he replied.

"We have in mind something much more involved in terms of cultural integration," Emma responded. I saw that she was unflustered by the man's nonverbal communication. "The transformation of outdated beliefs and attitudes about the roles of women, broader educational and business opportunities for presumed lower-caste members who are traditionally excluded, and a focus on empowered leadership."

"Our culture has been around for a considerable number of centuries," Sanjay said. Although, he didn't state it, I could tell that he was referring to Varanasi, which was considered to be the oldest city in existence. "It has worked as well as possible for everyone, given our population pressures. Why should we change, or as you say, transform it?" He ended with a decided look of superiority, not based on ethnicity but on gender.

"Because we have been living in the dark ages and thinking we are enlightened, that's why. If you want a sense of what I think we should be aiming for, I have copies of 'The Seven Principles of Social Equality' to share with you." Emma gave copies to everyone, including me, with a callous look on her face.

Sanjay and his colleague had seen the Seven Principles document. They had dismissed it as something that would not work for India, in spite of a strong underclass of support for it. Sanjay said to me invitingly, "Dr. Bradley, what are your thoughts about what we've discussed so far?"

I steepled my index fingers, adopted a look of natural sincerity, and began. "First, I would say that you are both right on track in terms of what you are initially expecting from each other. Second, if you are serious about this confederation, no partner ever gets everything they want—like Christmas." I smiled, but no one joined me, even though I knew that Christmas was treated as a secular holiday among many Hindus. I continued, "Third, you are attempting to do something quite extraordinary that has never been done peacefully in the history of this planet: true cultural integration. However, I tend to agree with Mr. Krishnamurti that such a transformation of his culture, which has evolved over centuries, will be very difficult to accomplish."

Emma was smiling until my last statement. She looked as though I had stabbed her in the back. Both Sanjay and his business colleague looked quite pleased with my conclusion. Emma suggested that we had accomplished as much as possible for a start and had learned much about each other's prioritized projects. She suggested that we conclude the meeting. Everyone agreed. Emma looked at me disappointingly and exited the room.

Sanjay extended his hand to me and said, "Maybe you would like to visit us in India and meet my extended team who are working on this project."

"I would indeed," I said.

"We'll set it up," he replied.

28

THE VISIT

Several weeks prior to the initial meeting with Sanjay and his business colleague from India, Emma had experienced a series of startling events. It began with a sequence of highly emotional dreams about her childhood. Her mother had died shortly after her birth, so Emma had frequently played alone as a child. Her father started giving her complex puzzles and toys to play with that focused on her cognitive learning.

As the puzzles became progressively more complex, she sensed an adult playmate whom only she could see, and who taught her how to solve the difficulties she experienced. The dreams she was now having were so vivid in detail that she felt as though she were re-experiencing the events from childhood. In these present dreams she noticed that the visage of her invisible playmate was familiar to her, which interested her more than frightened her.

Emma now recalled that as she had grown older, she began to lose conscious contact with her adult playmate because she didn't need her as much to cope with her life challenges. On special occasions she would secretly request the help of her playmate, whom she now thought of as her guardian angel, and by morning the solution to a dilemma or problem she was dealing with would be downloaded like a software document. She never took these events too seriously but had simply attributed them to lessons she had learned from childhood.

Now, her most recent series of dreams involved the visage of the woman she now vaguely remembered as her childhood playmate. As a matter of fact, the face was strikingly familiar.

Over the period of a week or so, Emma's dreams took on a definite theme. In one dream, she was in a familiar setting with people she knew, and in another, she was with unfamiliar people and was meeting them for the first time. In both types of dreams, there was the vague outline of a sinister character that scared her. She felt more secure and confident in the former setting than in the latter. As the emotional content of her dreams intensified, she wondered whether she should see someone about her psychological state if the dreams continued.

Over the following weeks, Emma experienced her dreams with even greater visual intensity than before. In these dreams, the visage of the patient and caring woman came into the greatest focus thus far. She was tall, about five foot nine, with the body of a model, in a dress that outlined the curvature of her body. She had European features and piercing green eyes framed by dark auburn hair.

During one of her dreams, Emma suddenly opened her eyes and saw the woman from her dreams sitting in a chair near her bedside. She was speechless and yet unafraid because she was, in fact, looking at a mirror image of herself. But it couldn't be a mirror, she surmised, since she was lying in bed and the woman was sitting in a chair. The woman smiled and said, "Hello kiddo. Long time no see."

Emma was speechless and didn't know how to respond. First, she wanted to make sure she was awake and not still dreaming.

"No, Emma you're not asleep. You are fully awake," the woman said.

"I don't understand. What's going on? Who are you?"

"Look, Em, I know this unexpected reunion is a lot to process, given how long it has been since your childhood here on Earth."

Emma blurted out, "Am I dead?"

The woman laughed and said, "Em, please don't get dramatic on me; you're very much alive. However, I need to explain some things to you. Then we can get on with what we need to do. Okay?"

Tentatively, Emma said, "Yeah, okay. An explanation would be nice."

"I am your twin soul, identical in both vibrational frequency and wisdom. Being in a human body somewhat limits how much you can recall because the channel to how much you know is so narrow. The name I have taken for this visit here on Earth is Lara Headley."

"My twin soul? What does that mean?"

"Come on, Em. It really hasn't been that long. Yes, we are two peas in a pod," Lara said with a laugh. In spite of her confusion and anxiety, Emma managed to smile when the download revealed events she clearly recalled.

"In fact, we are two identical peas in a pod—in every respect except personality; I couldn't duplicate that characteristic with a human body. I chose to make us identical human twins for what I have in mind. Now, I need to get to the point. I am here on a mission to help capture and neutralize a rogue Pleiadian who is in opposition to everything you are attempting to accomplish."

"Sounds like a movie. Is this a dreamland movie, Lara?"

"I wish it were, Em. Unfortunately for earthlings, it's very much real life."

"Is the rogue guy the sinister character in my dreams?"

"Yep. That's him."

"I don't understand."

"You know, Em, I think you need to go back to sleep. After you awake in the morning, process our meeting for the entire day, and then I'll meet up with you tomorrow night to explain the rest. Okay?"

"Yeah, okay," Emma replied tentatively. She was still trying to understand what was going on.

"Look, if you need me during the day to get a pinch-yourself test, I'll be there."

In the next instant, Lara was gone.

When Lara appeared the following evening, Emma wasn't asleep. She was waiting for Lara's arrival because her mind was filled with questions. She was much more centered than the she had been on the previous evening when Lara had first arrived.

"Good evening, Em. I hope you had a pleasant day and have begun making sense of the distinction between your earthly existence and your Pleiadian origin."

Emma began to feel natural in conversation with Lara. "What do you mean by my Pleiadian origin, and how does it relate to the mission you mentioned last night?"

"Em, we have been sending emissaries to Earth for centuries, trying to get earthlings to the next level of evolution. Our efforts have not worked in the past. As twin souls, we were sent to infiltrate an ultra-secret organization called the Consortium in order to capture and neutralize its Chairman."

Emma looked confused and said, "I still don't understand. I'm a member of the Consortium, but I don't know of any Chairman. Lenhard Rieser heads the organization."

Lara went on to explain the existence of the Consortium executive board, which was headed by the Chairman. She explained that his main objective was to prevent the people of Earth from living more compatibly in order to ensure their survival.

"Why?" Emma asked, astounded. She began to realize why the Seven Principles had not been more readily adopted.

"We believe he wants to maintain control of planetary events by influencing their dominant way of thinking. And he has been very successful at it so far. At present, he has considerable influence among the balance of those who might revert to a world of fear and conflict, as well as those who outright resist changing in any way that would benefit others. So, it's very simple from a Pleiadian perspective. We are responsible for his being here and, in part, for what he has become.

He must be captured and neutralized. That, in essence, is our project."

"How do we go about capturing and neutralizing him?" Emma cautiously asked.

"First, I need you to invite Dr. Bill Bradley to become your top aide in establishing Eurodia."

"I am aware of him and his efforts to bring about global understanding, and his support of the Renaissance Communities," replied Emma. "But how do those activities fit with the formation of the Eurodia Confederation?"

"Bill's real role will be to form a close relationship with Sanjay Krishnamurti, at your expense. So be prepared. We know from surveillance work that Sanjay is a member of the Consortium's executive board. He can be a direct connection to identifying and capturing the Chairman. Justify Bill's role in whatever way you need to. Okay?"

Emma replied, "Okay, I'll try to make it work, but this project is coming at me really fast."

"We can work on that so you are more comfortable with what we are trying to accomplish. Just keep in mind that you are the coordinator and Bill is your top aide." Pause. "Okay?"

"Yes," Emma reluctantly replied.

"By the way, Dr. Bradley is also one of us."

"What do you mean, he's one of us?" asked Emma.

"He belongs to our family. The Guardians."

"The three of us?" asked Emma.

"Yes, the three of us, and many more."

Just when Emma thought she had everything under control, Lara added something new.

"Are you with me so far?" asked Lara.

"Yeah, I think so."

"Okay. Your job will be to 'work' Lenhard Rieser. We believe he is the direct link to the Chairman, since, as you know, he is executive director of the publicly-known Consortium."

"I don't think I can work Lenhard Rieser. I know he has antiquated ideas about the role of women, but I don't think I would be credible going that route. The first woman selected for the Consortium is reportedly in his pocket."

"You don't have to worry about Rieser. That's where I come in. I'll work Rieser in your place. We are identical. Remember?"

"How?"

Lara smiled and said, "I have my means. And he might be quite surprised. So remember, Bill's primary job will be to endear Sanjay to a friendship. From there he knows exactly what to do."

"And what is that?" asked Emma

Lara explained.

"I can't wait to meet Dr. Bradley," Emma said.

- - - | | | | | - - -

During the following week, Lara, Emma, and I assembled at the Pleiadian safe house in the Netherlands. The occasion was to make introductions and plan the identification and apprehension of the Chairman of the Consortium.

"I guess it's probably difficult, at first, to realize that we are one family—the Guardians," Lara began. "More specifically, that we all share a common objective that has guided our life activities." She turned to Emma and said, "Em, this is Bill Bradley. He has earned his stripes in terms of life-threatening human drama as well as being raised when he was a child by John, his Pleiadian mentor. As you were raised by me. In essence, this is more like a family reunion."

I looked at Emma, then at Lara, and saw no difference in their physical appearance. They were perfect examples of the word *identical*. In terms of personality, Emma was an expressive, and Lara was more of an introvert but firmly in control of situations that involved her. As a result, I was certain I was only seeing the tip of the iceberg where Lara was concerned.

"I am pleased to meet you, Emma," I said with a warm handshake. "And I'm looking forward to working with you."

Lara picked up again. "You might wonder why we have taken such a direct role in dealing with the Chairman. The answer is that he is—or was—one of ours: a Pleiadian. We believe we are responsible for the considerable influence he has wielded over global Earth affairs."

Emma asked, naïvely, "So if he is one yours, why don't *you* identify and neutralize him? Why do you need us?"

"We are certain that the original emissary, who is now the Chairman, we sent to assist in Earth's transformation no longer exists, at least in his original form. We believe he changed his identity and has successfully shielded himself and his Consortium activities from everyone except his board. We also have good reason to believe that Lenhard Rieser, executive director of the Consortium, is the connection between the board and the membership body, and the most probable direct connection to the Chairman. That's why our initial approach at identifying the Chairman is through Lenhard Rieser."

Emma was still trying to grasp the overall picture of what was happening since her disturbing, or enlightening, dreams when Lara said, "In addition to the Lenhard connection, we also have a backup plan to use Bill through a relationship with Sanjay Krishnamurti."

29

CONNECTIONS

Sanjay Krishnamurti returned home to New Delhi, India, to confer with his prime minister regarding the initial meeting with Emma Rushland. "Ms. Rushland will not be an easy person to deal with. I do not know the extent to which Dr. Karl Christen supports her position, but I will find out."

"What is her priority?" asked the prime minister.

"I think she is quite serious about the idea of cultural transformation, meaning fundamental changes in the way we have functioned for centuries in spite of the influence of the British."

"What does that mean in terms of her perception?" he asked, attentive. The prime minister was a pensive individual who paid attention to the detailed way his interactions occurred with others. In essence, he was skilled at reading their nonverbal cues.

"She believes strongly in the Seven Principles of Social Equality, which begins with the given, not assumption, that all humans are equal, in terms of personhood, by virtue of birth."

"That could be a problem," the prime minister said to no one in particular.

"More like intractable," added Sanjay. "Can you ever imagine yourself to be equal to a Vaishya? An artisan merchant, or farmer, or an untouchable for that matter?" he asked, as though the question itself was distasteful. Sanjay laughed at the thought; the prime minister was pensive. He did not answer. He wondered what *he* really thought, particularly in light of how he had changed as a result of the two Great Tragedies.

"What else do I need to know?" he asked, his mind already running ahead to other matters.

"Her top aide, a Dr. William Bradley from the US, was also present. He didn't say much until the very end of our discussion," replied Sanjay, reminding himself how focused the prime minister was to everything that had happened. "I don't think he is 100 percent in alignment with her views. In fact, I wonder if we might invite them both for further discussions here in India. I could get a better read on him, and possibly more," Sanjay said, an idea beginning to form in his mind.

"Good idea," replied the prime minister. "Do it." He rose to attend his next meeting, his bodyguards in tow as he departed their meeting.

- - - | | | | | - - -

Emma Rushland received a secure communication from Sanjay expressing his appreciation for the opportunity they had to begin sharing views of initiating the Eurodia Confederation. He concluded by extending an invitation for us to have a follow-up meeting in New Delhi, and indicated that the prime minister was also looking forward to it.

She summoned me to her office to convey the contents of the invitation.

"Hi, Bill. Have a seat, and take a look at the latest missive from Sanjay." Emma and I had begun using first names after Lara introduced us. It was more like reuniting with an old friend.

I scanned the communique twice and handed it back to her. "What are your thoughts, Emma?" I asked.

"I think he wants to engage us. He's probably anxious to get funding for the business ventures they have planned."

"Probably."

Emma said, "I'm interested in spending time with the prime minister. I was impressed with his statement at our introductory meeting. He seems to be deep and introspective. Did you notice how observant he was of everyone, particularly Dr. Christen?"

"Yes, I did. Why don't you wait a day or so and then suggest a visit three weeks from now. Meanwhile, you can meet with Lenhard Rieser to bring him up to date. I wouldn't be surprised if you heard from Dr. Christen shortly thereafter."

"Good idea, Bill." She paused. "What about dinner tonight? We could continue brainstorming our strategy."

Before I could think about it, I blurted out, "Of course. That's a great idea." Then another thought came as quickly afterward: *What about Gala? What would she think? No problem*, I convinced myself. This was only a business dinner.

"I know of a quiet place near here where we can talk and actually hear each other," she said, smiling. "And it's a fish restaurant."

I had to remind myself that a fish restaurant was just that, not seafood like we typically had in the US. "That's perfect," I replied. I'm sure she noticed the look of reluctance on my face.

"Don't worry, Bill. I'm a married woman. You're safe with me, okay?" She looked at me for confirmation.

"Okay," I said. I appreciated that we got this agreement openly resolved, more for my sake than hers.

The restaurant Emma chose that evening was perfect. The maître d' showed us to a quiet, secluded booth. Emma asked, "Does this work for you, Bill?"

"Perfectly," I said. The waiter magically appeared just after we were seated. I assumed they knew Emma from prior experience. I ordered Wild Turkey with a splash of Coke—sinful for such an expensive whiskey. Emma said, "The usual, Georges."

My impression was that Emma was a very expressive person who lived her life from the inside out. She was rarely receptive to compromising fundamental issues, particularly those that dealt with people who were determining their own fate and those involving equitable opportunity for participation and contribution. How to accomplish these? She also appeared to be flexible as long as those two elements were substantively upheld.

I just listened and sipped my bourbon. It was easy to keep everything going as long as I asked questions. Then she stopped and asked, "What about you, Bill? What drives you in terms of the work we do?"

I paused, thought about her question, and replied, "Helping us adapt to a new reality, where we learn how to live with each other in a mutually compatible way."

"What does that mean?" she asked, with greater interest.

"I mean, if we don't learn how to care about each other in the way we function, we'll be right back where we were before the pandemics. That's why I think Eurodia is the most visionary approach to cultural adaptation, and also the most challenging. It's much easier to work with people who are culturally alike, like the Tawhid Confederation is attempting to preserve."

"The real reason I suggested dinner for tonight was to ask you a question away from the office," she said. "Should I wait for Lenhard to contact me about the recent meeting with Sanjay, or should I propose to meet with him?"

"That's a good question." I said. "What has been your pattern so far? Does he generally wait for you to approach him, or the other way around?"

"We haven't established a pattern, as of yet. I think he's more concerned about the public perception of interfering or influencing the process with India than about protocol."

"Then I suggest you wait a few more days, then send him a memo titled 'Eurodia Update.' Propose a meeting somewhere private, where confidentiality can be assured. However, I have a feeling he'll contact you before you send such a memo."

"Okay, I'll take your advice and hold off. Now let's have a fabulous fish dinner and some excellent French wine."

"Amen. But before we do, I have question for you," I said, looking serious.

Emma looked surprised. "What is it?"

"What's the sole meunière like?"

"To die for," she replied with a smile.

Given my recent history, it took a beat or two before I smiled in return.

30

THE SWITCH

Emma Rushland received a secure memo from Lenhard Rieser two days after our dinner. She immediately informed me of the invitation she had received from Lenhard to meet privately at the official office of the Consortium in Genève, Switzerland. The memo stated that the purpose of the meeting was to update the Consortium body of affairs involving the evolving status of European business and economic matters. It also stated that the meeting would be informal yet private and confidential, so there would be no need for any formal preparation, particularly of a written nature. The memo concluded by indicating that the conversation would obviously be limited to the two of them, referring to the fact that I, her top aide for the Eurodia project, would not be accompanying her. This was strictly a meeting involving a Consortium update.

"I'll be right there," I informed Emma, not wanting to discuss this matter by telephone, even from an office down the hall from her.

When I was seated across from her, I silently pointed upward.

"Everything is secure. You can speak freely," she said, although I knew from experience that there was no such thing as secure.

"Okay, what are your thoughts?" I asked.

"He's interested; I'd guess more than interested. I understand he rarely extends an invitation to meet with someone unless he's instructed by a higher power."

"I agree it's a significant first step in what will hopefully be a chain of events leading to the higher power," I said, grinning.

"Right. I should be careful of running ahead of myself."

"What do you want to achieve from the meeting?" I asked her.

"I'm not sure, now that you ask me. Like his memo states, it will be an informal conversation. I think we'll be okay as long as we keep our objective in mind: identifying and possibly locating the Chairman," she said, referring to "we" as herself and Lara, her identical twin, and indicating the prior conversation she had had with Lara about the same questions.

"Just remember, Em," I emphasized, "steady as she goes; no rush. These guys know what they are doing. They've been doing it for some time now."

"I promise we'll be careful."

Approximately two weeks later, Lara Headley, posing as Emma Rushland, presented herself to the two receptionists at the official office of the Consortium. The actual office space was rather small and unassuming, considering the influence and reputation the organization wielded. The whole point was to be as nondescript and understated as possible. In spite of the modest floor space, the furniture was elegant and reflected a definitive masculine flavor.

In truth, the office was a front. The actual work of the Consortium was conducted at an extremely secure location in Liechtenstein, near the residence of the Chairman, Karl Gustav Christen. The communications system was as secure and impenetrable as any on the planet. It was designed by a Russian team from a black-market firm. By agreement with the head of the firm, the team disappeared shortly after installation.

One of the receptionists escorted Lara into an inner office, where she was warmly greeted by Lenhard Rieser. He asked if she preferred coffee or tea, or some other beverage.

"Just water, please."

Lenhard smiled warmly and began. "Emma, I am so pleased that you have become an active member of the Consortium. Quite frankly, we need new ways of viewing and adapting to world affairs. We honestly feel you represent that change in perspective."

Lara listened with rapt attention but couldn't help picturing a mouse about to be eaten by the cat. She smiled inwardly, knowing exactly where her focus would be concentrated. "Why, thank you, Mr. Rieser. I feel somewhat overwhelmed by the Eurodia project, and wonder whether it is a bit over my head."

"Nonsense," replied Lenhard. "We are confident you can handle it perfectly. It's just a matter of settling in." She could tell he regretted using the word "we," as it exposed the fact that there was another person involved.

"I'm pleased I have Dr. Bradley working with me, because he gives me a different perspective." He smiled at this.

The receptionist knocked softly and entered. She brought coffee, tea, water, and an assortment of condiments on a silver platter. She served Lara water and Lenhard coffee, and quietly retreated from the room.

"And how do you differ, Emma?" asked Lenhard.

"He is a strong supporter of the Renaissance Revolution. I tend to carefully consider the culture and history of a country before deciding on implementation." As Lara spoke, she had an intuitive feeling that she was being watched, although she could not detect or pinpoint a hidden camera.

She was correct. She was being secretly observed by the Chairman and had been from the moment she walked into the reception area. He noted how sophisticated she was and how she carried herself, as though she belonged at the highest levels of power. He concluded that she had matured professionally since his brief encounter with her at the meeting with the Indian prime minister and his coordinator, Sanjay Krishnamurti. Of course, taking on the responsibility she had been given, she either had to grow up fast or wilt on the vine.

As they exchanged ideas about the integration process, Lenhard became more comfortable with Lara, still believing she was Emma. She had a level of sophistication about her that he had not observed on previous occasions. Her continual smile put him at ease, and he even noted a stirring along his loins on several occasions. However, he knew that she was off limits because of the plans the Chairman had in mind for her role in establishing Eurodia. She had to be above reproach.

Then Lara asked a question that took him out of the groove he had drifted into. "Are there any ideas that I haven't considered? Or issues I might not have thought of from a broader perspective?" she asked. "After all, this briefing idea goes both ways." She smiled broadly as she hinted at a broader perspective for the first time. By this time, the Chairman had tuned out of their conversation and was attending to more important matters. Lara was aware that something had happened and that she was no longer being observed, once again using her advanced power of clairvoyant perception.

Lenhard stumbled slightly but composed himself and responded, "I'm not sure what you're asking."

"We have some pretty smart people who comprise the Consortium. I was just wondering if there were views beyond those that Bill and I have come up with. I don't think anyone would be concerned about where we got our recommendations from, and we wouldn't feel compelled to tell anyone anyway, as long as they were helpful."

"I'll give it some thought," he replied, in case the Chairman was still observing their conversation. He made a mental note that he would bring it up in the future even if the Chairman didn't.

When their meeting appeared to be complete, Lenhard said, "Well, I appreciate your journeying here. Is there anything I can assist you with?"

"Just a taxi, and I'll be good."

"I can have our car take you back to your hotel. Let me walk you out." He called the receptionist to page their limousine, and proceeded to escort Lara to their outer reception room.

When they reached the outer area Lara said, "Oh, by the way, I'm staying overnight. Can you recommend an excellent restaurant?"

"Of course. Would you like local cuisine?"

"Certainly," she replied.

"In fact, might I join you tonight for an early dinner?" He couldn't resist.

"Certainly," she replied again.

"I will come for you about seven o'clock."

"My hotel is the Angleterre."

He almost said, "I know." Instead, he replied, "I'll see you at seven, Emma."

Lenhard and Lara arrived at L'Entrecote Couronee and were immediately shown to a private table. He seemed lighter and more at ease; home turf. He took the lead and ordered a bottle of red wine, since beef was the specialty of the house. After testing the wine, giving a modest toast, and taking a few sips, he said, "That's excellent wine."

Lara smiled and replied, "I agree."

A comfortable silence ensued momentarily as Lenhard collected his thoughts. Then he offered, "Sometimes, I get frustrated with some members of the Consortium. You asked me about ideas and opinions. When I offer them, it's as though they already have their minds made up, and what I have to offer is ignored."

She didn't say anything, just left the space open for whatever he felt like saying, since she assumed he was most likely speaking of the Chairman. Her introverted personality was key to having others share information about themselves.

"Well, you're the executive director. I would think your opinion would be the most important. After all, you have the most hands-on experience of how things work."

"That's not always the case in terms of final recommendations," he slipped, but went on. "I have an advisory board of active members. We have to agree on matters of the highest importance."

"Again, you're on home turf," she said. "You can set the rules and the venue."

He took another few sips of wine, and the maître d' refilled his glass. "Not always. They like to move around, besides Switzerland—even Liechtenstein, of all places," he said, and quickly caught himself.

Lara pretended she didn't hear him and reached down to retrieve her handbag, "What did you say?" she asked.

"Oh, nothing," he replied, and felt relieved.

They ate dinner and engaged in light, nonsensical conversation. Lara began to sense his agenda, but he would never ask outright, given his position in the Consortium. As a result, after a wonderful dinner, he returned Lara to her hotel and concluded that the time was well spent with a woman of substance. He also thought, in retrospect, that the evening was more like he was reporting to her than the reverse.

31

EURODIA-INDIA

After Lara's visit to Geneva to meet with Lenhard Rieser, when she posed as Emma, we had begun to put some pieces together for identifying and locating the Chairman. All three of us—Lara, Emma, and I—were very excited. Lara had stood in as Emma to more effectively use her personality and psychic powers as a means of eliciting information from Rieser. Three probable pieces of the puzzle that Lara had concluded from her conversations with Rieser were:

1) Someone was listening to their conversation in Rieser's office— probably someone with authority over Rieser, most likely the Chairman.

2) Rieser admitted that his recommendations to the person he probably reported to made final decisions, most likely the Chairman.

3) Meetings with a senior person occurred in Liechtenstein, most likely the Chairman.

The population of Liechtenstein was approximately seventeen thousand after the two pandemics. The country's location and sparse population were a gift of manna—a gift from the gods. Given this information, we immediately turned the information over to perhaps the most powerful intelligence gathering agency in the world, the NSA, although the CIA might have questions about such a conclusion.

The NSA's job was to begin using their extensive resources, in addition to whatever means was typically used to achieve its objectives, to locate and identify communications and travel in and out of Liechtenstein consistent with the operation of an ultra-secret organization like the Consortium. We didn't expect a great deal from the NSA database, since Liechtenstein was not a country high on anyone's surveillance list. In addition, there were no airports in the entire country. The country's primary international activity was their highly secretive tax haven for the ultrarich, which they rigorously guarded.

The second part of the plan involved convincing Sanjay Krishnamurti that he was prepared to take on a highly influential leadership role in Asia, which would be based on India and China as the foundation economies, similar to the roles of France and Germany in establishing Eurodia-Europe. From this base and their combined global economic GDP power, Sanjay's influence could be as great as he chose on the global stage, as well as behind-the-scenes activities for influencing world affairs. Once he began to take such possibilities seriously, the Chairman would learn of his ambitions.

The ensuing situation was believed to be sufficient to lead to conflict, which I might use to learn the identity of the Chairman. The initial step in this process was for me to establish a trusting and respectful relationship with Sanjay. The obvious place to begin was the next meeting of Eurodia in India.

I had sent a secure note to Sanjay, with Emma's and Lara's knowledge, indicating how excited I was to exchange ideas about the future of Eurodia and world affairs, thus opening the door to his thinking that he should begin considering the global landscape.

Sanjay had chosen to personally meet us at the Indira Gandhi

International Airport. He was effusive in his greeting of our delegation, as if he and Emma had already decided to move forward in total agreement. As he greeted her arrival with a wide smile, he looked over her shoulder and winked at me—a good sign. I smiled imperceptibly to avoid anyone thinking we had a conspiracy underway. Sanjay didn't appear to care. I assumed he was probably in his element as the next decisive world leader. I wondered if I had laid it on too thick.

We were housed in the five-star Ashok Hotel near Parliament House. We each had a suite and a twenty-four-hour attendant, both of whom we naturally assumed were spies. It was irrelevant in my case, since I didn't have any official documents. Emma retained all such documentation that was approved by the European Federation. She kept these materials with her at all times, in a briefcase that would inflame the contents if it were not opened by Emma's fingerprint and a coded lock.

The reception meal was a six-course Indian dinner, and we agreed that no business was to be discussed then. We all sat on cushions in the elegant palace and conversed in hushed tones. Emma spent most of her time engaged with the prime minister, who appeared to genuinely enjoy her company. Sanjay and I exchanged thoughtful conversation and comments about the changing world situations since the two pandemics, presumably setting up our ensuing meeting together.

The following morning the four of us—Emma and the prime minister, and Sanjay and I—met, with Emma's and the prime minister's secretaries there to take notes. There was little in the way of significant disagreement between Emma and Sanjay this time. Emma confided in me that their conversation had more or less cemented the initial activities of Eurodia; timing was the only factor necessary for agreement.

Sanjay was cordial but appeared distracted, as though he was thinking of something else of greater importance. However, everything went smoothly throughout the morning session. The afternoon was reserved for separate, individual meetings between Emma and the prime minister, and Sanjay and me, as we had discussed previously.

When Emma met with the prime minister in the afternoon, her instinct about his depth of wisdom was confirmed. As she had concluded, the process of truly culturally integrating was not going to be easy. He was most concerned about how much the remaining Europeans had changed with respect to ethnocentrism. Were they ready to accept Indians as equals, or were their attitudes still colonial and condescending? Emma confided that she didn't know. She also said that if cultural adaptation did not take hold fairly quickly, she would have serious concerns about the success of the Eurodia Confederation. This concern was quickly followed by her declaration, "Failure is not an option!" They both smiled.

The prime minister said, "What equally concerns us is the history of Europeans in terms of money and conquest. These objectives have always overridden everything else, followed by redesigning the conquered culture in their own image."

"I understand your concern, though I do not claim to have experience of it," Emma said. "I assume that's an era long past and certainly out of date. The major difference at play here is that most of us remaining appear to have achieved global transformation to compatibility."

"Yes, that is encouraging," he replied. "If so, we can begin relearning how to live together and work together as equals. Of course, our concern is based on recent experience, so that we may be very sensitive in the initial stages."

"I understand," she replied again, wondering if she could think of a less apologetic and more empowering response. "All I can do is repeat my previous statement, that failure is not an option—for both of us."

"What pleases me most is that we appear to agree that what we should do and how we should do it are not the major concerns between us. But what we will be most challenged by is true transformation in how we view and accept each other as people."

"I guess that's the essence of the Renaissance Revolution—put into practice with the Seven Principles of Social Equality," Emma said. He smiled in cautious agreement.

I was in the precarious position of attempting to accomplish the opposite result from Emma's through my conversation with Sanjay, an individual who I presumed had not changed significantly in his attitude toward unconditionally accepting others. My justification—which I did not completely believe, because I sensed something genuine about him—was that I had to perform on his playing field and by rules that he understood. John did warn me in advance about the game involving my personal integrity, confirming Lara's admonition when we first met. Now I wasn't so sure I could pull it off. I also noted that I was actually more comfortable playing physically life-threating games than I was when I had to pretend to have an inauthentic state of mind, like conspiracies to undermine someone else. I later learned that Sanjay was much more expert at this game than I was.

Sanjay was excited about our having time alone to "share" ideas about his leadership role in the global arena. "Dr. Bradley, I am pleased that we can spend time together to exchange ideas about the changing world. Situations move so fast that I can hardly keep up with them—like the confederations."

I did feel composed and centered when I wasn't lying, so this opening was probably perfect. "I agree about rapid change. I guess that's what happens when a void is created. It seems to fill of its own accord."

"That's an excellent description of what preceded the formation of the confederations," Sanjay said.

"I guess we tend to revert to our natural historical connections first, unless there are significant overriding factors," I said.

"You mean like the Eurodia idea," he offered. "We have a real need to mutually connect and succeed with Europe."

"Yes, the Tawhid Confederation appears to be an attempt to redesign the British Empire culturally, politically, and economically," I suggested. "I think the assumption is that they expect little upheaval in terms of cultural acclimation."

"I think they are wrong!" Sanjay quickly interjected. He stopped momentarily, regretting, I suspect, not the essence of his statement but his strong emotional reply. After all, the East Indians did have extensive experience with the British Empire as a conqueror.

I waited, assuming he was getting his thoughts together to moderate his reply.

"What I meant was, even before the pandemics there was building discord and tensions from people of color in the United States, Britain, and Australia. I don't think the formation of a confederation is going to make these divisions go away. What do you think?" he asked, putting me back into explanation mode, which I was trying to avoid.

Again, thinking of our relationship of integrity, telling the truth was easy for me. "I think you are probably right." Then I quickly changed tack. "That's why I think the success of Eurodia is the most important partnership of all the confederations."

"Why is that?" Sanjay asked.

"It's one thing to change our dominant way of thinking to authentically accepting others. It's quite another to redesign our way of living and working together in order to preserve our mutual existence." My intent was not to propose anything but to establish the conditions for human preservation as the driving force, keeping in mind that Sanjay, by experience, was a product influenced by Oxford and Stanford.

"I'd like to reflect on your ideas and then resume after I've had time to think them through," he said.

Sanjay and I resumed our conversation an hour or so after our initial time together. He began by saying, "I think we stopped when you suggested that the success of Eurodia was the most important experiment. And something about preserving our existence."

"It's simple, from my perspective. You are trying to integrate two very different cultures based on their having equal footing. That's never been done before in modern history. A world based on domination and power always has a winner and a loser, a master and a servant."

He waited, apparently deep in thought.

"Your confederation will have to resolve a broad range of differences and preferences related to ethnocentrism in order to be successful in your collaboration ventures. These are issues I am certain you are aware of," I said. I was thinking, *such change begins at home*, although I didn't state it.

"Yes, we are aware," he replied.

"My real point, which I sent to you, is the void in leadership created in Asia after transformation."

Sanjay looked at me intensely, as though he was not sure what I was implying, since the conversation was moving significantly beyond the Eurodia project.

"What exactly are you implying, Dr. Bradley?" he asked, now looking genuinely surprised.

I took the leap. "I'm implying a leadership role waiting to be filled. And it will be filled fairly soon. Why not you?"

"Have you talked with Emma about this?"

"Of course not; not yet. If this role is not of interest to you, we can drop the conversation here and now, and pretend I never brought it up." I looked at him with the same intensity with which he was observing me.

"Why me?" he asked.

"Why not you?" I asked. "You have the Western pedigree and your Indian status. All you have to do is gain credibility with China."

He continued to stare at me, looking as though he was asking himself, "What is it he wants?"

"Look, part of my responsibility as global emissary is to be on the lookout for possible future global leaders. I think you are one. Give it some time to incubate. As I said, if it feels right, we can discuss it more; if not, let's move on with the success of Eurodia. Okay?"

"Okay," he said hesitantly.

Anxious to get beyond this exchange, I said enthusiastically, "Now, I am ready for another six-course Indian dinner."

As I began to walk away from Sanjay, a thought popped into my mind, one I had been thinking since I first met him. I returned to the conference room, where he was still sitting and appeared to be deep in thought. I knocked lightly on the open door, and he turned toward me with a broad smile. "Did you forget something, Bill?"

"No. I was just wondering if I might ask you a question."

"Ask away," he replied, smiling.

"I know India is a very large country, but I was wondering if you are in any way related to Jiddu Krishnamurti, the Indian philosopher of the last century."

"Yes, I am," he replied. "I am related in lineage through his brother. How do you know of him?" he asked.

"When I was a professor, one of my postdoctoral fellows who was Indian gave me his book as a Christmas present."

"What book was that?" he asked.

"*The Awakening of Intelligence.* It was probably the most influential reading in my process of self-exploration. It totally transformed my perception of reality."

"Ah, yes, that is probably his best work."

"Well, see you tonight at dinner." As I walked away, I experienced a change in my perception of Sanjay, one involving genetic transference—from the same lineage of his famed ancestor.

32

INTROSPECTION

The following morning, after the departure of the Eurodia-European team, Sanjay arranged a meeting with his mentor, the prime minister. He began by relating the conversation he had had with Bill Bradley, with an emphasis on Dr. Bradley's suggestion of Sanjay leading the recovery of Asia. The prime minister listened patiently as Sanjay recounted the exchange between him and Dr. Bradley.

The prime minister asked, "What do you think is his motivation?"

"I am not sure. There were periods of absolute authenticity, and yet every now and then there was doubt on his part, as though he was not sure of what he was trying to accomplish." Sanjay laughed.

There was a long pause as he waited patiently for the prime minister's reply.

"He is certainly correct; both the Tawhid Confederation and the West European regions have declared leadership. At present, Asia, north and south, is dormant, as though waiting for someone to step into that role."

"What do you think?" Sanjay asked with contained excitement.

The prime minister replied, "It's not so much the opportunity as it is your preparedness for such a role."

"What do you mean?" asked Sanjay, surprised there could be any doubt.

"I mean your vulnerabilities. The rules for you will not only be different, but they may require a much higher standard for global acceptance and influence . . . from a Western perspective," he added as an afterthought.

"Why is that?" asked Sanjay.

"For obvious reasons. We may have transformed as people, but we have not established the rules for going forward or how competitive we still might be."

"What do you feel are my greatest vulnerabilities?" Sanjay asked openly.

"Don't you know?" asked the prime minister.

"I have an idea."

"You have more than an idea," the prime minister said sternly.

"Others have described me as arrogant, based on a sense of superiority," he offered.

"And?"

"Ambitious, based on a desire to exceed the accomplishments of others. But I always thought this was a desirable trait."

"Where arrogance is concerned, appearing to be humble creates a mystery about us. Both Karl Christen and the US president have learned how to create mysteries about themselves. These mysteries make them bigger than life as well as reality."

"And ambition?" asked Sanjay. "A strong desire to achieve something?"

"That's a tricky one," replied the prime minister, smiling. "I would suggest that genuinely achieving your ends through others keeps you out of the spotlight and endears you to them. Ultimately, everyone knows the real source. You can clearly see that both of these characteristics played perfectly into Dr. Bradley's hands by his suggestion of Asian leadership for you."

"You think he knew this about me?" asked Sanjay, surprised. "The two traits?"

The prime minister laughed heartily and said, "Of course he knew. He is very perceptive. Now, we have to find out why he has selected you."

This question created a sense of anxiety inside of Sanjay, the reason for which he couldn't put his finger on.

- - - | | | | | - - -

During our flight back to the Netherlands, Emma and I got together to share notes about our separate meetings. She began. "The prime minister was absolutely delightful, Bill. His depth of wisdom was everything I expected and more."

"Is he receptive to the Renaissance idea?" I asked.

"Yes, I think so. At least, in principle. Putting it into practice in India might be a push, but I think he plans to leave those details to Sanjay. What about Sanjay?"

"He's an enigma, and a moving one at that."

"What do you mean?"

"We pretty much know he's a member of the Consortium Board, which has done some horrible things over the years. However, it's possible that neither he nor Li Jong is aware of its history. I suspect Sanjay agrees with you on most issues related to Eurodia. Your differences are probably related to prioritization and timing. He is not accustomed to a forthright woman like you, Emma."

Emma smiled. "I picked up on that, too. But I don't plan to act meek just to please him. I can be straightforward without appearing to be aggressive."

"That would probably work, although it's not easy to accomplish when you feel strongly about something," I replied. "But what about the Chairman's identity? I could relay to Sanjay that there is a secret group that has opposed everything we're trying to accomplish, and see how he reacts."

"I would suggest you tread carefully with that approach. We don't want to make him suspicious or scare him off. Let him make the next move, and you just follow your instincts," Emma said.

"That's probably the best approach. General Maxwell and his cyber team at the NSA are still working on the information Lara provided. Maybe they will come up with something that I can use to guide my approach."

- - - | | | | | - - -

After thinking about his conversation with the prime minister for several days, Sanjay decided to follow up on his initial meeting with me. He sent me a short communique inquiring about a private meeting during the following week. I assumed the "private" designation meant alone—or more precisely, without Emma.

I responded the following day, indicating that I thought a private meeting would be a good idea. The premise, I said, was that if I could understand Sanjay's vision for Eurodia-India, I would be better able to influence Emma in her decision-making. I also said that I would inform Emma of our meeting, in spite of the fact that it would involve only the two of us. In a like manner, Sanjay responded that he would inform his prime minister.

At Sanjay's suggestion, we met on the tropical island of Mauritius, at the famous Villa Resort and Spa. The all-villa hotel was located on the western shore of the island, which provided easy access to the walking paths within the Casela Nature and Leisure Park and the Black River Gorges National Park. The two parks allowed us the flexibility of holding our most important conversation outdoors.

Sanjay seemed surprised at how easy it was to be with me. Perhaps it was because I didn't appear to have any hidden agendas. As in our first conversation, I was slightly distracted every now and again. Sanjay's comfort and openness, from my perspective, was mutual. In some ways, I felt that I was experiencing an earlier version of myself.

I began by sharing with Sanjay a brief synopsis of my work with the Quest, omitting any reference to John, my Pleiadian mentor. Sanjay shared his experiences at Oxford and Stanford. Mostly he shared that he had never felt at home at either place but more like an honored guest.

"What do you mean?" I asked.

"In subtle ways, the Brits always made it clear that they had occupied us, which meant I was not and could never be equal to them."

"In what way?" I asked. "Your academic performances at both Oxford and Stanford were exceptional."

"Equal as an academic colleague," he said openly.

"Have you ever considered that you might be seeking something from both the Brits and Americans that they can't give you?" I asked.

"What do you mean?" he replied with greater intensity. In such moments, I had flashes of his ancestor Jiddu Krishnamurti's writings, and wondered how much of the man's wisdom might be in Sanjay's bloodline.

"I mean, the sense of equality we feel about anyone comes from within us. Our personhood of equality cannot be bestowed upon us by any person or written document. The written declaration of our independence and their treatment of us, as individuals, is a *confirmation* of our own authenticity."

He stared at me as though he was recovering a latent revelation.

I continued, "The real test to understanding what I am suggesting is to examine how you classify and treat people you consider inferior to yourself." He continued to stare intensely.

I concluded, "Once you resolve your equality with them, you won't have any problems with Brits or Americans. Equality or not will be their problem, not yours."

"How do you know this?" Sanjay asked.

"Obviously, by having gone through the experience myself," I said, smiling.

"Why don't we meet up again in an hour? There are a few things

I have to attend to," he suggested, clearly introspective about his own experience.

"Fine," I replied.

I began to notice that Sanjay liked to mix in periods of reflection whenever we talked about certain subjects involving introspection, particularly when there appeared to be a personal reference.

When we resumed our conversation, Sanjay asked, "Who are you? And what do you want from me?" remembering the prime minister's question.

I paused, our eyes locked, and a stream of thoughts of how I should respond ran through my mind. He didn't appear to be uncomfortable with my silence as I fast-forwarded to what I wanted to know by the last day of our three-day meeting. He would detect any diversion or smooth justifying here. I felt I had to come clean, so I decided to go with my intuition, as Emma had suggested.

"With respect to your first question, I am just one person committed to ensuring that the transformation that has occurred as a result of the two pandemics is not reversed—in spite of our initial efforts to resist it."

He continued to look at me with his penetrating eyes. I had the impression that something was happening to him, too.

"I was approached by a man who helped me to discover my passion for life, and the rest is history, as the saying goes," I said.

"Is that it?" he asked, knowing that there was more.

"Not exactly. The success of Eurodia is the key to bringing about an example to the world of what we need to achieve in integrating cultures. That's why Emma chose me. By 'integration' I don't mean the loss of one's unique identity, but thinking and working in a truly inclusive way—whether one is of Indian or European descent—moving smoothly between the two cultures without pretense."

"And my second question. What do you want from me, Bill?"

"Before we get to that question, what is your commitment to cultural integration and the Seven Principles?" I asked.

"Frankly, I am in process. A month or so ago, I was very clear about what I wanted and how to get it. Now I'm not so sure." Sanjay reflected on his encounters with Emma, the subsequent conversation with his prime minister, and now what he was experiencing with me.

"Once you are clear about your commitment to the success of Eurodia as I have described it, I'll answer your second question. Okay?"

"I'm glad we have three days," Sanjay replied. "I think I'll use room service tonight. Let's resume tomorrow morning."

That evening before going to bed, I had an extensive conversation with Emma regarding my exchange with Sanjay; I assumed that Sanjay had one with his prime minister, as well.

33

A ROCK AND A HARD PLACE

Sanjay Krishnamurti and I met for breakfast the second day of our private retreat. He appeared to have had a restless night. I didn't look much better. We had both apparently experienced separate emotional processes involving personal issues in the sleep state. Sanjay had tea, and I had coffee with cream. Neither of us had an appetite for food.

I finally said to him, "You look disheveled."

He replied, "You mean terrible. You don't look much better yourself."

I smiled. "Yeah, I certainly had stuff going on that I didn't expect. At least, not consciously. What about you?"

"The same, I think. But it's mostly about me, I am fairly certain. Hey, why don't we get out of here and figure out what's going on. I think I can handle it if you can."

Famous last words, I thought as we headed out. *Shit, I think I'm beginning to like this guy. No matter; what's important is that I get an ID of the Chairman.*

We headed for the walking path at the Casela Nature and Leisure Park and set off at a brisk pace. We talked very little since we were both still processing our conversations from the previous day. When we returned about an hour later, we were both recharged and ready to engage.

"Where did we leave off yesterday?" asked Sanjay.

"I believe we left off with a question I asked you. Are you committed to the change that is going to be required to make this partnership work, and to implementing some form of the Seven Principles? I think both are crucial to Asian leadership."

"The truth is, until this process began, I was committed to getting out of this deal the business resources and partnerships that will help establish India as being as powerful as any economy in the world today. Since I began negotiations, I have begun to see a picture bigger than my own ambitions. I don't think I've arrived yet, but I'm close. I think that's what last night was all about."

I suspected his indecision also involved his association with the Consortium Board. How would he reconcile the commitment question with the wishes of the Chairman? "I am going to go out on a limb," I said, wondering if I was being too impulsive. I figured we would get to this point sooner or later, anyway. "Before I answer your second question, about what I want from you, I want to give you an update with respect to a hyper-secret organization. Shortly after World War II, this secret organization was formed with new leadership. Since that time, it has orchestrated most of the major events, such as economic upheaval, local conflicts, and wars, that have occurred in the world."

Sanjay started to become visibly uncomfortable and had to consciously resist the urge to ask a question as a diversion. I put my right palm up to stop him and indicated I would entertain questions when I was concluded.

"The individual who leads this organization appears to be in opposition to the changes necessary for working together in a committed way. The first step in achieving this way of functioning was the Quest, whose purpose was to transform the Earth's consciousness from survival to compatibility. It has succeeded, in part, because of our efforts in favor and in spite of this individual's efforts in opposition. As you might guess, the major success was the aftermath, in terms of human selection, of the two pandemics. I guess human crisis is a necessity for expanding consciousness.

"As we move to the implementation stage, we want to ensure that nothing happens to reverse this transformation, that would take us back to using our old survival way of functioning. We believe the Seven Principles provide the guidelines for moving forward. That's also why the success of Eurodia is so vitally important. It will serve as an example of cultural acclimation to all the other alliances. In one way or another, they will have to face the resolution of deep cultural differences. Now, your questions, Sanjay."

"How do you know about this secret organization and how it functions?" Sanjay asked.

"We have known about it for some time now, although we don't know how it functions. However, we do believe the leader has an agenda separate and apart from the members of its broad membership. We draw this conclusion from events that have happened in the past."

"Who is 'we'?" asked Sanjay.

"Mainly those individuals who proactively work to have the Quest and the Seven Principles take hold. We are at a critical juncture in moving forward."

"Well, I can assure you that India will do its part to make Eurodia a success. In short, our future depends on it," Sanjay said.

I had the impression that Sanjay did not want to continue discussing the secret organization. However, as they say about the legal process, he opened the door for more in-depth discussion based on his questions.

I asked, "Have you ever heard of such an organization in your business transactions?"

"No one has ever mentioned such an organization to me."

Cute; accurate answer, I thought. "Do you know if such an organization exists?" I asked pointedly.

His eyes moved rapidly from left to right and back again, as though he was trapped. "Why would you ask me a question like that?" he asked, clearly uncomfortable.

"Because we believe you are a member of the secret board."

"I don't know what you are talking about. I am not a member of any secret board," Sanjay replied, almost pleading. He was probably wondering how someone could have discovered his membership on the Consortium Board.

I looked at him, clearly indicating that I knew he was lying.

Absolute silence followed his denial. He stared down at his clasped hands resting on the table.

"We believe you are relatively new and not aware of the history of the organization. So now to your second question, what do I want from you? It's very simple: I want the identity and location of the leader of your group."

"I'm sorry, Bill, I can't help you." Fear replaced defiance. I could only imagine the consequences for a member who revealed identities in the group, particularly the leader.

"The problem for you is that it was the American NSA that discovered your involvement with the group. I have no idea how they will use this information or what actions they might take."

On the verge of tears, all Sanjay could think about was that he was trapped between the NSA and the Chairman—both of whom dealt with such situations in "permanent ways."

"If what you say is true, do you know what would happen to me?" Sanjay asked.

"I can guess. So anything you say will be between us only," I said, which he knew was a lie. It was the first outright lie I had told him.

"All I can say for now about the Chairman is that he is hiding in plain sight."

"That's it?" I asked.

"Yes," he said emphatically. "I must first talk with my prime minister before answering any more of your questions."

"Okay," I said. "I understand." Then, as an afterthought, I asked, "Do you want to meet for breakfast?"

"I'll let you know," he said, and got up and walked away.

"Oh, by the way," I called after him. "I am still serious about the leadership of Asia. Discuss it with your prime minister. We will support you."

"Are you serious?" he asked with a strained smile.

"Of course I am. You might just find your true calling."

- - - | | | | | - - -

"I apologize, Prime Minister, for awakening you at this hour of the night."

The prime minister knew that Sanjay would not call if it was not an emergency. He was accustomed to late night and early morning awakenings. "What is it, Sanjay?" he asked simply.

"I am in a tenuous situation that I can't discuss, even over this secure line."

"I understand," the prime minister said calmly. "The transport will be ready in one hour to return you back to Delhi. Be sure to gather everything of significance. Do not rush or panic. Remain calm. Do you understand me?"

"Yes, Prime Minister. I understand."

Exactly one hour later, the sleek private jet took off from Sir Seewoosagur Ramgoolam International Airport heading northeast for its eight-hour-and-twenty-minute flight to Delhi, India.

34

DISAPPEARANCE

The following morning, I waited in the restaurant for Sanjay's arrival at our usual meeting time for breakfast. I figured that whatever the previous night was like, last night had to be worse. When he was a half-hour late, I phoned his room, but no one answered. I inquired at the front desk and was told that he had checked out. I asked when, and received a stone-faced reply of silence. The man followed with a terse reply. "Sir, we don't give such information to anyone about our guests' departure times." The essence was, how could you ask such a question at this hotel? So much for my experience and panache at such an exclusive resort.

I returned to my villa room and called Emma. "Hi, Emma, this is Bill. Our friend departed, probably in the early-morning hours, as a result of our conversation yesterday afternoon."

"Do you feel you made progress with regard to moving forward with the Eurodia program?"

"Yes," I replied, recognizing her veiled question. "Significant progress." Then it dawned on me that I shouldn't take a chance on the possibility that we were being monitored. "I feel he was anxious to return home and begin organizing."

"That's great news, Bill."

"I'm not surprised by his early departure. He indicated he wanted to report to his prime minister as soon as possible. He told me he felt we had made substantial progress and that he might be leaving early this morning."

"We'll make arrangements from here for your return. Why don't you be at the Ramgoolam Airport in about two hours? Your transport has been on standby awaiting your return. Everything should be in order by that time."

"Great, I'll be there. Overall, I think our talks were a great success. Thanks, Emma. See you soon."

Less than eight hours after takeoff from Mauritius Island, Sanjay's jet landed safely in Delhi, India. He was immediately taken to the prime minister's private office. The prime minister welcomed him with a hug and a kiss to both cheeks. Although Sanjay was tense and frightened for his future, the prime minister smiled broadly and gestured for him to be seated on a soft pillow. Tea was immediately served to both men, which provided an opportunity for Sanjay to relax.

"You must be exhausted after such a long flight from your retreat," the prime minister began.

"Er, yes, I am," Sanjay distractedly responded. His mind was racing ahead, mentally practicing how he would explain everything to the prime minister. Then he moved toward the prime minister, buried his head in the man's lap, and began sobbing uncontrollably.

The prime minister rubbed his head gently and said, "Tell me everything from the beginning, and we'll see how to best sort out the present state of affairs."

Sanjay sat up and began to recount how everything had started with his invitation to join the publicly known Consortium, of which the prime minister was aware, and from there, how his ambition had taken over. He had been invited to become a member of the Consortium Board—which he had not known existed until then—and sworn to absolute secrecy. He also shared the consequences of revealing anything about the board. Finally, he mentioned Dr. William Bradley's revelations of the previous evening involving events instigated by the board.

The prime minister raised his hand and cautioned Sanjay in no uncertain terms. "Do not tell me the identity of anyone on the Consortium Board or its leader." He was adamant. "What I don't know, I cannot reveal to others nor lie about."

Sanjay continued to sob softly. All he could think about was how his career was over. He was brought back to reality when the prime minister said, "We must have you disappear completely and construct an explanation. Your absence could be at least two years, and probably more."

Sanjay replied, "But what about my career?"

The prime minister responded sternly. "You should be more concerned about your life!" The prime minister had had Sanjay secretly followed and surveilled. He had anticipated that the situation was imminent.

Then he softened, as he would to his own son, and said evenly, "It has already been arranged. You will be working to improve the plight of the untouchables. There is a village in the rurals where no one will recognize you, once you are dressed appropriately. I will be putting you in the hands of one of my most trusted brothers of the poor. Your survival will depend on how intensely you focus on improving their lot and providing whatever they need. In essence, you must learn how to become invisible and then experience humility. First, we must do a makeover, which will take three or four months. In the meantime, we will invent a story for your disappearance."

With the prime minister's final statement, Sanjay was led away, a broken man—at least, the prime minister hoped so. He knew from experience that the road to greatness was never a straight line. And it was certainly not reserved for the wealthy, irrespective of the advantages they were afforded.

- - - | | | | | - - -

I arrived in the early evening to Schiphol Airport, approximately nine miles from Amsterdam. I was transported by a private limousine to the Netherlands NSA safe house, where Emma, Lara, the NSA, and the president's Special Projects Team leads awaited my debriefing. As the net began closing in on the Chairman of the Consortium, General George Maxwell, head of the NSA, and Colonel Darin Thomas, head of the SPT, became involved—one for surveillance and location, and the other for the capture mission led by Lara Headley, respectively.

Everyone was looking forward to my debrief, since I couldn't say anything substantive over the secure phone. I began slowly and deliberately. "In not so many words, Sanjay admitted to being a member of the Consortium Board. I am fairly certain that he and Li Jong knew little about the board's history."

General Maxwell interrupted me and asked impatiently, "Did you find out who runs the board and who the members are? We couldn't care less about Sanjay or his sidekick, Li Jong."

"The closest I got to the Chairman's identity was Sanjay's statement, 'He's hiding in plain sight.' He didn't give me a name."

"What about the others?" asked Colonel Thomas.

"He didn't reveal anything more about their identities, either. Between the Consortium and the consequences of being identified by the NSA, I think he was extremely frightened. I suspect the Chairman is equally unforgiving in this respect."

"You sound like you are sorry for him," said General Maxwell. "I hope we aren't dealing with Stockholm Syndrome"—a situation where the good guy sympathizes with the plight of his adversary, the bad guy.

I immediately replied, "No, General, you're dealing with a 'Human Syndrome.' I didn't consider myself to be part of an elimination squad. When he was trapped between the sources of consequences, the only person he could think of was his prime minister, who is his mentor."

"I'm sorry, Dr. Bradley. I'm just caught up in capturing this Chairman guy and want nothing more than to ship him to another galaxy."

Colonel Thomas looked to General Maxwell and asked, "Did we pick up the phone conversation between Sanjay and the prime minister, General?"

"No, he used a highly secure phone that we were unable to intercept. In any case, he probably wouldn't have revealed anything by phone. I suspect he was instructed to hightail his way back home, as Dr. Bradley has confirmed."

Just then there was a soft knock on the meeting room door. "Dammit, we're busy!" General Maxwell shouted. In spite of his outburst, the soft knock came again. Emma raised her hand and cracked open the door to see her secretarial aide, who said in a soft voice, "I think you should see this." She handed Emma a piece of paper and quickly withdrew. Emma read the note and turned to see everyone looking at her expectantly. She read the communique out loud.

"It says, 'To the Global Diplomatic Community: We want to inform the global diplomatic community that the air transport returning Mr. Sanjay Krishnamurti from a meeting with a member of the Eurodia-Europe corps apparently went down over the Indian Ocean. A massive recovery effort has been dispatched from India to begin the search for survivors. We will keep the world informed of our progress. Please keep Mr. Krishnamurti and his crew in your prayers. The Prime Minister of India.'"

General Maxwell said, "I doubt if we'll ever see Mr. Krishnamurti again."

"He is as good as dead, isn't he?" asked Emma.

"Not likely. He's too valuable."

"Then where is he?"

"Probably being woven into the fabric."

Emma looked at General Maxwell, confused. Lara assumed a look of neutrality, thinking she would inform Ravi Patel, the Pleiadian assigned to the transformation of India, of the general's remark via their psychic communication network.

- - - | | | | | - - -

When the prime minister had received the call from Sanjay, he decided it was time to put his plan into action. He had dispatched a team of agents to take over the Indian air control system and the navigation and safety of Sanjay's transport over the Indian Ocean, across India, and into Delhi. Sanjay was then dispatched by a blind limousine to the prime minister's residence. The remainder of his plan involved mere details once Sanjay reached his private office.

The following afternoon, the prime minister sent out a follow-up communique for worldwide distribution.

To the Global Diplomatic Community:

As an update to yesterday's communique regarding Mr. Sanjay Krishnamurti's air transport, we have not been successful in locating his airplane or any survivors. We will continue to search a wider sector of the Indian Ocean. Please keep Mr. Krishnamurti and his crew in your prayers.

The Prime Minister of India

When word reached the Chairman about Sanjay's missing air transport over the Indian Ocean, he immediately summoned Lenhard Rieser for a meeting at the castle in Neustadt, Liechtenstein.

35

IDENTIFICATION

In his unofficial role as liaison between the executive board and the broad Consortium membership, Lenhard Rieser regularly traveled from Geneva to the Consortium Communication Center in Neustadt, in northern Liechtenstein. At the Chairman's request, he immediately arranged for travel to the CCC. The secretaries in Geneva arranged a mid-morning flight to Zürich as well as Rieser's usual limousine transport to the CCC, about an hour and a half drive from the airport. Such arrangements were rarely made using secure communications so as to avoid any suspicions of the Consortium staff.

After spending a few hours at the Consortium Communication Center updating the status of Sanjay Krishnamurti and other business of the Consortium, Rieser summoned the limousine for travel to the villa overlooking the town of Neustadt. As was custom, travel to the villa utilized a hidden route that brought him to the rear entrance. He was met by the Chairman's manservant, Sean McIntyre, formerly trained by the British SAS, who escorted him to the Chairman's office suite.

Rieser and the Chairman talked briefly about the Chairman's responsibility with respect to the Cancer Research Center near the capital of

Vaduz, located along the Rhine River in southern Liechtenstein. The Chairman indicated that the operation essentially ran itself, with his top senior scientist in charge. The scientist had been recruited from the German Cancer Research Center—DKFZ—in Heidelberg. The two men discussed the Chairman's more active role in leading the recovery of Western Europe and possible expansion eastward. They agreed that a greater focus in this role was best for the present.

"That brings us to the discussion of Eurodia, and more specifically, Sanjay," the Chairman said.

Lenhard replied, "I stopped by the CCC on my way here to get an update regarding the search effort in the Indian Ocean. It appears there has been no report of a sighting of survivors or aircraft debris. I have the impression they may call it off in a few days."

The Chairman stared out of the floor-to-ceiling window to the town below. "I had had Sanjay in mind as a possible successor to Sir Charles Ethan. I know he was young and had rough edges, but I figured the more we got him involved in our future activities, the better we could decide whether he had long-term potential or not."

"No question he was the brightest and most intuitive of the remaining board members," Lenhard said. "There was something special about him that went beyond his business acumen."

"I don't like our board members going missing without us having something to do with it," the Chairman said, smiling menacingly.

"Should we do our own investigation?" asked Lenhard.

"You read my mind. Let's make sure we've covered all possibilities, especially where board members are concerned."

"And," added Lenhard, "where there is no body for confirmation."

Moving on to another agenda item, the Chairman asked, "What did you think of your meeting with Emma?"

"I found her quite composed. I think she will handle Europe-Eurodia quite well."

"I agree," replied the Chairman, sounding skeptical.

"What?" asked Lenhard, recognizing the Chairman's questioning look.

"There was something about her. My perception of her at the announcement and at your meeting was different. When meeting with you, she was not only composed but also perceptive. I can't put my finger on it, but she reflected an air of great sophistication."

"I'll keep tabs on her," said Lenhard, not wanting to reveal her effect on him the evening they had dined. "Too bad we don't have Sanjay to keep us informed."

"What about Dr. Bradley as her aide? Anything there?" asked the Chairman.

"No more than we already know. You approved of him, based on Emma's recommendation, to keep her in our confidence. I'll follow up on Sanjay's disappearance and keep an eye on Emma for anything unusual. Too bad we can't consider her as Sanjay's replacement."

That comment perked the Chairman's attention.

There was a soft knock on the door, and the Chairman said, "Enter." Sean quickly walked over, handed him a folded note, and immediately departed, as though he was never there.

- - - | | | | | - - -

After Dr. Bradley's debriefing, General George Maxwell had immediately returned to his US office to confer with his cyber team. He hit the "open" button to his highly secure global SAT phone at his Fort Meade office. "Maxwell."

"General, I think we may have something here."

General Maxwell recognized the voice of Colonel Darin Thomas, head of the president's Special Projects Team.

"As you suggested, we surveilled the movements of Herr Lenhard Rieser and connected with your people for hacking any travel he might have in mind. We were able to learn of a trip he suddenly planned from Geneva to Zürich by air and then to Neustadt, Liechtenstein, by limousine. Using 'tag and go' with my team along the A4 west to Vaduz and then north, we followed him to a location just outside of Neustadt. We waited more than three hours for his next move, but the limousine did not exit. So we spread out and surveilled Neustadt."

General Maxwell broke in and said, "Get to the point, Colonel."

"We lost him, General."

"How could that happen, Colonel?" asked Maxwell. "It's a goddamn village."

Rather than answer Maxwell's question, Colonel Thomas continued his report. "In spite of our oversight, I struck up a conversation with a local and said that I was touring with a few friends, then asked if he knew the touring hours of the castle up on the mountain. I asked if the villa next to it was part of the tour. He said no, that the villa is the home of their most famous citizen. 'Who?' I asked. Well, guess who, General?"

That's what Maxwell liked about Thomas; he didn't take things personally. Maxwell calmly asked, "Who?"

"None other than Dr. Karl Gustav Christen."

"Could it be him?" Maxwell asked.

"That's my question to you, General. Your intel people have been looking for someone from Liechtenstein who is well known and hiding in plain sight. We had better be right about this one. I suggest your team focus in on the site where Herr Rieser went. I'll send you the coordinates."

General Maxwell smiled at Colonel Thomas's comment about being right and said, "I'll be expecting them." He paused a moment and then said, "Let me make a call and get back to you. Meanwhile, hold tight, and keep a look out for Rieser's limo."

After hanging up, General Maxwell buzzed General Kenneth Clarke, the president's chief of staff. "Hey, Ken. Thomas and his team followed Rieser to Neustadt, Liechtenstein. They lost him there, but they did discover the residence of its most famous citizen."

"Who is he?" Ken asked excitedly.

"None other than Karl Gustav Christen."

"No shit," Ken replied.

"Could it be him?" General Maxwell asked.

"I'm convinced he tried to poison the president when they disagreed on global recovery. I didn't like him the moment I met him. Something sinister about him."

"Well, we'd better be right before we call in Lara for neutralization. Talk it over with the president, and see what he wants us to do," the general said.

General Clarke immediately put his people to work, searching everything they could about the life and history of Karl Gustav Christen and his family heritage. There was an incredible amount of recent information regarding his cancer research work, public service, and generous donations made on behalf of Liechtenstein. Then they hit a wall for the time prior to World War II, where Christen's family appeared to be just another privileged aristocratic family dating back over several centuries. Everything seemed to have started with Karl Christen's appearance on the scene shortly after World War II. There was nothing to hint at or confirm his activities as Chairman of the Consortium but also nothing to contradict it.

- - - | | | | | - - -

The Chairman calmly read the folded note from his SAS manservant, then turned to Rieser and said, "It appears you might have been followed to the Comm Center."

"What do you mean? I used our normal precautions."

"A stranger in town inquired about touring the castle, and asked about the adjacent villa. One of our loyal locals proudly told him it was the residence of our most famous citizen: Karl Gustav Christen. What do you make of that?"

Before Rieser could reply, the Chairman calmly picked up his phone and pushed a button. Sean McIntyre answered immediately. Karl was certain that his identity as Chairman of the board had been compromised.

"Ready the helicopter. We'll be leaving in twenty minutes."

"Done, sir," Sean said. He dialed the downstairs recreation room, where the helicopter pilot was lounging. The pilot was one of the two who were on standby 24/7. The pilot hurried to the outside concrete platform through a basement exit, boarded the helicopter, and began the checklist countdown.

Precisely twenty minutes later, the Chairman retrieved a briefcase that had been prepared for such an occasion. He and Sean headed out of the office to the back entrance that Rieser had used earlier. The limo driver was instructed to head back to the Zürich airport with Rieser as his lone passenger. Rieser got in, immediately raised the tinted windows, and they headed south to Vaduz to connect to the A4 west back to the secret entrance at Zürich airport.

Meanwhile, the Chairman boarded the waiting Sikorsky UH-60 helicopter and headed due west to an undisclosed location along the Swiss Alps. He thought, *Although the timetable is speeded up, it's time to set the project into motion.*

36

||||||||||||||||||||||||||||||||||||||||||||||||||||||||||||||||||||||||||||||||||||||||||||||||||||||||||

THE HUNT

Kenneth Clarke interrupted a meeting of the president and his national security advisor, and indicated that an urgent matter had arisen. The president was aware that Ken would not have taken such action if it were not something of the highest priority. The advisor was also aware; he quickly collected the papers he was discussing with the president and made his way out of the Oval Office.

After his departure, Ken established the highly secure conference line with General Maxwell over at Fort Meade—NSA headquarters. "Hi, Mr. President, Ken. We have a few decisions to make. I'll explain what they are as quickly as possible." General Maxwell explained to the president the events involving the SPT tracking and surveillance of Lenhart Rieser, and possibly the Chairman, in the limousine.

"Are they monitoring the limousine?" the president asked.

"Yes," replied General Maxwell in a clipped military tone. "They tried to put the slip on us again by using a secret road, but we were on to them this time. They have about an hour before the limousine arrives at the Zürich Airport."

"Have they confirmed the visual of both Rieser and Karl Christen?"

"Rieser was confirmed in the identical limousine en route to

Neustadt. Karl Christen has not been ID'd as a passenger. The limo windows are tinted, so external visual is not possible."

"So Christen, and possibly Rieser, may still be at the villa?" the president asked.

"Yes," replied General Maxwell. "However, our surveillance team thought of that possibility and left Colin Roberts, responsible for logistics, in one of the surveillance vehicles in Neustadt."

"General, at this point, have that individual go to the villa and ask to see Dr. Karl Christen, possibly as a tourist. Who knows, he might come to the door. And have him look around for whatever else he might find. What do you think?"

"I think all we have to lose is confirmation that we are actively looking for him. Truth is, he may know anyway."

"Okay, call us back when Colin returns."

Twenty minutes later, General Maxwell called the president's office at the White House to report that the resident butler had politely invited Colin in but had informed him that Dr. Christen was on an undisclosed business trip. He would gladly take a message and pass it on. The butler had also offered Colin a tour of the villa since it was considered an historical site, although not officially a part of the castle tour. Colin declined when it appeared that the Chairman wasn't present. However, he had "accidentally" taken the wrong way out when he left and drove to the back of the villa. He had observed an empty helicopter pad and the smell of avionics petroleum-based exhaust fumes. As logistics coordinator for the SPT, Colin was also a helicopter pilot. He thought he had heard a helicopter flying west during his surveillance.

"What conclusions do you draw, General?" the president asked.

"Sir, Rieser is probably in the limousine that initially headed south to Vaduz en route to Zürich, and the Chairman took a helicopter heading west toward Switzerland."

"Should we contact Lara and have her advise us as to what the next steps should be?"

"I think so, especially where capture and neutralize are concerned. In truth, if he is Pleiadian, we may be dealing with someone who is more elusive than we think."

The president said, "General, do whatever you have to, to make sure we find him and neutralize him." As his statement hung in the air, the president disconnected.

The president next put in a call to Lara Headley at the Netherlands safe house. She answered on the first ring in the office she was assigned to.

"Hello, Mr. President," Lara said. "And greetings to you, Chief Clarke." Lara assumed that "Chief" was short for chief of staff.

It unnerved the president and Ken Clarke to have someone know who was calling by using clairvoyant perception. However, they were both adapting to Lara, as she constantly reminded them that such extrasensory skills were readily available to them all once their scientific establishment gave them permission. She had even jokingly suggested a change in the name of a word game from "Simon says" to "Science says."

"Hello, Lara. We have a situation here."

"Yes, I can tell. What is it?"

"We think we have identified the Chairman of the Consortium."

"Wonderful," replied Lara. "Who is he?"

"We are fairly certain he is Dr. Karl Gustav Christen, head of the Cancer Institute in Liechtenstein and the official leader of the West European Recovery Project. He is quite popular and charismatic."

"How certain are you of his identity?"

"About 80 percent. If we are wrong, then the consequences of our actions could be severe, let alone embarrassing."

"That would be low-risk collateral damage considering the situation we're attempting to address. No one would ever know. He would simply be here one moment and gone the next," Lara said.

The president was becoming aware of an aspect of Lara's personality he had not previously sensed. "Well, Lara, we would prefer not to be wrong in that case."

"I understand, Mr. President. But we have ways of confirming his identity. Where is he?"

"That's just it. His residence is a villa in northern Liechtenstein, in a town called Neustadt. We think he took a helicopter in the direction of Switzerland from there about an hour ago. So, we have no idea where he is presently."

"We can assist you in locating him, now that we have his identification," Lara said in a tone that matched the president's.

"Who is 'we'?" the president asked.

"I will summon the capture team from Pleiades, along with a pod for the Chairman's long-term residence."

"What do you mean by a capture team? And what is a pod?"

"The capture team is a two-person crew who is able to identify and apprehend the Chairman using advanced technology from Pleiades, of course. A pod is a simple but highly sophisticated programmed space-travel vehicle for isolated navigation throughout the galaxy."

"Why can't *we* locate and capture him? I am apprehensive about involving you in our planetary problem."

"The capture team has powers similar to the Chairman that you do not possess. We can pick up the search and capture him whenever you grant us permission, Mr. President," Lara explained. She guessed that insisting would only move the president into a more staunch position. "Or you can pursue him yourselves and inform us when you have his location. It's up to you to decide what role you would like us to play."

"Let us try to locate him first, Lara. And we'll let you know whether or not we are successful."

"Okay, Mr. President. Let us know when you would like our involvement."

Lara clicked off and sent a psychic communication, which traveled beyond the speed of light, to the Pleiadian Council apprising them of the situation. The council responded that they would send the capture team and a pod in anticipation of locating the Chairman. It was clear that earthlings had no idea who or what they were dealing with in terms of conventional—though sophisticated by their own thinking—armament and telecommunication systems for locating and capturing the Chairman.

Now that the Pleiadian team had his probable identity, locating him should be easy. Capture and neutralize was essentially a job completed. Lara thought of an eighteenth-century human saying: "The best-laid plans of mice and men often go astray." She hoped her spontaneous thought was not an omen.

- - - | | | | | - - -

General George G. Maxwell, director of the US National Security Agency, had earned three of his four stars in the field of combat in the Middle East and Asia. The fourth star was honorary, and was awarded in accordance with his appointment to head the NSA in alignment with his intelligence peers, who were all four-star generals. Maxwell knew the importance of intelligence when dealing with a formidable adversary. He had a history of taking action in anticipation of what might happen, yet the Chairman of the Consortium had been calling the shots so far, and they had been in reactive mode.

Recalling the president's directive to "do whatever it takes to find him and neutralize him," he picked up his secure line and made a call to Colonel Darin Thomas. "Colonel Thomas, we're going to take an alternative approach to capturing the Chairman and find out what's going on."

"What do you have in mind, General?"

"We need the secure capture of Herr Lenhard Rieser. We also need a safe capture during which there are absolutely no witnesses. I understand you are in the final stages of following his limousine, probably to the Zürich airport."

"Affirmative, sir."

"I have made arrangements for you and your team to have private jet service for Herr Rieser from Zürich to Bern, where we anticipate he will be returning to."

"We can confirm that with the tower, sir."

"Excellent," replied General Maxwell.

"Sir, permission to ask a question?"

"Go right ahead, Colonel."

"Sir, we ordinarily take orders directly from the president of the United States. Is this op ordered by him?" There was a pause, then a reply.

"Yes it is, Colonel. I take full responsibility for this action."

The last statement was code for "You have a choice, Colonel. Call the president directly to confirm, or proceed with my order." Either way, Colonel Thomas would be off the hook. In addition, this was an action the president shouldn't know about in case it went south.

"Your orders are sufficient for me, General. Simple chain of command. Just for the record, I would never second-guess you, sir." Colonel Thomas reminded himself that General Maxwell had been his handler in the field. Taking orders from the national security director was second nature. Personally, he believed that the capture ordered by the general was an opportunity they couldn't afford to lose if they were going to locate the Chairman.

"Okay, I appreciate that, Colonel. Remember, what we need to know is where the Chairman is and what is going on."

"I understand clearly, sir."

"Keep me informed, Colonel." As an afterthought he added, "Take care of the delicate package."

"Affirmative, sir. Every step along the way." The delicate package was the general's daughter, Monique Rashad, second in command of the Special Projects Team. She was hardly a delicate package.

When Lenhard Rieser's limousine arrived at the Zürich airport, he began his well-accustomed journey to his flight to Geneva. His name was called on the public address system, and he was told there was a private jet service at the VIP gates. He assumed it was a chairman's perk. When he arrived at the VIP gates, he was told that private arrangements had been made for his flight back to Geneva, with a verbal note of thanks. Rieser felt that he was finally getting the acknowledgment he deserved all along, although there was a nagging feeling about this perk from the Chairman.

The attendant on the private jet was a Zürich beauty with a wonderful smile. She asked, "Would you like some champagne or something else to drink, Herr Rieser?" As she placed a cup of nuts in front of him, she bent to reveal her perfect cleavage, leaving the rest to his imagination.

"Yes, I'll have some champagne." His spirits began to rise.

She momentarily returned with his glass of champagne, and again revealed more of her cleavage as she instructed and assisted him in buckling his seatbelt. Shortly after a few sips of his champagne, he was soundly asleep.

It was a short flight from Zürich to Frankfurt, Germany, where the NSA European Interrogation Center was located. When Rieser was brought back to full consciousness, someone asked him if he was hungry or thirsty.

"No," he replied. Looking around, he demanded, "Where am I?"

"You're at a remote site," his NSA interrogator replied, unperturbed by Rieser's demanding tone and authoritarian attitude.

He was becoming clear about the sting that had been perpetrated. "I assume you are aware of who I am and what can happen to you?" he asked the interrogator.

The seasoned interrogator ignored Rieser's questions and informed him that he had two choices: one, answer two questions and be safely transported to his home in Geneva; or two, refuse to cooperate and be returned to his job with full disclosure of pictures of him and the beautiful attendant on the private flight. When he was shown the photos, he saw that his facial shots were prominent but not hers. Their various naked positions were phenomenal. Some were positions he had never experienced before—but the photos showed that he had enjoyed them immensely. The interrogator informed him he would be given an hour to decide, and left the room.

After an hour, the interrogator returned and asked what his decision was. "They are both a no-win for me," Rieser said confidently, in spite of his compromised position.

The interrogator then informed him that they planned to exercise a third choice in vivid detail, whereupon Rieser cried, acknowledging that he hated pain and loved life more.

"The Chairman is somewhere in northern Switzerland," Rieser began. "Where? I honestly don't know. I have never been there nor have I ever been invited to visit." In addition to the motivation that choice number three gave him, he also believed he was not included in the future plans of the Consortium anyway, even after all of his years of loyalty to the Chairman. But he kept these thoughts to himself.

"I don't know what is going on exactly, except that robots, androids I believe, and advanced artificial intelligence are crucial elements to the future of the Consortium. My job has been to secure the administrative personnel associated with a secret research facility in Switzerland." At this point, Rieser wanted to know what they might do to secure his future.

The interrogator replied, "Essentially, witness protection. Anywhere you want to be that's safe for you. You will simply become a missing person. If there is no body, it's too complicated to investigate. You'll be set for life."

Unexpectedly, Rieser said, "If you throw in the flight attendant, I can give you the key to the bank."

"Okay," the interrogator said. "What is the key?"

"I'm in charge of securing the new administrative hires for the Switzerland research facility. They are currently in search of a new director of administration."

"We can give you the flight attendant's cousin for six weeks. After that you're on your own in terms of what she decides to do. Will that work?"

"Deal," said Rieser, unaware that the woman's "cousin" was one of the most skilled inquisitors—man or woman—of an individual's deeply held secrets using drug-induced sexual fantasies. Someone like Rieser could become a gold mine of information about Consortium projects over the years, as well as those from the Consortium who were involved.

"Oh, I naturally assume I'll get all the photos and digital negatives of me in compromised situations," Reiser requested as an afterthought.

"Of course," replied the interrogator. *After all, with the cousin in residence, the photos will be unnecessary*, he thought. The old ways of disposing of people were outdated and unnecessary. Men like Rieser, and some women, were more easily controlled using sex, reputation, and wealth. Most of all, who could he tell what happened to him without more stringent consequences?

37

GOING DEEP

When I returned home to Salt Lake City to take a break from my adventures in Mauritius, I received a note from my significant other, Gala: "We need to talk." I don't know why that phrase always gave me anxiety, as though a reckoning were imminent. It usually involved a situation I had chosen to put on "parking lot." I immediately consulted my mental Rolodex of unresolved issues I had chosen to ignore. Meanwhile, I sent a reply informing her of my return from the island in the Indian Ocean, and that I looked forward to our conversation.

I guess I felt uncomfortable about the question I suspected she would raise; it would probably involve the direction of our relationship. When was I going to give up this whole thing about changing the world? According to Gala's thinking, it was clear that the world had no intention of changing, and wherever we were headed, we were headed! Unless, as with the pandemics, we were forced to change. We should try to get the most out of the time we had left. That's what most people were thinking, I felt she thought, in spite of the fact that they rarely, if ever, talked about it.

Then I thought, *perhaps she's right*. I often felt as though I were trying to put out a forest fire with a glass of water with no ice cubes. What was it that drove me to continue with the Quest and its aftermath? The more I followed this line of thinking, the more I felt a rumbling deep in my gut, along with a sense of hopelessness.

In spite of this feeling, I sensed that I was getting close to something, because I was experiencing an all-out alert simply by reflecting on our previous conversations. Surprisingly, it was about something deeper than my relationship with Gala. I felt the alert leading me into unexplored territory within my inner self, so I decided to let go and enjoy the ride. What began as mild exploration in preparation for my conversation with Gala rapidly turned into a deep-dive process down a chute. In order to gain clarity about what was happening, I decided to engage a spontaneous imagery-word exercise I had learned from working with Pat Christensen, my mentor for in-depth exploration. The words that sequentially appeared on my inner screen were:

- Guilt
- Commitment
- Obsession
- Fear

Then I added the phrase, "Stepping over the line." The word *commitment* got stuck in my throat even though I was only thinking it, not saying it. After exhausting my triggered emotions about Gala, the feeling was still there, stronger than the initial state. I knew that if I peeled back the layer one more time, I would see the whole thing. So I did.

There it was, fully revealed and totally obvious! The question was, did I want to take it on? That was the true source of the fear I was experiencing. I decided to retire for the night and pretend it would all be fine in the morning. I felt that I had done enough deep-dive exploration, with no idea where I was headed or where I would end up.

As I moved through the initial stages leading to deep sleep, I experienced a state of unexpected relaxation. That's when the movie spontaneously began in my mind—except that it was more like a virtual reality experience.

I suddenly awakened in a peaceful, calm state. I had total recall of what had occurred during my spontaneous virtual reality experience. I lay there attempting to feel my seamless bodymind linkage, which was slowly returning to normal. When I felt connected again, I decided to call Pat Christensen. I related my dream-movie and the emotional events preceding it. I explained that what I had experienced was more like reality, not a dream.

Pat was very familiar with what I had gone through. She had, in large part, mastered the out-of-body skill of astral projection when she had participated in the government's Star Gate program. The program had used people like Pat to clairvoyantly travel to distinct locations to gather information and intelligence about what was occurring there. She referred to it as "clairvoyance at a distance."

She said, "Most individuals spontaneously experience this phenomenon when certain mental pathways are opened—commonly through deep emotional trauma—and the fear that blocks a situation one had previously refused to 'see' is overcome." She paused, then continued. "The most common spontaneous trauma is an existential crisis—literally an emotional crisis that redefines a person and what he or she is capable of experiencing once the pathway is opened."

"Do you mean that what I saw occurring is actually what's going on?" I asked.

"Before getting to that, tell me the emotional challenges that are going on in your life right now."

"For the past week or so, I have been sleuthing a person who was subsequently killed in a mysterious airplane crash. I did an imagery word exercise, and the word on my inner screen associated with this person was *guilt*. The second word on my inner screen was *commitment*, probably with respect to my relationship with Gala. That one causes me the greatest emotional conflict, like a deep, throbbing pain. Simply put, she wants marriage and I don't. And she is the love of my life!

"The third word was *obsession*, probably with the Quest and its aftermath, that has turned into the Renaissance Revolution and the Seven Principles. Oddly enough, that one is the least conflicting within me. It's simply what I have to do. Period. The final word was *fear*."

"Sounds like a perfect storm to me," she replied, detached. "The intersection of the person, Gala, and the Quest probably triggered your deep dive. The word *fear* was probably not about any of those events but your fear of crossing the line into a deeper level of exploration. Somehow, your mind knows there is no return once you cross it."

"What is my fear about crossing the line?"

"Like all existential crises, fear of the unknown. You have no idea of who you will become once you transcend your fear and the line disappears." I could hear her chuckling as she shared this revelation with me, which I didn't think was funny. "That is, in terms of meaning, purpose, and what's important to you in your life. But all of that usually works out over time."

"Okay, I think I understand all of that stuff." I didn't, but I didn't want to discuss it just then. "Back to my original question: is what I saw the reality of what is happening?"

"Most, if not all, events have probabilities associated with them when dealing with mental projection. Nothing is absolute. However, given all we know about the Chairman and his extraordinary abilities, I would guess that what you clairvoyantly experienced has a very high degree of probability of being reality." She added, amused, "You now have a new arrow in your quiver."

"What do you think I should do?"

"There is only one thing to do. Tell the president. Also mention the Star Gate program and my participation. It'll make you more believable. I'm sure my records are sealed pretty tight by the DoD. You might also call John and get his take on your experience and what you should do.

In the final analysis, it comes down to you and the reality of what you experienced."

"Thanks, Pat."

She disconnected. After a moment or so, I called John.

He picked up on the first ring and asked, "What do you want to do?" I was still not accustomed to his automatic reception of my emotional projections.

"Meet with the president," I replied brusquely.

"I'll set it up," he replied. "Also Tony?"

"Yes," I said. *The first domino has been pushed*, I thought. And there was no going back.

--- | | | | | ---

Gala arrived at my home looking tired and red-eyed. I assumed she had been crying, as though she had already gone through the script of our conversation. She got straight to the point. No preliminaries.

"Why do you have to solve everything?" she asked. "The president has General Clarke, Dana, the NSA, the FBI, the CIA, and a hundred other alphabet agencies. Why are you so important?"

"I can't answer that. But I can say that he decided to fill the void with the Seven Principles. You know how much I had to do with its writing and implementation."

"Bill, where do we go from here?" she asked wearily.

I noticed that I didn't have the same level of anxiety that I would normally have had, since I had just gone through a traumatic experience that was much more confrontative.

"The truth is, I think we are heading toward a resolution of this thing, where I can probably be used for what I am good at instead of for life-threatening stuff," I lied.

Her eyes lit up, and she heaved a strong exhale of relief. "Now that's something worth hoping for."

The moment she said that I knew I had made a huge mistake, but I couldn't help giving her a sense of hope, even if it was only partially true at some level, just not at the core. The truth was, I didn't know what was in store for me, given the revelation of my dream-movie.

- - - | | | | | - - -

Two days later, John, Tony, and I met with the president in the Lincoln Room. The president was impatient about meeting, since he had no idea why we had requested an audience. John had simply informed him that I had insisted on meeting at his earliest convenience. The president figured he was too busy to meet with no agenda, but too much was going on to refuse. So here he was, stuck with the Three Wise Men from the East. "Well?" he asked as an opening.

Both John and Tony looked at me as though they had no clue why we were there. But they knew why. In fact, John had confirmed again that what I had experienced in a semi-dream state had a high probability of being reality.

"I'm responsible for this meeting, Mr. President," I said. He looked at me as if to say, "This had better be good."

I began, and ended twenty minutes later.

The president looked at me, dumbfounded and speechless. However, what I had presented to him made such sense that he asked, "What are we going to do about it?"

"Well, for starters, we have to find him."

38

THE ALLIANCE

The president began considering a possible clandestine armed intervention of the research facility, based on Rieser's and Bill's information. Such an event would present complications—*even if the entire operation occurred to perfection*, he thought. First, other countries with highly sophisticated surveillance and intel systems would soon learn of the event. Even if it was successful, the United States' strongest allies would not only be angry but possibly be unforgiving for their lack of knowledge and inclusion. Its adversaries would be angry in any case for not being informed and offered inclusion, which they would have declined anyway—not to mention a secret armed intervention in another country without their permission. On the other hand, inaction was unacceptable. The stakes were too high to simply hope that the activities of the Chairman involved nothing hostile—they most probably did, and possibly planetary.

He picked up his highly secure satellite phone, which he kept with him 24/7, and dialed the red-coded line to the prime minister of the United Kingdom.

A mildly stressed voice immediately answered. "Hello." Businesslike and serious, she asked, "What's the situation?" This particular phone line was reserved exclusively for critical world events that required immediate decision-making.

"Hello, Christine," the president replied evenly to the prime minister. "This is Ted."

"I know who you are," she replied, annoyed at his introduction. "What is the situation? I am alone."

"Nothing involving an immediate world crisis," he said quickly.

Christine Richardson, as leader of the British Labour Party, had earned a reputation for her quickness and intelligence, particularly in highly threatening situations.

"Then why are you calling me on the red-coded line?"

"Because I'm about to inform you of a red-coded decision you will have to make before this conversation is over. Although the event is not imminent, your decision is crucial."

"I'm listening," she replied curtly.

Where should I begin? the president thought. He went directly to the point of the call. "We have good reason to believe we know the source of the two global pandemics. We also believe that the individual who is responsible for them is planning something much more devastating for the future of the planet"—both wasn't quite the truth.

Christine was silent for five seconds, then asked, confused, "Like what?" She couldn't imagine anything worse than the two events that had reduced Earth's population by more than half.

"We don't know exactly, but we are convinced it involves artificial intelligence and the unscaled production of androids."

"You mean like Star Wars? Or aliens?" Aliens had frequently been in the news lately.

Ignoring her questions, the president said, "In any case, we believe the individual planning the large-scale production of these androids is much further along than we had imagined. We also believe that if he is successful, it may lead to our loss of control of planetary governance."

"Ted, you keep saying 'we' believe. What does that mean? Who is 'we'? And what do you expect of me?" She felt it was time to cut to the chase and get to the essence of his call.

"I know this isn't going to be easy, Christine. However, I want you to believe me when I say that we are dealing with a global crisis in the making. We want your involvement in a clandestine armed intervention to maintain control of the planet. That's it in a nutshell."

Christine did not immediately respond as she processed Ted's statement.

"You mean, you want our involvement in case what you believe is not accurate. Then you have an ally to help absorb the global condemnation that will follow."

"Or credit," he interrupted. "I guess it comes down to whether you believe me or not, and whether we are an extension of what you would do if the situation were reversed—no matter how hard we try to be independent of you."

"Don't use that one on me, Ted," she replied with a chuckle. "Suppose I decide not to be part of your intervention?"

"Then we go it alone," he responded definitively.

"Okay, we're in," she said, equally definitively.

"Thank you, Christine," he said with a huge sense of relief. "I will inform you of the details of the operation we have in mind, but we are thinking of a Special Forces op involving our Seals and your SAS people."

He paused. She could sense there was more he wanted to say. "What is it, Ted?" she asked in a serious tone.

"What you should also be aware of is that once this situation is resolved, our Tawhid Confederation is just a transition stage, as are the others. It is the foundation for the next era of planet Earth. That's why the success of this operation is so critical."

"What do you mean, Ted? Now you are truly confusing me."

"My intent was not to drop everything on you at one time, but where we are truly headed is toward a One Earth Federation."

"What does that mean?" she asked, unable to let his comment pass.

"Something like the founding of America from thirteen colonies, or what Woodrow Wilson had in mind with the League of Nations after World War I. That culminated with the formation of the United Nations, promoted by Franklin Roosevelt during World War II. It's interesting to note that both organizations for international cooperation were proposed as a result of global armed conflict."

"How soon?" she asked, feeling a sense of anxiety.

"Sooner than you can imagine."

"How will we get there?" She was unable to let go of all of the questions he had prompted in her mind, because she had recently been thinking along the same lines.

"Hopefully not as we have done in the past, but rather by the widespread acceptance and implementation of the Seven Principles."

39

THE CAPTURE TEAM

The capture team deployed from Pleiades was instructed to use the vortex to enter our sun's solar system but remain undetected by Earth's surveillance technology. It was clear that the most advanced human technology, combined with humanity's poorly developed extrasensory system of consciousness, was ill-equipped to detect the capture team's cloaking technology, or to locate, identify, or capture the rogue Pleiadian. However, the Pleiadian Council wanted to provide the opportunity for the advanced Earth systems to lead the process of capturing the Chairman—and discover its futility.

The capture team brought with them an Infinity Pod. The pod was a self-propelled spacecraft designed to travel the Milky Way Galaxy, fueled by the galaxy's infinite sources of energy. It comfortably accommodated a single entity. It was the ultimate form of imprisonment for someone found guilty of an occasional capital crime on Pleiades, especially those involving interplanetary violations that threatened other civilizations. Such violations were considered to be the highest form of capital offense.

The punishment for such crimes was based on the fundamental galactic principle of connectedness. This principle was true of every extant entity and object in the universe, whether animate or inanimate, by the inherent possession of consciousness. Denial of the expression of connectedness through isolation for an undefined period of time often led to in-depth introspection and transformation, and occasionally, transcendence.

For living entities to express these connections through life activities was not only mutually sustaining but also a natural life existence. On Earth, such activities provided joy, happiness, and success, driven by passion and love. To be without the dynamics of connectedness was to be void of being fully alive. Such disconnections brought on loneliness, despondency, and depression—irrespective of one's wealth or possessions.

A historical example was the common practice by indigenous tribes of turning their backs on a condemned person to imply that he or she no was longer part of their group or even existed. Such practices were considered to be worse than death. In contrast, the Pleiadians, as an advanced civilization, considered killing another entity to be characteristic of ancient, barbaric societies, and unthinkable as an appropriate form of behavior or punishment, regardless of the violation. For them, imprisonment was about reformation designed to create a higher level of consciousness, such that an individual would never again be vulnerable to the dictates of lower forms of relationship.

The ultimate objective was expansion to an irreversibly higher-level of consciousness consistent with Pleiadians, and possibly Arcturians. Their focus was on forgiveness and rehabilitation in consciousness, and ultimately, the individual's return to his or her existing society, having experienced transformation or even transcendence to a more expanded spiritual state.

In the case of the Infinity Pod, which provided isolation, the only essential element for a Pleiadian's sustenance was energy, which was abundant in the universe. Thus, an entity, or prisoner, could literally "live" forever in a perpetual state of suspended isolation. In most cases, the isolation would lead to meditative enlightenment and eventual return to Pleiades, since crime on Pleiades was an incomprehensible act practiced by lower forms of consciousness.

PART SIX

IDENTITY

40

CIRUS

Nestled along the northern reaches of the Swiss Alps was a string of small villages in the valleys below. Most of them had been forgotten by time and nearly all of the luxuries of modern living. One day folded gently into another, periodically interrupted by the changing seasons of temperatures, colors, and human activity.

The most exciting activity near one of the remotest villages had been the construction of an elaborate, high-tech weather monitoring station at the top of one of the highest mountain peaks. Although the station had taken several years to construct, limited in part by the seasonal weather, the time duration wasn't long by the villagers' standards. What surprised them was that continual improvement was part of its regular operation. New equipment and supplies arrived on a monthly basis. The villagers were told that year-round monitoring, as weather would allow, was a vital function of the monitoring station. The villagers couldn't care less, since they were given a generous annual stipend for road usage and improvement, but most of all for their confidentiality regarding the construction project. They were told that the weather station was a top secret project sponsored by the United Nations to facilitate both weather monitoring and global communication.

At the base of one of the mountains, about twenty miles from the village, was an old mine shaft, forgotten by most of the villagers since it represented another time and hardened memories of lost jobs when it was closed. The entrance to the long-abandoned mine shaft looked the same as it had for the last seventy-five years: strewn with boulders, cobwebs, and a less-than-daunting barrier with a sign that read: "Geben Sie Nicht—Extreme Gefahr!" (Do Not Enter—Extreme Danger!). Not far from the closed entrance was a camouflaged steel door wedged into the mountain. It could be opened and sealed along horizontal channels by pneumatic control.

The inner tunnel was at an angle to the original mine shaft, and merged with it several hundred feet into the main entrance. At this point, the original shaft, with modern reinforcements, became a warren of pathways leading to administrative offices, facilities, ultramodern research laboratories, and testing facilities. The research work being conducted at this highly secure laboratory involved studies of robotics and android technology. It was part of the project named Cirus by its founder, the Chairman of the Consortium. Its name, meaning "far-sighted," was derived from Old Persian.

Cirus was the next-generation continuing work of the Consortium to influence the major activities on Earth, albeit to create a much more smoothly functioning global society, now that all-out nuclear confrontation appeared to be something of the past. The destruction of nuclear warheads was proceeding at a rapid rate, as was the conversion of the accompanying technology to peaceful purposes. These activities pleased the Chairman, since he was acutely aware of the threat to Pleiades from exposure to radioactive fallout. In spite of these activities resulting from the achievement of the Quest, the lingering fear of humans reverting to the restoration of nuclear weapons was ever-present. However, Cirus was far more ambitious than the prior efforts of the Consortium in generating a permanent solution.

In accordance with the accelerating technological trend on Earth, the Consortium envisioned a reorganized global society. The vision was a three-tier framework with the pre-pandemic values, structure, and objectives for the future governance of humankind, as well as an army of androids for administration—and enforcement, where necessary. The three tiers of society consisted of the primary tier of Andies, short for androids; the secondary tier of Techies; and the tertiary tier of those remaining, referred to as the Others.

The Chairman had amusedly been reading an article on the internet that 70 percent of Americans fretted that their country was losing its identity. What they were really worried about was the radically changing values as a result of the influx of immigrants—hence the backlash and the corresponding self-imposed isolation. Many countries had simply banned the immigration of those from war-torn regions altogether. *Well*, the Chairman thought, *wait until they see what I have in mind for the future of humankind, not just Americans.*

All three tiers of society were to be directed by the Controllers, who would replace the Consortium's executive board—with the Chairman as Control.

The Andies were artificially designed androids built to physically and aesthetically resemble human beings. Each one was a unique mechanical, inorganic construct designed for a specific purpose to secretly operate within the Techie and Others populations.

The Techies comprised the bulk of the human population. They were addicted to smart information technology devices to varying extents, and used them on a daily basis.

The Others were human beings who had realized early in the evolution of smart IT devices how enslaved they could become to its usage by choice, job, or peer pressure. As a result, a few, but not all, used IT devices in moderation or only as necessary. The Others assumed that 24/7 monitoring of all humans was already a reality. This group dominantly consisted of middle-age and older individuals. The Chairman's strategy was that they would soon die off anyway.

The major values the Chairman anticipated—domination, control, and power—already existed as a result of the Consortium's operation prior to the two pandemics. With new and projected technology, these translated into domination of all resources and inhabitants of the planet, including the Techies and Others; control of how resources and people were utilized and programmed to think, respectively; and the power to orchestrate major activities, both terrestrial and extraterrestrial. The most important aspect of the exercise of these values was that they be executed by the power of influence—a much easier and more efficient process with the popularity of social media and networking.

The overall objective, consistent with a recent highly popular book, was that technology become the elixir for humankind's greatest desires: immortality, agelessness, and pleasure. The ultimate illusion, from the Chairman's perspective, was for humans to believe they had achieved the power to not only create any reality they chose but also to do so through advanced technology. For the average person, the illusion, if not the reality, could be experienced using virtual reality. The Chairman's role as Control would be as the facilitator of endlessly pursuing that dream. The three tiers of existence were the framework that was designed to facilitate the process.

- - - | | | | | - - -

The recent adventure with probable US agents at his Liechtenstein villa had advanced the Chairman's timetable for the final design and testing stages of the army of androids. The Chairman wanted to ensure that he had ultimate control of the Andies and the chain of command for their actions and deployment. The critical feature he wanted to ensure was that they were undetectable when dispersed among the Techies and Others. That is, in their various roles, they would dress and behave similar to the Techies and Others in their infiltration. This meant that, in addition to sophisticated computer programming, a wide variety of roles and personalities had to be designed using AI. The present status was the repetitive process of testing each prototype and refining the computer-controlled programming before going into mass production.

The scientists and engineers who worked at the Cirus Research Center were told that they would be working on a top secret energy project sponsored by the United Nations.

41

‖‖‖

INSTITUTE FOR THE STUDY OF HUMAN CONSCIOUSNESS

The work of the Institute had found its focus: the integration of higher levels of consciousness into present and future human forms. The purpose was to create and enhance human beings with not only greater physical and mental abilities but also greater intelligence and wisdom through access to expanded states of consciousness. In simple terms, this meant the integration of body, mind, and spirit to produce entities capable of exceptional performance governed by humanistic concepts, practices, and behaviors, as opposed to the conceptual development envisioned by the Chairman: the creation of androids programmed with artificial intelligence to follow his dictates, in his role as the Control, in administering and overseeing the members of society.

The Institute's research focused on retaining the essential organic elements of humanism, whereas the Chairman's vision involved a totally synthetic entity, presumably limited by the consciousness of those involved in its construction. Regarding the latter, the Institute believed that it was not possible to artificially build an entity that exceeded one's own level of consciousness evolution, particularly by simply programming ideal behavioral responses driven by human consciousness.

The initial project toward achieving the Institute's objectives had begun with humans who had already transformed from survival-based thinking to compatibility. This objective involved the work of Dr. Catherine Wang and Dr. Frances Wilkerson in conjunction with the Technology-Based Learning program at GBI, which had become known as Myra's Legacy.

The president and CEO of GBI, Myra Westbrook, had acquired the backing and active support of her board to institute a special program in three phases: recruit, develop, and employ a wide variety of untapped science, technology, engineering, and mathematics (STEM) human resources from within the United States. These resources included people of color, recent immigrants with US citizenship, women, and a variety of other groups who were lost in the shuffle of exclusion, such as white males from low-income backgrounds. As Myra had previously suggested, the impetus for the program was the discussion at the White House of the rapidly declining primary resource of exceptional Chinese and East Indian students. The decline was due to the fact that their native countries had begun to develop their own outstanding university STEM programs and, in the case of India, the Eurodia Confederation.

While the underutilized US human resources were readily available, most science and high-tech organizations saw little need to design and institute serious programs to attract, develop, and retain them. Now that the decline appeared to be permanent in nature, the industry viewed Myra's Legacy as the test case of what might be administered nationally, if successful.

The major elements involved in the recruitment phase were identifying, qualifying, and selecting the initial class in the GBI human restoration program. The initial emphasis was on those resources that were highly probable for success, similar to the early admissions program instituted by Dr. Benjamin Mays at Morehouse College during the 1950s and 1960s. GBI had little difficulty in instituting this phase; after all, these human resources had always been there. The essential element in their selection was their transformation from survival to compatibility. A major objective in the initial stage was to select individuals with a high probability for success.

The second phase, develop, was one in which high-tech organizations and others experienced and widely practiced the Institute's major impact. The impact experience began with an Institute board meeting during which Gail Erickson asked Frances Wilkerson, "What could people of color do on their own behalf that no one else could prevent or do for them?" Their exploration of this question led to a startling realization, which turned out to be the key element for the success of the entire GBI program. In practice, it was accepted, to varying extents, by a majority of the selected members of the program. It involved the invalidation of the illusion of superior and inferior individuals by the nature of their being, and resulted in the realization of personal human equality as the nature of human existence.

The Institute team of Wang and Wilkerson facilitated the statements:

- You are equal, by virtue of being, to any human who exists.
- Equality cannot be earned by the attainment of goals, although the achievement of goals can serve as visible confirmation of successful conversion.
- Equality cannot be granted by anyone, although others can limit equitable opportunities for the full expression of another's capability.
- Equality cannot be made a reality by a written document, although it may convince oneself and others of that inherent reality.
- Equality becomes reality by how one thinks, behaves, and achieves in concert with these propositions.

Facilitating these statements as reality for the class participants turned out to be the key element in adopting a mindset of success.

This mindset, when authentically practiced, became a way of being. Authentically adopting this way of being was subsequently identified as the turning point for the successful class participants, since most of them had been laboring under the impression of inferiority in some unique way: birthright, color, sex, religion, selectively chosen intellect, ethnicity, lifestyle, wealth, heredity, and most of all, artificially ingrained value systems. The vital conclusion drawn from this phase of the program was that it was not possible to perform to one's potential without fully recapturing one's inherent equality as a way of being.

The final phase, employ, involved well-known experiential learning processes, commonly referred to as project-based learning. The most important assignment for all of the participants was significant, hands-on learning experiences that involved in-depth challenge and opportunity, which became essential elements in becoming employed by GBI. The most important learning experiences in the employ phase were extensively integrating differences for interactive learning, organizational compatibility, and group success.

The first-phase program achieved 60 percent success. The program facilitators, Frances Wilkerson and Catherine Wang, were not surprised but were highly encouraged. After all, they concluded that they were attempting to invalidate centuries of mental programming involving the reality of the superior/inferior illusion.

Another project the Institute took on was the integration of the Minnesota township with the neighboring Renaissance Community. The township had decided to move slowly into the integration process—a typical human reaction to avoid radical change in the absence of a crisis. This decision was not unanimous but sufficient to stall the process, although most of them sensed there was trouble on the horizon. As most crises occur, the one involving the township had begun happening all over the country. By their ignoring the rate of change, it was the initial vector to another perfect storm.

The second vector was the decrease in taxable income resulting from the reduced population in the wake of the pandemics, in addition to unemployment for a significant fraction of their workforce. This also meant that most people had only enough money for the absolute necessities.

The third vector of the perfect storm was the rapidly increasing disparity in wealth between the haves and the have-nots, tending toward a totally unregulated free enterprise system, similar to the system that existed in the early 1900s. Now, a true immediate and inescapable crisis faced the township front and center.

The townspeople held an emergency town meeting to discuss what could be done to save the town and its inhabitants. One suggestion was to simply give up and move to a metropolitan area. Arturo Alvarado, the town's director of human capital, quickly pointed out that the same fate awaited larger cities; they were simply buying time. After continued discussion of stop-gap solutions, someone asked Arturo what did he suggest.

"I suggest what I have been recommending all along," he replied. "Learn from our neighbors, the Renaissance Community. They are not experiencing this crisis."

"What are they doing?" someone else asked.

"They are using the guidelines of the Seven Principles of Social Equality, which we have discussed with the town leadership for more than a year. I suggest we start there."

Curious, a woman asked, "How are they doing it?"

"That's the beauty of the Seven Principles. It suggests what needs to be done, but the how is left up to us."

"Can you give us an example?" another asked.

"Of course," Arturo replied. "One of the principles states, in essence, that we as a collective provide the basic resources of food, shelter, and clothing necessary for everyone's survival."

"Isn't that communism, or at best, socialism?" a stern townsman asked.

"Do you provide the basic resources of food, shelter, and clothing for your family?" Arturo asked.

"Of course I do. It's my basic responsibility to take care of my family, whether they are able to work or not," the townsman said emphatically.

"Then, do you run a communist household? Or a socialist one, at best?" Arturo asked, smiling.

"No—I mean, I don't know. I'm obligated to take care of my family's welfare."

"In the crisis we currently face, could you extend that way of thinking to others in our community?"

"I guess so, but only after my family is taken care of."

"How we do or don't meet the needs of our families and everyone else is, again, up to us. However, we absolutely must decide on which of the statements of the Seven Principles we are willing to adopt first, if any. Then move to implementation."

Arturo allowed a moment or two for quiet thinking before moving to his final statement.

"If we decide to proceed according to these principles, fully or in part, I know a great person from the Midwest who can help us. Her name is Gail Erickson. She can work along with me in our deciding on the Seven Principles as well as their practical implementation, if we invite her assistance."

- - - | | | | | - - -

David and his team at the Institute had also concluded that information technology, robotics, and artificial intelligence were expanding at a rate that could not be ignored. They were inevitably going to become an essential part of the future human identity.

Gail Erickson's integration of research in the areas of metaphysics, and Pat Christensen's expanded states of consciousness, brought a powerful new dimension to the evolving fields of enhanced and virtual humans. The model the Institute had chosen to pursue in the short term was a cyborg, a human being whose physiological functioning was aided by and sometimes dependent on mechanical electronic devices—essentially, a combination of human and artificial body parts. The intent was to retain the natural human nature of the person. Pat's work had strongly suggested that the two essential body parts necessary to retain natural authentic human functioning were the brain and the heart.

"We must also ensure a human reproductive system," Gail had pointed out, to which they all agreed.

"As naturally as possible," she added. They laughed.

"The brain is necessary to interface with the mental plane of consciousness for the accurate interpretation of human interaction, as Pat has suggested," David explained. "It's the ability to distinguish survival or truly life-threatening experiences from illusion."

"Followed by the authentic and appropriate emotional expression interfaced through the heart chakra," Pat chimed in. "The corresponding natural human emotion is the result of interfacing with the causal plane. Mastery of these two planes is the doorway to more advanced levels of consciousness and the acquisition of greater wisdom."

The Carrington and Christensen team concluded that the next-stage human being, with all the appropriate artificial enhancements of eyesight, strength, quickness, agility, stamina, intelligence, and functioning, could easily be designed while simultaneously conserving the human heart and brain, along with its inseparable human mind. Therefore, the next prototype virtual human being was dependent on the recruitment of a significant cadre of human beings to continually evolve to higher states of consciousness.

42

||||||||||||||||||||||||||||||||||||||||||||||||||||||||||||||||||||||||||||||||||||||||||||||||||||||||||||||||

THE LINCOLN ROOM AGENDA—
IN HARM'S WAY

I had gone beyond suspicion of special invitations to the Lincoln Room, especially when there was no apparent explanation. My suspicion was elevated to fear when the suits showed up with light-adjusting glasses and a look of destiny. I, of course, knew the routine since we had gone through it on several occasions. At least I would be in first class, with any seat I chose. Drinks were free but limited.

On my way to Washington, DC, I had visions of the Last Supper and who was appointed to kiss me—certainly not John, Tony, or Lara. They were above biblical dramas. The only other person I could think of was the president. He was fearless in his decision to sacrifice others, even though it appeared to pain him.

When I arrived, the regular cast was there—Lara, Tony, and John—with one surprise: General George Maxell, the director of the National Security Agency. He rarely smiled about anything, so I wasn't surprised by his "mission look." The president smiled and quickly turned away. That was a bad omen for me, I guessed. On the other hand, I was free to make any choices I wanted to—at least, in theory. The president took on a serious air and said, "Hi, Bill. Glad you could make it."

"I'm always available to assist you, Mr. President, in any way I can," I replied, trying to keep a straight face.

"I think I'll let General Maxwell brief you first. And then we can decide what the best course of action will be. He'll bring you up to date on where we are with respect to the Chairman and what we think he's up to. By the way, your surprise meeting with me led us in a direction we hadn't anticipated. That's why we invited you here tonight." He turned to General Maxwell.

"General?" the president said to the NSA alpha male.

"A week ago, we learned of a top secret United Nations-sponsored facility that had been constructed in Switzerland to provide a new energy source for the entire planet," the general said. "And as with the research findings of the Cancer Institute, the director of the facility was planning to freely contribute their invention to all the nations of the planet. In fact, we have good reason to believe that the facility is an ultra-modern laboratory for the design, development, and production of robot androids. Our source informs us that it is the brainchild of the Chairman."

Now I connected the dots between the revelation of my dream-movie and the president's information.

"We were fortunate to identify a source who oversees human resource planning for the facility," the general continued. "He informed us of his willingness to appoint any individual of our choice to this position. Of course, he's being more than adequately compensated for this favor." At this point, I guessed the only person with such authority would be Lenhard Rieser. But why? What did I not know about what was going on?

The president took over again, like a tag-team match, and said, "The clincher here is that the director of the laboratory would be delighted to have someone with a scientific background as the new director of administration."

I was beginning to feel trapped by the carefully orchestrated presentations.

"The director of the laboratory is a long-standing friend of the Chairman from the Czech Republic. He and his entire research team of twenty-five scientists and engineers were hired to conduct research and development. The Czech Republic is a world-renowned pioneer in robotic androids. They both share the vision of a robot-orchestrated world under human control."

The president seamlessly took control of the conversation again. "Based on everything we know to this point, General Maxwell and his team have suggested that we need an internal resource to confirm our suspicions of what is going on inside the research facility so that we can take the appropriate action based on accurate intel. If we are wrong in any way about our suspicions, then taking action would be disastrous for the United States, and would project the Chairman into the role of a global philanthropic leader. You can see how delicate and precarious this situation is." The president paused and looked at me. I was more uncomfortable than at any time since I had arrived.

"However," he continued, "we have good reason to believe that the actual research going on at the secret facility involves the mass production of humanoid androids. We naturally assume that if this is true, these robots are not designed for the energy needs of humankind. We obviously need confirmation."

Finally, I asked, "I'm pleased to be privy to what you have shared with me, but I don't know why you invited me to this gathering." Wrong statement.

The president assumed the mantle of commander-in-chief and responded. "Well, Bill, we thought you might consider being the internal resource to confirm our suspicions. You obviously fit perfectly."

"Seriously Mr. President, this is a CIA or NSA operation, not a job for a former scientist with no experience in clandestine operations," I said, smiling.

No one else laughed or even smiled, not even my trio of friends.

"I beg to differ," replied the president, discarding his inviting persona.

"You were first to alert us of what you suspected was going on. You know the background of the entire affair involving the Chairman. And you have considerable experience as a scientist-administrator—in spite of your reference to lack of experience. I won't mention the operations you and John were involved in during the past three years, but they do qualify as clandestine."

My Pleiadian trio of friends bowed their heads and pretended they had no voice or opinion about the obvious direction the invitation was going.

"Before considering your internal resource idea, I'd like to talk privately with my friends."

"Fine," said the president. "Why don't the rest of us take a break and let them talk privately for as long as they choose."

After the president and General Maxwell departed, I turned to my "friends" and asked, "So, what's going on here? Why me? And do you all agree with using me as a sacrificial lamb?"

None of them responded, which appeared to be a combined yes.

"You know that if I went, the chances of my coming out alive would be close to zero."

They all nodded, which was clearly another unanimous yes.

"You know that all they want from me is visual confirmation of what's going on and the layout of the security involved. Then they can attack the compound at will, regardless of my safety!"

Lara said, "We know. You have to decide if it's worth it for the rest of humanity."

"So all of you agree with this assignment for me?" I asked, disappointed.

"Yes," they replied in unison. John said, "If you can be rescued, I'll be there for you. However, you must know that capturing the facility is the highest priority."

"Thanks," I said. I had never felt so alone in my entire life. It appeared that I had no choice but to "volunteer" for a suicide mission.

"Oh, by the way, do all of you know what's going on in the research facility?"

Tony said, "Yes."

"Then why don't you tell them!" I shouted.

"The president wants this to be a US-UK operation. Also, this is too close to determining your planet's destiny. He's still upset about the decision to allow the Pleiadian immigration. However, that was the Council's decision on behalf of their own survival. So, we've all agreed to remain silent. You are responsible for deciding your destiny. It's as simple as that."

I stood there looking at the three of them and remembered what Tony and John had said from the very beginning: *We are not here to save you. We are here to assist you in saving yourselves.*

The president and the others returned to the room. "Let me tell you what we have in mind, Bill," the president said, "and you can give us an idea of what works best for you. However, this situation goes way beyond any one person. General Maxwell's plan is to give you a different name and keep your credentials as is, including your administrative background at the university and as a small business owner. The name we have in mind is Dr. Walter Gordon." The president smiled, apparently assuming my approval.

I remained stone-faced.

"Our source in charge of hiring will authenticate an extensive background check, including your university credentials. Fortunately, your research work has been in a field completely different from the research and engineering director from the other side of the world. He'll play down your specific field of research and provide you with documentation to use on your arrival."

"The objective is relatively simple," said General Maxwell. "We get you in as an administrator. You will confirm what is going on and as much as you can about the internal security. On your trigger of an undetectable signal, a team of Seals and SAS British Special Forces will assault the facility."

"Where is the facility, the entrance, and my exit protocol?" I asked.

"Rieser has given us a pretty good idea that the facility is located in an abandoned mine shaft near a small town at the base of the Swiss Alps, which we have confirmed using satellite tracking. Once we get your information, we can have a better idea of how the assault team will enter. We know the town and the entrance to the old mine shaft from satellite tracking. Any other information you can provide will be crucial to our success. However, the team's first priority will be to locate you and secure your safe exit."

I stood there reviewing my life and all the people I owed amends to, and came to the conclusion that my survival depended solely on me. I was not trained as a Special Forces professional, but I was trained to use my verbal, mental, and creative skills. I could also use my abilities involving other states of consciousness and extrasensory skills, if necessary. When considering all of my assets, I experienced a false surge of confidence while feeling a corresponding reduction of fear. I thought, somewhat foolishly, *I got this!*

43

THE EAGLE HAS LANDED

Over the next two days, I was dispatched to the small town near the mine as a single passenger aboard a Citation X midsize jet. I was met by a security team of two smartly dressed individuals, male and female, with armbands disclosing UN Energy Resource Project. With an inviting smile, the man requested my documentation from Herr Rieser. I reached inside my briefcase and gave the papers to him. He told me that I was replacing the previous director of administration, who had departed after two years of service.

About twenty miles outside of town, the driver of the BMW station wagon I was riding in surprised me by passing the old boarded mine entrance and stopping shortly beyond it. A well-camouflaged metal door began to open on rollers to reveal a highly supported metallic cave that, upon entering, eventually merged with the original mining cave. Just inside the metallic door was a huge generator that I guessed was used to power the laboratory utilities.

After mounting the golf cart inside the mine shaft, we headed for my new quarters. I asked the driver if we could stop at the nearest rest station, since I had not relieved myself since leaving Zürich. "Too much coffee," I offered.

He smiled and said, "Sure," although I sensed that I had interrupted his mental schedule. He took a quick left turn and then right, and stopped abruptly. "Right through that door. Make it quick. We have a schedule to keep."

I entered, went to a stall, and pulled out the tiny transmitter I was given by the NSA. I quickly typed: *Two entrances adjacent old metallic merged* and pressed send. Six words, about ten seconds. I washed my hands and returned to the cart.

My driver said, "I didn't mean to rush you."

"No problem, I just needed to relieve myself." I hoped he hadn't heard me flush the toilet instead of a urinal.

After a few quick turns, we entered the housing quarters for the five administrative staff. These quarters, as well as the entertainment and eating facilities, were separate and apart from the research and development segment of the operation. Each staff member had an offsite hotel apartment in town for alternate weekends, provided by the laboratory. My golf cart driver stopped in front of one of the doors at the end of a hallway and said, "I'll wait. You have about ten minutes to freshen up for your meeting with the director of R&D. Let's not keep him waiting."

I dismounted the cart, retrieved my briefcase and one piece of luggage, and entered the housing unit. It was more spacious than I had imagined—more like a three-room apartment with a bathroom. I didn't unpack but simply washed my face and combed my hair. I assumed the apartment had previously been occupied by the retiring director of administration.

When I returned to the cart, my driver said, "Thanks for your promptness. When we return, I'll show you how to set the code for your room. You will have the codes for all the other administrative staff. Of course, no one, including me, will have yours." I doubted that. "Except the director of R&D." With a snide smile he added, "He's God."

The entire floorplan of the facility was unfolding exactly like I saw in my astral time-travel observation that I had shared with the president.

I was both excited and scared that I might make a mistake. In addition, I had given only cursory thought to my astral projection skill and the ethics of having it. However, I couldn't think of that now. I whispered to myself, "Okay. It's showtime," to help relieve my anxiety. As the president had implied, I should certainly have no problem conversing with a scientist or an engineer.

We arrived at the administrator's—or rather, my—office before going on to see the director of R&D—a good sign, nonverbally communicated by my driver. We entered the office, where the driver repeated the same instructions about coding and then exited. Abruptly, a decisive knock on the door came, and the director entered without a verbal invitation. He filled the entire doorway. He was about five foot six, stout, and had a head of tousled brownish-gray hair, which looked as though it was never combed. His eyes bored into me through his circular eyeglasses. Then he broke into a broad smile, which was more like a sneer, and said, "Welcome, Dr. Gordon. I can't tell you how excited I am to have a scientist in this position. I can speak normally, as I do with my colleagues, without having to translate into civilian language." He smiled again, which turned into a laugh when I indicated I understood exactly what he was talking about—and I did.

The Czech director seated himself to clarify who was in charge. However, I also sensed a collegial respect in terms of the research work that Rieser had communicated I had done. "I'm here to greet you and answer any questions you have regarding your responsibilities with us."

"I don't have any questions about administration. I assume Ms. Cartwright will introduce me to everyone and generally advise me as to how this job is done." I ended with a smile.

He laughed again and said, "That's the most important decision you have made so far."

"I do have one question, though," I said. "I understand from my briefing that administrators do not have access to the R&D sector. Is that correct?"

"Yes, that is correct." He paused momentarily and then said, "However, I will have someone retrieve you tomorrow morning at nine o'clock for us to have a more private conversation about the energy work we do here. Given your background, I am interested in your thoughts. That is really why I am excited about your assignment with us."

"I look forward to learning more," I said.

He abruptly got up, headed for the door, stopped, said, "Tomorrow then," and walked out.

--- | | | | | ---

The following morning I met with Ms. Gabrielle Cartwright at eight o'clock. I had already learned that Ms. Cartwright was the daughter of an American scientist at the University of Zürich and his Swiss research colleague, Dr. Helga Gutzwiller Cartwright. I began our conversation by saying that I was here to learn about the position and that she would be my teacher. She smiled and replied, "I understand you have a nine o'clock meeting with the director. You will probably be retrieved at precisely 8:50, so don't appear surprised. There is a general opinion around here about American scientists and promptness."

"And what is that opinion?" I asked.

"It's a guideline," she replied. I smiled but didn't reply.

"Do you have any other questions?" she asked.

"Yes, can you give me any advice about the meeting? Maybe what I can expect?"

"I think he wants to know how committed you are to the work we do here."

"Very," I replied immediately.

She looked at me skeptically and said, "Just do more listening than talking, and ask more questions than make statements, and you'll be fine."

"When I return, you can introduce me to the staff."

She smiled again and said, "I look forward to everyone meeting you and introducing you to what they each do." She got up and left.

At promptly 8:50, someone knocked on my office door and waited for me to say, "Please enter." A tall, serious-looking East European man entered and said, "I am Peter Glauser, here to escort you to the director's office."

"I'm ready," I said, and began to pick up my notepad.

He said, "You won't need that. Your conversation will be informal."

"Okay," I replied, and proceeded to follow him through a double security system—one electronic and the other manned with two armed security guards in a booth—that separated administration from research.

My escort walked me a short distance past security through the laboratory entrance, turned right down a passageway, and knocked on an office door. I heard a voice say, "Enter."

The director invited me to be seated in a small work area across from him, and asked if I wanted something to drink. I replied that I had already had two cups of coffee.

"I hope you enjoy your work here," he said.

"I am certain I will," I replied.

"For the locals, we have emphasized the service we provide for the weather monitoring system. For those of us associated with the research facility, we are performing highly classified work."

"What kind of classified research?" I asked.

"Dr. Gordon, the research we are conducting here will have a major impact on the world in terms of clean energy for the entire planet." He then went silent, as if to let his statement sink in.

"Rieser told me that I would be pleasantly surprised by the work you are conducting here."

"Our discoveries will be freely available to the entire world."

"Really?" I blurted out. Then I remembered Ms. Cartwright's advice and said, "Tell me more. I'm really interested now, but I must warn you, I've been away from my research for some time."

"Once you are involved with our overall approach, you'll catch on quickly." He paused, looked upward momentarily, and began.

"Clean energy is one of the world's greatest challenges. Most think it is decades away. Not so."

This time I waited for him to continue. I was catching on to how his train of thought worked.

"But control and distribution are equally important, as are how and who we use to manage them."

Continuing with my naïve persona, I asked, "Are you already at the management stage? Is the clean energy source a foregone conclusion at this point?"

He waved his hand, smiled, and said, "Yes."

"I supposed the UN would be handling much of the how and who, although getting the Security Council's approval for anything requires a Houdini act."

He laughed and said, "Exactly my point. Since the last pandemic, many of those remaining are trying desperately to recreate the management systems they had before."

I quickly recognized that he was talking as though I wasn't there anymore, so I just took in as much as he wanted to say.

"Instead of focusing on the future and implementing the wonders of technology and artificial intelligence." He stopped as abruptly as he had started, and said, "I get excited sometimes about the future and the work we are doing to meet those challenges."

He quickly focused his intense eyes on me again and said, "I understand you previously had a robust research program. Didn't you do some work in AI, toward the end of your scientific career? I remember reading something about it in Rieser's brief."

"Toward the end of my active research career, I partnered with some of my colleagues in computer science and the medical school to do some work on limb repairs and replacements. Since that time, the work in this area has exploded. However, I still follow what we started."

"See!" he exclaimed. "That's what I was referring to yesterday: once a scientist, always a scientist!"

I smiled broadly because what he said was true. No acting was necessary.

"Well, that's it for today. I have to get back to work. So much to do and so little time. I'll be in touch." He added as an afterthought, "Maybe next time we meet I'll tell you more about the advanced work we are doing here. It's truly extraordinary."

He rose abruptly and pushed a button. My escort magically reappeared, and the director said, "Dr. Glauser will take you back to your office to get adjusted with administrative stuff," as though it were distasteful to even say the word.

As Glauser walked me back to my office, I noticed one of the researchers staring at me and then hurrying on his way. For a fleeting moment, I thought I recognized him. *Not a good sign*, I surmised. I wondered if I had been made.

Although Dr. Glauser still wasn't friendly, some of the tension I had initially felt seemed to have lessened.

Just before meeting with Ms. Cartwright again, I sent off another message, remembering that they were to be no more than six words: *Administration security research secret stealth communication*. When the NSA IT people had warned me to not exceed six words, they told me that it had something to do with the algorithmic package, not the number of digits.

44

PREPARATION AND ANXIETY

General Maxwell had received the first six-word communication from the mountain research facility: *Two entrances adjacent old metallic merge.* He and his team had begun deciphering its meaning. The first three words were easy to interpret. There were two entrances to the original mine that were relatively close to each other. That made sense, since the reconnaissance done by satellite tracking showed the original entrance relatively untouched; even the warning sign was still in place, off to the side. The last three words were not so easily understood: *old metallic merge.* After repeated efforts by the NSA deciphering team, one of the brightest young analysts, Shelley Minor, who had no knowledge of the operation, was called in to give her take on the six-word message. The general described the message as a puzzle they were playing with. She looked at it for about thirty seconds and broke into a smile.

"What?" General Maxwell asked.

She turned to him and said, "One entrance is old, and one is probably new. I don't get the fit of the last two words, *metallic* and *merge*."

"Maybe a metallic detection system from the inside," someone offered.

Shelley turned to the general and asked, "Is that it, General Maxwell? I have a deadline to meet on an important project for my section chief that's to be sent to you, but I'll continue to think about your puzzle over lunch," confirming that she had no knowledge of the context of the "six-word puzzle," as she had described it.

During lunch with her Millennial friends, they discussed the wedding attire of one of their nontraditional friends. One of them said jokingly, "Something old, something new, something borrowed, and something blue." Then they all fell out laughing. "That's it!" Shelley shouted.

"What's it?" one of them asked.

"The director's little puzzle," she replied. "They merge! Like a marriage!"

Once Shelley shared her revelation with General Maxwell, it was easy to surmise that the "new" door she referred to was metallic.

General Maxwell, at the president's directive, had assigned one of his top aides to assemble a joint Seal-SAS assault team—the Special Air Service was the British Army's most renowned Special Forces unit, similar to the Navy Seal teams. The president had been in constant contact with the British prime minister, Christine Richardson, since his recent telephone conversation. He had convinced her that any plan to apprehend the Chairman would be a joint effort between the Americans and the Brits.

Although the American component consisted of Seals, the overall assault team leader was Colonel Darin Thomas, a former Seal. As head of the president's Special Projects Team, Colonel Thomas reported directly to the president. The SPT was not only off the radar, but for congressional funding and approval, they were nonexistent. Colonel Thomas and other members of the SPT were to be known only by their association with the Seal Special Forces unit. In fact, all the members of the SPT had passed Seal training with the exception of Monique Rashad. However, they had quickly determined that she had equivalent talents, and then some, based on her training by a French Special Forces commando and the Black Ops with the SPT.

The British component, the SAS, comprised seasoned veterans of black operations, most of which were known only to the British prime minister and one or two in the British SIS, the Secret Intelligence Service of MI6. Several members of the combined American-British team knew each other from the joint ops project named Destroy the Islamic State.

As the joint teams discussed their approach to penetrating the two tunnel entrances and dealing with the inside security forces, they determined that the metallic door, probably stainless steel, appeared to be the most formidable entrance challenge.

Darin decided that he would lead the Seal team in the assault on the metallic door, which he guessed was probably on rollers. He assigned Monique to the British team as second-in-command. The two teams began preparing for the major assault on the entire complex by practicing their separate entrances on the basis of connecting as a team where the two passageways merged. Monique fit perfectly with the SAS team as they got to know her, particularly with her accuracy involving firearms and quick reflexes in response to unexpected events.

The two teams were dealing with so many unknown factors that much of their success would depend on experience and quick response to surprises as well as pulling a few surprises of their own.

In the interim, the second message from Bill Bradley was received: *Administration security research secret stealth communication.* NSA's brain trust for resolving coded messages immediately began interpreting the six words, and shared this information with the British MI6. In the process, they noted that they were attempting to interpret coded messages from someone with no experience in clandestine operations. This excuse did not sit well with the general. He ran a 100 percent responsibility, results-oriented system, the same as the results he expected from combat operations.

Since the assault team needed intel, his patience was wearing thin, particularly since he knew a younger-generation analyst was readily available as a backup: Shelley.

- - - | | | | | - - -

Bill Bradley's trio of friends were struggling with their decision to avoid directly interfering with the destiny of Earth. The decision was not theirs but were original orders from the Pleiadian Council. They had offered to handle the situation with their Infinity Pod, but the president and his team had insisted on being in control of locating and capturing the Chairman. The president conceded that he would leave neutralizing up to them.

Of the three—John, Tony, and Lara—John struggled most with his commitment to protect Bill. They had been through so much together since John's arrival some years ago. And now here they were again, probably at the most critical point in their pursuit of the Chairman. Both Lara and Tony were acutely aware of John's struggle, but the decision as to what he would do was John's to make.

While going through this mental conflict, John noted a cell phone call and excused himself from the other two Pleiadians. Not surprisingly, it was Gala.

"John, where is Bill? I haven't been able to contact him for the last forty-eight hours. I thought he was home for a rest after his last assignment."

"Bill is on a very important mission."

"What does that mean?"

"The mission is very dangerous."

Gala sighed. She had been on an emotional roller coaster since her last conversation with Bill. She commonly processed difficult situations through her emotions rather than verbally. However, such processing always left her drained and with no recourse but to face reality. The process was also humbling. At some level, she envied the fact that Bill wholeheartedly embraced challenging verbal exchanges that constantly changed his perception of a situation. The difficulty she experienced was the fact that such processes were unpredictable and usually led to something being exposed over which she had little or no control. This was a thought process she preferred to do alone, but only at the completion of her emotional roller coaster ride.

She couldn't help but ask, "Could he be killed?"

John simply said, "Yes."

"Could you get a message to him?" She felt she knew the answer before John replied.

John paused.

She persisted. "Tell him I love him. And that we can make it work no matter what it takes." She paused and then finally blurted out, "That I'll never leave him, no matter what."

Finally, John spoke. "I promise to pass on your message to him." To help allay her fear, he said, "He always seems to have more than nine lives."

"Just tell him, John," she said, being in no mood for jokes.

"Okay, I will," and he clicked off.

Inside the research facility, Bill had been clairvoyantly sensing that something was about to happen, but he had no idea what it would be. It was like the experience of the warming effect as a prelude to a snowstorm, or being in the eye of a hurricane. Something dramatic, or even violent, was imminent. He had zero faith in the president's briefing that an assault would begin on his signal and that his safety would be the first concern of the Seal-SAS team. Most of all, he felt a deep sense of fear about himself, as though something was incomplete. He reflected on the researcher whom he suspected recognized him, but nothing had happened to expose his cover—so far.

Then he suddenly received an overwhelming telepathic thought-form. He knew immediately that it was from John—a soul-to-soul connection. He instantly received John's holistic communication as well as the attending emotion Gala had communicated.

45

SHOWTIME!

The Chairman couldn't put his finger on it; there was something not quite right about the energy around him. He knew he was safe and secure from any system of surveillance near him. However, whenever he felt this sense of unease, he knew instinctively that it was time to move to another location. He had more than twenty safe havens around the planet, all of them secure from any detection.

However, he was presently near the research facility in Switzerland because mass production was about to begin of the variety of androids that would be dispersed into the world's population. The human-like androids were to be used in conjunction with the subliminal programming used on all social media and practically all downloading IT devices. Programming involved anything from the popularity of Karl Gustav Christen for global leadership to messages of when and how to either save and invest money or to spend it to keep the economy in proper balance. *These combinations are the perfect solution for managing a planet with a significant number of humans who, collectively, have little or no interest in mastering inner wisdom to properly balance their technological advancement*, thought the Chairman.

Most people were unaware that every time they downloaded a program or an application, the opposite automatically occurred: information was collected on them. In-depth information on potential leaders and influential individuals, as well as their philosophies, were collected. The process of brainwashing predisposed empowering ideas, and reprogramming a leader-led global mindset began with the first tech device given to a toddler. Then, when that device was played, the suggestive content was subliminally communicated.

Over time, users fell into one of four categories: tech-averse, tech-in-moderation, tech-compulsive, and tech-addictive. The latter two categories were similar to common addictions involving alcohol, drugs, and compulsive personality disorders. These software programs and information storage technologies were designed to be run from the Consortium Communications Center, located near Neustadt. The ultimate objective was for IT devices to become a natural part or an extension of the human anatomy, whether a hand extension, a watch, or remote connection. The near future would involve the implantation of a chip administered as a vaccination shortly after birth.

It was the function of the army of androids to circulate around the planet in a variety of functions and jobs to ensure that all the Techies were actively engaged with a daily menu of programmed ways of being, thinking, and behaving. A major function of this army's responsibility was to institutionalize the belief that a Techie would experience a panic attack if their IT device was lost or became inoperative. Much of the original information collected from social media, collated as marketing profiles, were freely contributed by users through social networking programs. Global functioning was dependent on the mass production and dispersal of the highly sophisticated androids throughout the world. They, in essence, would begin to replace both high-level and middle human managers.

- - - | | | | | - - -

The Seal-SAS assault team was housed, along with NSA support personnel, about sixteen miles from the mountain research facility. The team was on twenty-four-hour alert for whenever the Chairman, Karl Christen, was sighted or entered the mine laboratory. These were the real signals to apprehend or attack, respectively, whether Bill signaled or not. This order was contrary to the assumption that Bill's initial extraction was of the highest priority.

The support personnel consisted of NSA interrogators, a safe-house security team, a fleet of six SUVs, and a Blackhawk helicopter for quick exit. The wait provided them time to become involved with the interpretation of the second six-word message, even if a word became obvious during the attack.

The intel team at NSA headquarters was becoming better at the civilian decoding process after Shelley shared her approach based on playing numerous video games. They had interpreted the first three words as linear spatial locations of the facility, which set the strategy for the initial stage of the assault. *Secret* and *stealth* referred to the work and mode of attack, respectively. *Communication* was the most difficult word to decipher, since they were informed by the townspeople that the mountaintop tower was used for weather monitoring and information collection. Communication was still a mystery.

The objectives were still the same: to find out where the Chairman was and what was going on inside the mine. Dr. Bradley's intel was the only "eyes" confirmation they had, although he still had not been invited to observe the research being conducted—only the android production from his clairvoyance-at-a-distance dream-movie.

On the third day of the team's deployment, an alert was communicated about midnight of a black SUV moving toward the mine. It stopped in front of a camouflaged metallic door. The door was opened. Two individuals, identified as males, entered the research facility, and the door was immediately closed. The point of the SUV's debarkation was identified using global satellite tracking, and was continually monitored after its discovery. The NSA security team was dispatched to the residence, and the occupants were questioned and secured. It was confirmed that one of the SUV's occupants was Dr. Karl Christen. The residence was a villa-like dwelling, and the occupants were his service staff.

The Seal-SAS team was immediately dispatched by helicopter to near the mine entrances to await further orders from the NSA Command Center. General Maxwell was still concerned that the communication intel had not been decoded, so as a last-ditch effort, he called Shelley again. When she arrived, she was excited to be helpful, but she began to wonder if the word puzzles were more serious than a training exercise.

As in the previous message decoding, the first four words were a no-brainer. Then she asked the director, "Is this a real operation, General?"

He hesitated and then said, "Yes, it is, Shelley. Very real."

"Gee, I'm sorry, General. I thought this was like a word sequence that we commonly use in our game called the Mole."

General Maxwell broke into her explanation and said, "That's quite all right, Shelley. Could you just take a crack at the last two words?" He shared with her what they had deciphered of the first four words.

"I don't know about the fifth word, but I would take the last word literally. In this case, the sender would be talking about their communication, not ours." She paused, looked at the general, and asked, "Which is what?"

General Maxwell was rarely at a loss for an explanation with respect to an op, particularly where intel was concerned—in this case, a lack of basic operational intel associated with the word *communication*. Reacting to Shelley's question, the associate director whispered privately to the general, "How do we know for sure what kind of antenna is atop that mountain, General?" Then General Maxwell said out loud, "Get that helicopter to the top of the mountain and check that antenna for communications or weather! If it's communication, then be ready to cut it on my command!"

"Yes, sir," the aide responded, and immediately initiated radio contact with the helicopter support crew that had transported the Seal-SAS team.

The general switched to communication with the assault team and said, "Get your team in place for entry as soon as we determine the function of the antenna at the top of the mountain facility."

Both assault teams approached from opposite sides of the entrances, minimizing any monitoring observation from the 180 degree approaches.

Silent explosives were deployed on the front metal door roller channels as well as the top and side braces, so that the door would fall forward.

The SAS team discovered that behind the wooden barrier and no-trespassing sign was a heavy wooden door, which they similarly loaded with explosives at vulnerable positions. If the silent explosives didn't work, they were planning on a heavy dose of C4—a powerful explosive that would make a highly noticeable sound but would ensure entrance through the wooden doors. In this case, a stealth entrance to the research and development sector would be voided. If the silent explosives did work, the teams were armed with silenced machine guns and machine pistols, ensuring a somewhat stealth assault.

Colonel Darin Thomas awaited the communication from General Maxwell at NSA headquarters while simultaneously messaging that the explosives on both doors were in place.

General Maxwell said to himself, "At least we will have answers to both questions: where the Chairman is—trapped inside the tunnel, hopefully—and what is going on inside of the facility. We'll find out for sure once we capture those inside."

About the same time, the helicopter landed softly on the mountaintop. The pilot said to no one in particular, "What a beautiful topside view."

The general responded, "Get on that goddamn antenna and find out what it transmits!"

The tech pilot approached the buzzing antenna. It was about ten feet high, which was the first tip-off. There was also a weather detector and a transmitter for barometric pressure, solar radiation, wind speed and direction, humidity, and temperature. However, the wires to the control unit hung, unattached and swinging in the wind. The ten-foot antenna was a highly sophisticated communications device that was also satellite compatible. The pilot activated his mic and spoke directly to the NSA command center.

"General Maxwell, sir, I ain't no expert in transmission antennas, but I do know the difference between one for weather and one for communications, courtesy of my old man," he said. "The cables for weather transmissions are dangling in the wind."

"Son, are you telling me that the weather antenna is not connected and the communications antenna is?"

"Sir, yes. That's exactly what I'm saying. And the communications transmitter is buzzing."

"Thanks, Sergeant. On my command, disconnect or sever the communication cables."

"Yes, sir."

The general switched to the other channel and said to Colonel Thomas, "Colonel, communications to and from the R&D facility will be cut on my command, followed by 'Go' with your mission."

"Roger that, sir." As an afterthought, he asked, "What about the signal from Dr. Bradley?"

"Son, you know as well as I do, plans for this type of operation change as a function of intel and opportunity. Now, get ready for the assault on my command."

The general began the countdown to the sergeant topside on the mountain: "Five, four, three, two, one, cut!"

The topside sergeant severed the three wires.

The general said to Colonel Thomas, "Go!", which was also communicated to the SAS team.

All of the silent explosions went off simultaneously. The small wooden door to the mine immediately fell inward. The SAS leader led the team inside and secured their position where the two entrances merged.

Meanwhile, the huge metal door detached but failed to fall. Darin quickly led the team and began pushing it inward. It teetered and then fell with a crash. They heard gunfire ahead, meaning the SAS team had encountered armed resistance.

When Darin's team approached the merge from an angle, his team outflanked two resisting guards from the security checkpoint and quickly disposed of them both with silent machine-gun fire.

The SAS team was up and advancing into the administration sector, where there was no armed resistance since security was dealing with the loss of communication. Bill Bradley was wildly waving his arms as he directed his staff to proceed to their rooms and remain there. Then he locked all five doors with his master coding information. He quickly approached Colonel Thomas and informed him of the two security positions and that the staff was not a threat.

To Colonel Thomas, everyone associated with the enemy operation was a threat. He ordered two men, one from each team, to accompany the staff out of the mine and secure them. He instructed the two men to contact the security team at the safe house to send an SUV to retrieve the administrative staff and begin questioning them for logistical intel.

Then he asked Dr. Bradley, "What's behind the two security checkpoints?"

"I don't know exactly, but I have a good idea from a diagram I saw in the director's office," he lied. "We weren't allowed there, but I suspect it is highly secure and probably not associated with energy research."

Unbeknownst to the attacking Seal-SAS team, the two research security teams housed at a nearby location were on a twelve-hour rotation. The resting team could be activated at a moment's notice when contacted by the deployed security force. If this team was alerted, the Seal-SAS team would be caught in a pincer, with the team on duty and the resting security team at their back. They would also probably be outnumbered by the attacking security teams. Fortunately for the Seal-SAS team, the communication's shutdown prevented contact with the off-duty security team from inside the mine—at least for the present.

46

THE STALEMATE

When the external communication wires were severed, the Chairman's British SAS manservant, Sean McIntyre, knew something had been compromised. He instructed the security force of eighteen armed veteran mercenaries to take up their prearranged positions to guard the research laboratories and assembly line. Exposure of their true research was to be avoided at all costs.

There was only one R&D employee working at the site at that time of night. His main responsibility was to oversee the readiness of the system for the morning's operation. The Chairman had planned this time, since he wanted as few researchers as possible to be present when he secretly visited—preferably, none. This was to be his last visit before going into full production of the androids. The Czech director would be in charge of mass production and continuing research.

None of the R&D personnel and security forces had been allowed to view the Chairman's entrance as Sean guided him to a secret office, when he met with the director. They had hardly begun their two-hour discussion when they were interrupted by a hard knock on the office door. Sean entered without the Chairman's permission, which was rare. The Chairman was visibly upset at being disturbed. He instructed, by finger movement, for Sean to handle the situation, then he turned to continue his discussion with the director.

Sean exited but returned in a matter of minutes. He just stood there. Finally, the Chairman turned to him, annoyed, and asked, "What is it?" Sean informed the Chairman that external communication had been disrupted and that there was an armed assault on the research facility.

The Chairman's sense of unease from earlier that evening was confirmed. There were still performance matters and production priorities he had to discuss with the director before the Chairman permanently left the site. He asked Sean, "Can the assault be contained? I need more time with the director."

"I think so; it doesn't appear to be an all-out attack with massive numbers."

"Determine what our situation is and how we can make contact with the off-duty security shift," suggested the Chairman. He thought, *There's no major problem except saving the facility for mass production. In the final analysis, I could always use the fail-safe solution and continue the work elsewhere. The crucial research findings have already been completed and scientifically recorded.* "Keep me informed if we are forced to evacuate."

The Chairman resumed his debriefing with the director regarding the status of research and development involving the variety of androids and the timetable for mass production and global distribution. He appeared to be relaxed and unconcerned about the assault on the facility.

The director said, with greater anxiety, "Shouldn't we be considering our escape instead of having this discussion?"

"Oh, I think we're fine," replied the Chairman. "Our forces can contain them. Let's continue with the wonderful progress you've made, in particular with the new AI algorithms that make it almost impossible to distinguish our newest androids from a real person."

Meanwhile, the administrative personnel had been taken to the nearby NSA safe house by the SUV Colonel Thomas had requested. They were made comfortable as a team of NSA interrogators prepared to interview each of them. Their stories were pretty consistent: They were hired to oversee typical administrative duties involving payroll, benefits, personnel problems, family communications, and insurance. They were all paid salaries significantly higher than the current market in exchange for guaranteed service of at least one year. Agreed-to income and benefits were for life. Most importantly, they were sworn to a signed secrecy agreement, which, if violated, would void their lifetime income and benefits, and result in immediate dismissal.

They had also agreed to remain in their sector of the workplace and not engage in conversations with the scientists and engineers about their research and development work. They were informed of its highly confidential nature involving an energy source to satisfy the world's continuing demand, and told that the sponsoring organization of the laboratory planned to give the invention freely to every country that chose to use it. This last condition solidified their commitment to work in secrecy at the facility.

The NSA interviewer who interviewed Gabriella Cartwright, Dr. Gordon's administrative assistant, was a woman. The two connected with ease, although Gabriella was initially guarded and suspicious of the interviewer's questions. They spoke easily about Gabriella's upbringing and having an American father. Gabriella offered that it helped to dispel a lot of myths that she had heard about Americans while she was growing up. Finally, Gabriella revealed that she had been employed by the research facility for several years and was the most senior of the administrative staff. She further revealed that she had found Dr. Gordon rather naïve about what he was getting into but had concluded that he was probably chosen because he had been a famous scientist. "He was obviously the director's choice," Gabriella suggested.

The NSA interviewer finally asked Gabriella, "Is there anything you can tell us about the operations or the facility that could be helpful in locating the director's boss?"

"The who?" asked Gabriella, looking baffled.

"The person who the director reports to."

"I've never seen or met whoever that is. The director runs everything and only reports to the UN and the sponsoring corporation. I know because we prepare the reports that are sent to them. The director has no boss that I am aware of."

"I see," said the interviewer, deciding to take a different tack. "What about visitors?"

"I do know of the entrance and exit for the research staff and deliveries that go directly to the R&D sector. We are not allowed there, and I am the only administrative staff member who knows it even exists." She paused momentarily and then continued. "I think it is probably also used for important visitors to come and go without being seen by the staff or other scientific personnel."

"Can you draw a description of how we might locate it?" asked the interviewer.

Gabriella paused, fearing she was close to violating the code of secrecy. Then she asked, "Something is not quite right, is it?"

"Yes, we think the research that is being done there has nothing to do with energy but will probably be used for other purposes."

"What other purposes?" Gabriella asked.

"Honestly speaking, we're not sure. That's why we're investigating the site, to find out for sure."

"I suspected as much," said Gabriella. "All that secrecy, and the money we were all getting for life. It was too hard to pass up, as long as nothing obviously unlawful was going on. My parents were worried about the secrecy until I eventually told them about the energy project and giving it to the world. I told them that that was all I could say for the present. In truth, I don't know much more."

"Can you draw a diagram of the deliveries entrance and where it is located?"

"Sure, give me a pen and some paper," she said.

- - - | | | | | - - -

After taking over the two security positions leading to the R&D sector, the Seal-SAS team encountered a barrage of fire power when they attempted to enter the six-by-eight-foot entranceway to R&D. The security team appeared to have superior numbers and was definitely not rent-a-cops. They were seasoned professionals, possibly Special Forces turned mercenaries, Darin surmised.

I reminded Colonel Thomas and the Brit team lead that I thought I remembered the R&D layout, if that would help.

Colonel Thomas said, "That would be helpful, Dr. Bradley. We have nothing else. We're lucky so far that none of us are down."

"R&D has three major operations side by side and is divided by two major aisles: one operation for R&D, one for development and design, and the third for production. There are a series of nine offices in front and nine at the back of these laboratories. They appear in this arrangement just beyond the wall with that single entrance." I used my finger to diagram it on the floor.

"How do you know this amount of detail," asked Darin, "given you weren't allowed in the R&D sector?"

"I told you, I saw the diagram in the research director's front office when I met with him," I lied. "Each of these lab operations was labeled," I said with confidence.

The two team leaders looked at me skeptically.

"I would guess that the Chairman is in one of the offices at the back," I concluded convincingly. *No matter if they believed me or not*, I thought, *they don't have anything else to go on.*

- - - | | | | | - - -

Darin received a prompt on his communication receiver from one of the two team members stationed at the metal door entrance. He answered and quickly retreated to the facility entrance to receive an outside call.

The female interviewer from the safe house was calling to inform Darin of the secret deliveries entrance, which was originally a narrow parallel shaft for emergency exit from the mine in case of an accident. She described how to find it by starting at the main entrance and doubling back in the direction of the original old mine entrance. In the low light of the cave, the entrance to the shaft appeared to be an alcove in the wall. *Neat way to camouflage it*, Darin thought. The SAS team probably went right past it.

When he returned, Colonel Thomas and the SAS team lead agreed that the Brits would double back and enter the research and development facility from the deliveries entrance. "Once you assess your position, we can coordinate our attack for entrance into the R&D sector," Darin said.

"Sounds like a plan to me. We'll contact you as soon as we are in position." The SAS team lead gathered his squadron and double-timed in retreat to find the alternate R&D entrance.

About this time, the off-duty security force team lead was becoming concerned. He hadn't heard from the on-duty team for about forty-five minutes. He put in a call to check. He was unable to make contact after several attempts; he was just getting static. *Probably that damn comm tower again*, he thought. High winds atop the mountain were the most common cause of damage to the webbed antenna. However, they were usually quick about getting it fixed. He decided to doze off a bit more before calling in again.

47

JUST THE BEGINNING

The SAS team found the emergency escape tunnel without difficulty. If they had been paying attention on their way in, they would have noticed it. As they quietly made their way through the tunnel, they came to a loading dock that was probably used for deliveries and removals. They could hear voices down a short hallway through the closed double swinging doors. By a stroke of fate, the short hallway came in behind the two elevated positions of the security force.

The SAS team lead retreated to the tunnel and contacted Colonel Thomas. He communicated the situation and their position. He proposed a twenty-second silent countdown to initiate his team's attack. They had discussed the plan in the case of a pincer situation: "Just be ready to enter the R&D sector on my team's actions." The team leader used hand signals for specific members of his team to attack one or the other of the two positions, each manned by the eight security personnel.

On the finger signal countdown to zero, two of the SAS team members stepped out of their hiding positions and threw concussion grenades at the two positions, then quickly retreated. The grenades went off simultaneously, temporarily blinding, disorienting, and confusing the laboratory security team members. As they began to recover, they realized that they had not been injured by shrapnel fragmentation.

As the SAS team rushed the dazed security team, a security team member's gun fired a burst, and the SAS team leader went down. Monique Rashad, second in command, immediately shot him through the forehead and shouted for the others to throw down their weapons and lie flat on the floor. When another security team member realized it was a woman who had killed his compatriot, he was so angered that he swung his machine pistol toward Monique. Before he got his weapon into position, a bullet hole opened just above his left ear. Monique stood fully upright and asked, "Any more?" The others were silent and proceeded to lie flat on their stomachs.

As soon as the concussion grenades exploded, Darin and his team rushed through the main entrance and spread through the laboratory's two aisles. They made their way to the elevated security position with no resistance, since the mercenary security team members were recovering from their disorientation. After hearing gunfire, the first person Darin looked for was Monique. She was standing there smiling, knowing the question on his face.

"Anyone of ours down?" he asked when he didn't see the SAS team lead.

"Yes, the team lead," she replied. Before he could ask, she continued, "Good thing he had a vest. He did sustain a serious shoulder injury that will need medical attention."

Darin looked at her and smiled.

"Those two are not so good," she said, turning her head toward the two dead mercenaries. "I never go for the body if there is a choice."

Darin quickly called one of the two Seal-SAS team members assigned to the administrative personnel who had remained at the mine entrance. He requested three SUVs for prisoner removal and medical attention for the wounded SAS team lead.

The prisoners were handcuffed with tactical handcuffs and hinges, and their feet were tied for the time being. These were not typical prisoners they were dealing with. In truth, most of the SAS team would have preferred a final resolution, where prisoners would be unnecessary. These prisoners would probably be free within a month and in confrontation with a Special Forces unit again before the year was out.

Shortly after the removal of the prisoners, the injured, and the expired in the SUVs, one of the two Seal-SAS team members assigned to the mine entrance calmly put in a call to Colonel Thomas. "Sir, two incoming helicopters. Not ours!" Darin instructed them to immediately rejoin their respective teams. He turned to Monique and an SAS team member and said, "Hell of a way to find out about the back-up security team. How many do you estimate?"

The SAS team member took a step back and allowed Monique to reply, "Between fifteen and twenty, I would guess. About the same size as the group we just encountered—eighteen and probably a team lead."

"If they don't use the emergency tunnel, we could have another pincer situation," said Darin.

"Don't bet on it," Monique replied.

"Let's station my team here and your team inside the entrance of the emergency tunnel."

"What about the Chairman?" she asked.

"Let's take care of him now. There's no other way out except the two entrances we have covered."

As they made their way through each of the offices behind the R&D sector, they finally came to one that was occupied by the director of the laboratory, who was alone and waiting to be apprehended. He was asked about his visitor. He replied that he was the only one remaining. They secured him with hands and legs bonds, as well as a simple mouth gag, and left him in the office.

After repeated attempts to contact the on-duty R&D security team, the group leader of the back-up mercenaries decided that not only was something amiss but was probably a code-red—which would mean that the facility was under attack.

The two Black Hawk helicopters split on approach to the facility; one came from the north, and the other, the south. Upon touchdown, the mercenaries split into three teams of six each. They had night vision goggles on; as expected and confirmed, the mine's entrance was completely dark.

One team entered over the fallen metal door, confirming that the complex was under attack. Another team entered through the original mine shaft and headed toward the emergency tunnel. The third team held in place. The team that entered over the fallen metal door stormed into the administration sector, their night vision optics giving them full visibility in the darkness. They were surprised when Bill Bradley, aka Dr. Gordon, turned on the lights, as instructed by Colonel Thomas, and were suddenly blinded. But most of all, they were completely exposed to the Seal team, who immediately downed three of the six entering mercenaries.

One of the surviving three quickly retreated toward the entrance of the shaft. Within a minute, the complex was completely dark again, and Bradley and the Seal team had no night vision equipment. The mercenary had obviously cut the major generator supplying electrical energy to the entire research complex. Colonel Thomas immediately ordered a retreat to the R&D sector, which the Seal team was quite familiar with. They used pin flashlights to set up their defense for the second wave of the attack. If Monique's SAS team didn't hold the emergency tunnel, they would be in a world of trouble—the same as they had done, by fate, to the on-duty security team. Colonel Thomas's team, of course, was not depending on fate. So far, there was only one seriously wounded casualty: the SAS team lead who had been taken away for medical treatment. Since the Chairman and his manservant, Sean McIntyre, had not been located, two team members were assigned to cover the backs of the Seal team from the emergency shaft.

The attack on the emergency shaft began high-low. One of the mercenaries dove in and lay flat on the floor of the cave, and the other was using an indentation in the wall for protection. They both scanned the cave. Monique and an SAS team member were on opposite sides, she in a crouched position, and he standing fully upright. Using his night vision goggles, the attacker in the low position had clear visibility of the standing Brit. He fired at the Brit, and the sounds of a groan and a fall followed. Monique aimed slightly higher than his muzzle position, fired three rounds, and heard the attacker's rifle fall into the dirt.

Her shot was followed by a barrage above her head, forcing her to seek cover. She decided to use her eyes for muzzle fire and her heightened sense of sound for location. She also aimed high to hopefully hit the neck or head area, since she automatically assumed the attackers had protective vests. When the muzzle fire paused, she took a relaxing breath and then fired three rapid rounds. Two bullets missed, but the third went through the attacker's throat and exited. Monique momentarily considered attempting to retrieve one of the night vision goggles. Fortunately, caution prevailed. As she began her slow retreat, she sprayed the entrance of the tunnel and moved to the other side to check her teammate. She confirmed he was dead. She removed his remaining concussion grenade and cautiously moved backward, covered by her other five team members who were positioned further along the tunnel.

Darkness became their strength and light was their weapon, Monique reasoned. The next wave involved three mercenaries; two came in peppering the cave left to right, and one focused on sighting the SAS team members. As they approached, Monique pulled out her wide-angle flashlight and adjusted it to high beam wide. It was the new military-style flashlight recently advertised for the public. She had only a few seconds for blindness and disorientation, since she would simultaneously be giving away her position. As the three mercenaries approached, fully confident of their highly visible vision shaded in green, Monique flashed the light on. They were momentarily blinded and stunned, but in such a confined space, they quickly recovered enough to begin firing wildly in the direction of the light. By this time, Monique had flattened on the floor of the tunnel. Deep breath, fire, and another one went down instantly. Her two teammates also fired during the moments of disorientation, and another mercenary went down. The third recovered and spotted the two Brits in vulnerable positions. As his muzzle went off, one was hit, and the other almost emptied his clip as he fired, dismembering the mercenary's arm. The remaining mercenaries from the tunnel team retreated, probably to confer with their team lead.

The mercenary team lead decided a more aggressive approach would be necessary to break the back of the resistance. Caution had not paid off. He conferred with his team and decided they would take on the strength of the attackers. They laid out a plan that might take a toll on their number but would ensure success once executed. The leader said, "It's time we showed these upstarts what true Special Ops are all about." Even with his emotional pep talk, he knew he was facing an exceptionally trained and experienced Special Forces unit. He was simply trying to communicate that some of them would have to die to achieve their objective. After all, this was what they had signed on for. His only hope was that they had superior numbers.

Darin and Monique conferred by their comm connection. She indicated that they had only five members left, but they were holding their own. Darin said, "You know the old saying, the best defense is a good offense."

"Yeah, in the movies!" She laughed.

"Let me tell you what I have in mind, and you can help me improve it."

"Okay, shoot," she said.

What he realized, again, was that they were both committed to what they did. It bonded them in a common cause. And although it could end tragically in an instant, they both lived in the moment and for the moment, in an inseparable bond.

48

UNFOLDING

For the mercenary team lead, the situation had become personal. It went beyond money or the director's cause—which he had never cared about. If Colonel Thomas's Special Forces team was victorious, it meant that the life he had turned his back on was superior to the one he had chosen for money. He was well aware that getting his emotions involved was dangerous for the task at hand, since he knew his team considered emotions to be a sign of fear. In addition, they believed emotions were unnecessary for seasoned professionals in the business of disposing of adversaries.

In contrast, the Special Forces team was collectively driven by a mindset of defending freedom and the American and British ways of life—no matter what the cost. In Monique's case, she had personal reasons for choosing sides, one tied to Darin and the other to her father, General Maxwell. In essence, they had become her family, or the closest she had to one. She secretly admired her father's leadership and military accomplishments. She often wondered what it would have been like to be raised by him. She was clear, however, that her combat skills were probably genetically passed on from him. Her mother's inherited soft skills had been shared with only two men: Darin Thomas and Jacques Lamoreaux, her French mentor.

Darin assumed that the two units were about equal in manpower, given the fact that the SAS team had eliminated four and his team had eliminated three at the outset of the attack. To offset the mercenaries' presumed advantage of night vision optics, they planned an unconventional approach based on disorientation, speed, and stealth.

The mercenaries divided into two teams each. They were stacked, three in front and three behind, with the team lead at the rear. They proceeded past the two security stations en route to the R&D sector. When the two point positions didn't draw any fire from the entranceway, the two stacked teams continued to move up the adjacent aisles of the laboratory, with the team lead closely behind the right-side team. When they reached the halfway point of the two aisles with no resistance, they had a feeling they were in no-man's land, simply by learned instinct.

At this point, two concussion grenades were thrown amid each of the two mercenary teams. As expected, the teams were disoriented and temporarily blinded—especially with their night vision optics—and pandemonium set in. Then the lights came on again, and a few attempted to tear away their night vision goggles.

Darin's team quickly emerged from the bank of offices behind the mercenaries and began firing at them from the back. Three members of each team immediately went down with little or no further movement. As the three in front began to turn in response, Monique's team peppered them with a similar volley from the front barrier position. When the shooting stopped, two mercenaries were standing, and several were in a dazed state—but most were lying unconscious. The mercenary team lead was one of those left standing. In his highly angered state, he swung his weapon toward Darin, but before he could fire, one of the Brit teammates fired a shot through his forehead. The other one standing immediately threw his assault weapon down. Darin shouted for each of them to throw aside their weapons and lie prone on the floor.

At this point, the semiconscious mercenaries realized that this was the first live machine-gun fire they had heard from their adversaries in the exchange. On closer examination, Darin noted that most of them were still unconscious or disoriented and semiconscious. It was only then that the mercenaries began to realize that they had been peppered with high-dosage tranquilizer bullets—some at more vulnerable places than others. However, as backup, the Special Forces unit was ready to use live fire if they felt endangered.

All the members of the mercenary team were quickly and efficiently secured with handcuffs. At this point, Darin congratulated Bradley on restarting the generator and the lights, his timing perfect as the concussion grenades were exploded.

- - - | | | | | - - -

At the beginning of the mission, Darin, the SAS team lead, and General Maxwell had discussed the delicacy of the unauthorized mission. First, it was occurring within an independent country that had its own law enforcement processes and procedures. Second, the security force for the laboratory was lawfully employed to protect its employees and the research being conducted, albeit under false pretenses. Third, the work being developed was probably a major threat not only to the United States and the UK but also to global security.

The most compelling reason for the unauthorized secret intervention, as determined by the United States and United Kingdom, was that the Chairman had to be captured and the nature of the research and development had to be determined in terms of its threat to the present and future global community. When all these points were discussed and considered, the mission was arbitrarily approved, for better or worse, by the heads of state of the United States and United Kingdom.

Under no circumstances was there to be an unauthorized blood-bath. The mercenaries were not terrorists, and were, in fact, lawfully employed. However, in the process of gathering answers to the two compelling questions, the Special Forces team was instructed to protect themselves at all costs. Therefore, in both of their encounters, fatalities were minimal, with the exceptions coming as a result of self-defense against one or more of the mercenaries.

The fact that lethal force was involved at all was one of the major reasons the three Pleiadians did not participate in the operation in any way. They considered it to be the typical barbaric way humans resolved conflict or disagreements—limited, of course, by their relatively elementary level of consciousness evolution.

To determine what was going on in the laboratories, the SAS team began exploring the labs and taking pictures. They tried several doors before they found one that opened, which seemed to trigger a master switch. The looming question still remained: where was the Chairman immediately after the final Special Forces and mercenary encounter? While the Seal team began a thorough search for the Chairman, they concluded that there was no way he could have escaped.

Shortly into the SAS team's laboratory exploration, they discovered a research engineer huddled in a hidden corner of one of the laboratories. He explained that he was there that evening to oversee that all systems were in perfect operating mode for the following day's work. He had remained hidden where he was once the commotion began.

The SAS team lead informed him that he would be interrogated and probably released to return to his native country. Surprisingly, he asked, "Might I be allowed to speak privately with Dr. Walter Gordon?"

The lead team member asked, "Why?"

"Because I have information that he might be interested in knowing."

- - - | | | | | - - -

Darin immediately requested that I have a private conversation with the engineer in one of the laboratories. I was unaware that he had secretly bugged the laboratory with a tiny magnetic-bond transmitter just prior to allowing us privacy.

The engineer locked the laboratory door so that no one could disturb us. "You don't remember me, do you?" he asked when we were alone.

"When I saw you after visiting the director on my first day, I thought I had seen you before. But I still can't place you, even though you do look familiar," I replied.

"I know you aren't Dr. Walter Gordon. You're Dr. William Bradley. I could never forget the great presentation you made some years ago at our international conference."

Keeping my pretense in place, I replied, "Thanks for the compliment, but I'm Dr. Walter Gordon. I may look like someone you met before."

"I was your host at the Chemical Physics Conference in Prague. A group of us even went out to dinner with you afterward."

The memories came flooding back, and I blurted out, "Matus Kozar!" He smiled.

I put my hands up, palms showing, and said, "Okay. I am part of a team trying figure out what's really going on at this facility. We're fairly confident it has nothing to do with energy research, and may even be a threat to the global community."

The engineer said, "The reason I requested a private meeting with you is that I started to think something really scary was going here as we began to develop highly sophisticated AI algorithms."

"Like what?" I asked.

He took on a serious look and said, "Highly sophisticated humanoid androids; mass production." He paused and then continued. "I'll tell you about that later, but I think I know where the director's special visitor is. I heard your colleagues talking about finding someone called the Chairman."

"You do?" I asked excitedly.

"Of course. I've been here since the start of this project. I know practically everything about it, especially from working at night," he said.

"Where is he?" I asked evenly, barely able to contain my excitement.

"I would guess in the storage area, off the platform, where you probably entered from the tunnel. There is a barely visible door behind it. It requires a code for entrance, as everything does here. When your people started searching the laboratories, I decoded the master switch so that the doors would open. Until then, the laboratories were locked throughout your encounters," he said proudly. "Of course, I didn't have to worry when the generator was disabled."

I was growing impatient for the answers I knew Darin wanted to hear, but I tried to keep my composure. After all, Matus still thought I was a scientific superstar. That's what I liked about Europeans. They never forget if you did great work. "What is the code?" I asked, matter-of-factly.

"I can give you the numbers, but you might have trouble with the administration," he replied.

I guessed he meant "administering it," so I asked, "Could you do it for us?"

"Of course. That's why I asked for you."

"Well, why don't we go to this private office and see if our special visitor is still there?"

Matus walked to the sliding laboratory door, deftly played his fingers on the numbers, and then pressed his right palm, the part next to his thumb—sometimes called the Mount of Venus—to the decoding plate. The door opened smoothly. Then I understood what he meant. Even the fingers he used to press the numbers were specific to memory of his fingerprints.

- - - | | | | | - - -

By this time, everyone except the SPT members, Darin, Monique, and me had cleared out to handle other logistical matters so that everything might seem normal in the morning. Of course, if necessary, we would inform the town's leader that we had a security practice run, but we expected that gun shots twenty miles away, inside of a tunnel, didn't awaken anyone.

By now, one of the questions had been answered. The facility had been designed to mass produce a variety of humanoid-like androids for dissemination throughout the world. We guessed that their purpose was to take orders from the Chairman by the daily use of IT devices, such that they would become indispensable to the public. The androids would probably facilitate, and in some cases enforce, the regular use of such devices.

Then the thought hit me: have we taken care of the Communications Center in Neustadt? That would be the brain of the subliminal programming operation. I immediately sought out Darin and asked, "What about the Communications Center in Neustadt?"

"Handled," Darin replied. "A raid of the Neustadt Communications Center by our team is planned for early in the morning, when everyone has arrived for work. It's expected that everything will be captured intact—including those employed."

49

THE DOWNFALL

Matus directed us to the storage room just inside the double swinging doors. He walked to an innocuous alcove with a decoding plate that was not visible by casual observation. He played with the numbers and then applied his right palm to the plate as he had done in the laboratory. The door opened, and there sat Dr. Karl Gustav Christen, absolutely composed. He smiled and said, "I've been waiting for you." He was alone.

I stepped forward and said, "Dr. Christen, we meet again, under quite different circumstances."

"Yes," he said, quietly composed.

"Allow me to introduce Colonel Darin Thomas and his second in command, Ms. Monique Rashad."

He shook hands with both of them, which Darin obviously found distasteful. Monique was neutral, accustomed to men who exuded power—both inner and outer—and existed in a realm beyond human judgment and justice, during her Middle Eastern upbringing.

"Should I call you Chairman?" I asked.

"As you please," he replied calmly.

"Mr. Chairman, I am perplexed as to why you have waged this campaign for so long to control events in opposition to human transformation, particularly with your Pleiadian background."

"Please, everyone, have a seat before we depart in a few minutes. It appears my journey has come to an end."

We sat in three chairs, situated as though he had anticipated our arrival. Darin was most disturbed and probably simply wanted to collect our criminal and leave. I had the impression that Monique was recalling her university days, and wanted to hear what he had to say—she had long ago learned that the demarcation between a criminal and a just person was blurred. It was mostly decided by the persons in control. That was what disturbed her most about the Chairman's casualness. I wanted to discover what I could learn of the human condition from his point of view. After all, he wasn't stupid and was once a Pleiadian, committed to our cause.

At this point, it became clear to me why the president wanted me to be part of this operation. He wanted Darin for strong-arm stuff and capture. Me, he wanted for interrogation and intel for possible future situations. And Monique fell somewhere in between.

The Chairman began. "What makes you presume that humans have the capacity and the intention for transformation unless they were literally faced with a so-called act of God? Like a pandemic? I know that humans refer to occurrences beyond their direct control in this way, but they certainly strongly influence those events."

"The aftermath of the two pandemics has had a transformative effect on a majority of those of us remaining," I replied confidently.

"You mean it took the selective elimination of more than half the Earth's population for you to conclude that self-annihilation was inevitable?" he replied without emotion.

When no one responded, he continued. "And now you are struggling with how to make the realization of compatibility a functional reality even though the answer is staring you in the face."

"This challenge can be achieved much faster without your interference. At least we've bought time," I replied.

He laughed and asked, "Do you know how long you have been operating in terms of self-interest, in spite of all your lofty declarations?"

"Centuries, I suppose," I said honestly.

"Granted," he said, "not one-dimensional. That's what is so perplexing about you as a species."

I could tell that Darin was becoming anxious and nearing the point of taking control of what he considered to be a stupid conversation. At some level, I also suspected the conversation was stirring something inside him. I had the impression that Monique was fascinated, given her upbringing in the Middle East. "What do you mean, we are 'not one-dimensional'?" I asked.

The Chairman looked at me as though the answer was obvious, then he replied, "As a species, you are an enigma. On the one hand, you look for external solutions for everything, and on the other, you are deathly afraid of personal exploration when that is the obvious source of your most perplexing problems. You build, and have sustained throughout your history, hierarchical systems of human relationships on the basis of superiority and inferiority. When you tire of killing defenseless animals for sport, you resort to killing each other as the ultimate means of conflict resolution." He paused and then continued. "I could go on endlessly about the human condition, but underneath it all is the basic foundation that must be either learned or facilitated: you don't really care about each other, except in true survival situations. I chose facilitation."

"Again, what did you mean that we were not one-dimensional?" I persisted.

"You also create and behave in unimaginably spiritual ways: music that stirs the soul, art that inspires the imagination, science that has eliminated true survival, medicine that relieves and cures human suffering, technology that is endless in its application for external exploration and expression, and on occasions, overwhelming expressions of love on behalf of each other."

Silence followed his statements. Then he added for emphasis, "Because of this duality, don't you conclude that this type of species should be controlled through the power of influence for its own self-preservation? That has been my life's work on Earth, since I gave up on your collective transformation."

Darin abruptly stood, meaning the conversation was over. I could not help but reply to the Chairman's statement. "Besides eliminating freedom of expression, your methods of influence have been worse than the conditions we have faced and overcome," I said, more in an attempt to convince myself. Monique looked at me and smiled.

The Chairman also smiled and replied, "As you say, if you want to make an omelet, you have to break a few eggs."

Darin walked up to the Chairman, who raised his left hand and stood while deftly slipping a tiny transmitter into his right coat pocket. We walked toward the R&D sector. As we approached the laboratories, the Chairman pressed the button of the transmitter, which activated an immediate explosion at the center of the R&D complex, circumventing the fail-safe mechanism. Darin, Monique, and I stopped abruptly and then began retreating toward the emergency tunnel. The Chairman continued as though he could outrun the collapsing ceiling. Then he stopped, turned, looked at us, and smiled as the ceiling collapsed on him.

Darin and Monique rushed back toward the emergency tunnel, with me in close pursuit. The entire R&D sector collapsed, filling with massive proportions of rocks and dirt. We rushed down the tunnel expecting it to also implode at any moment. When we reached the old mine exit, the administrative sector began collapsing. After several minutes, the entire mine had refilled, leaving it as it must have existed before excavation had begun more than one hundred years ago.

Matus walked up to us and said, "I guess you have concluded your work. Good riddance." He turned and walked a short distance away.

Darin used his comm pack and informed the safe house to send an SUV to retrieve us. Then he walked over to Matus and said, "Thanks for your help."

"I knew something very wrong was going on shortly after we started," Matus said. "I kept a journal of our work, including our research findings. Here it is."

Darin, surprised, took the journal and asked, "Is there anything we can do for you? Besides giving you a ride back to your living quarters?"

Matus replied, "You already have. You saved my life. There was no way he could let us live after mass production began."

Darin walked away from Matus and Monique, pulled out his SAT phone, and speed-dialed.

"Sir, it's complete. The mountain facility has totally collapsed, with the Chairman inside. We observed the collapse and his death."

"What about the delicate package?"

"Intact, sir." He paused and then asked, "Permission to comment, sir?"

"Yes."

"Your delicate package is not as delicate as you think."

"You don't think I know that, Colonel?" Then he clicked off.

50

||||||||||||||||||||||||||||||||||||||||||||||||||||||||||||||||||||||||||||||||||||||||||||||||||||||||||||||||||||

TIMELESSNESS

General Maxwell immediately relayed word of the Chairman's death to the president, who was delighted that such a long process, one that had frustrated his efforts for planetary compatibility, had finally come to an end. He thanked General Maxwell and informed him that he would update the British prime minister, Christine Richardson, of the victory. He said he would also inform her of the losses and injury suffered by the SAS team. General Maxwell then put in a quick call to General Kenneth Clarke, the president's chief of staff, apprising him of the team's success.

I called John to tell him to let Tony and Lara know what had happened—although I had the impression that they knew already. He said he would inform Gala that I was safe and would be returning soon. Then he passed the SAT phone to Lara.

"Hi, Bill," she said excitedly. "I understand we, or your team, finally brought an end to the Chairman here on Earth."

"Your team was extremely important," I quickly corrected. "However, I'm pleased it was a US-UK operation in the final analysis. The president and the prime minister will also be pleased."

"I'll be leaving immediately for Pleiades to present a report to the council," she said. "I am confident that your process of implementing the Seven Principles here will proceed much more smoothly from now on."

I blurted out, "You are returning to help, aren't you?" sounding desperate. I couldn't imagine continuing our work without Lara, and I told her so.

"You are far more resilient than you give yourself credit for. After all, your team of earthlings has already proven what you can do without our assistance," she offered, with a smile to John and Tony. "However, I'll see what the council has in mind for me and let you know."

I was silent for several seconds. Then I said, "We need you, Lara. We can't do this work without you. Especially this One World Federation that the president has in mind after his term ends. Please tell the council of our plans." I was almost pleading by now.

Finally, she said, "I will tell them," and clicked off. She was beginning to feel a slight increase in the emotions of her earthly body.

- - - | | | | | - - -

While the final encounter had been occurring between the US-UK Special Forces and the mercenary teams, Sean McIntyre had escorted the Chairman out of the emergency tunnel to the parked SUV he had hidden for their escape. As soon as they were safely on their way to the Zürich airport, the Chairman began to marvel at the performance of the first advanced android: Dr. Karl Gustav Christen. Too bad it had to be destroyed. The Czech director had done a marvelous job in terms of designing both perfectly humanoid looks and naturally programmed responses.

The Chairman had supplied the robot with the vital elements of his legacy, which he accurately guessed was what they would want to know. This was easy, since it was his true evaluation of the planet's progress. It also spelled out why his work was not yet complete and how he would take full advantage of the present situation—especially since they saw him "die," with eyewitnesses. He had taken the director's scientific notebook and could easily reproduce a new facility; this time it would be remote, secret, and hidden in plain sight.

When they reached the Zürich airport, Sean drove slowly to the parking area for private departures and arrivals. He showed the guard his credentials and the private aircraft papers he had reserved for their flight. Soon, Sean and the Chairman were in flight to the one place the Chairman assumed that no one would guess: his beloved villa in Neustadt.

Sean landed smoothly on the short runway outside of Neustadt and returned the Chairman to his favorite place on Earth. He would miss it when he relocated. After he was comfortably settled, Sean brought his favorite cognac, Hennessy Beauté du Siècle, for relaxation. It had been a trying and yet successful day. The Chairman began to envision a new era, which would probably require a new facelift, or more realistically, an entirely new history and body. After all, Karl Gustav Christen was officially dead. He had served his purpose.

The Chairman's final directive to Sean was to send an emergency email blast to all employees of the Consortium Communications Center to immediately execute Operation Disappearance and remotely destroy the CCC and its contents. Sean was also to inform them that they would be contacted in the near future to resume their present functions. In the meantime, they would be compensated as usual. Sean promised to handle the email blast the following morning and destruction of the center after sensitive information and records of secret consortium activities over the years were permanently erased.

Sean bid the Chairman good night and promised to wake him in the morning at the usual time, since the other villa staff had been permanently dismissed. The Chairman had already decided on his next permanent safe house on a private island in the South Pacific, complete with a new identity.

The following morning Sean came to rouse the Chairman. The bed was empty and still neatly made, as though no one had slept in it. Sean searched for his charge in every room of the villa. After exhausting himself, he sat in the Chairman's office and wondered if his boss had chosen someone else to attend to him in the future. Perhaps the Chairman wanted a completely new makeover, including a new manservant. Without executing any of the Chairman's instructions from the previous evening, Sean retrieved his private auto, headed for the Zurich airport, and began executing his plans for fading into the fabric.

- - - | | | | | - - -

The trio of Pleiadians, Lara, Tony, and John, had summoned the orbiting cloaked spaceship from Pleiades to the site of the Swiss encounter. They had been instructed to monitor the area for the Chairman's vibrational signature, and were informed that their roles would be to ensure capture of the Chairman in the event he eluded the Seal-SAS Special Forces team.

When the Chairman and Sean emerged during the final encounter, the orbiting Pleiades team immediately picked up his unique energy frequency. They called in to the Pleiadian team for instructions. They were instructed to follow the Chairman to his destination and wait for the appropriate time for his abduction, as instructed by the Pleiadian Council—when the Chairman was alone and unaware.

The orbiting team waited for Sean to retire. Then, without communication or fanfare, they appeared in the Chairman's office by teleportation. They teleported back to their ship and began programming the Infinity Pod for its endless journey throughout the Milky Way Galaxy. The Chairman appeared to be resigned to his celestial journey. One of the Pleiadian team members thought he noted a tear flow from one of the Chairman's eyes and a look of contentment on his face. A long and tiring journey had finally come to an end.

EPILOGUE

|||||||||||||||||||||||||||||||||||||||||||||||||||||||||||||||||||||||||||||||||||||||||||||||||||||||||||||||

CLEAN UP

The clean-up began, coordinated by General George Maxwell. The captured mercenaries were gathered into their two Black Hawk helicopters and flown to the American Interrogation Center in Frankfurt, Germany, for debriefing and ultimate release. They had not broken any laws but had simply acted to protect the research facility and its workers, for which they had been hired. No legal representation was necessary or requested when they were confronted with questions about the purpose of the work at the research facility.

The research staff was dismissed, and aided in their return to the Czech Republic without their director of research. The director was detained for further questioning about the research and development at the site. He willingly answered any and all questions pertaining to the work and progress of the android program. He declared, "In the final analysis, everything was destroyed, including my research notebook, which was kept in my research office."

The administrative staff was dismissed, and they moved on to various positions with no definitive knowledge or proof of what had been going on at the laboratory nor what they had been told. They were assisted by the NSA support people onsite as representing the sponsoring organization. They were each awarded a specific dismissal stipend based on length of service and a promise of secrecy.

The people of the village were told that during the night of the mine collapse, an experiment being performed had gone out of control. The condition of the mine had made total collapse unavoidable. The villagers were told that there had been only one person on duty, and he had fortunately escaped without injury. There was no mention of the security team. The township received a stipend as agreed, on a promise of secrecy. For most of the residents, it was good riddance. They were happy to regain the slow pace at which they had lived before the interference of the high-tech facility. They returned to their traditional way of living, and the weather station atop the mountain, which had been destroyed and removed, soon became a story of myth.

The Way Forward

The real test of human adaptation to a planet in transition began to occur. The one hundred Pleiadian immigrants were faced with a decision to remain or return to Pleiades. About 80 percent of them decided to remain on Earth because they believed their work was just beginning to be a difference. They had also established close relationships, some intimate and some friendships. Most of those remaining had never experienced human lifetimes.

As with most change in human consciousness, there is always a testing period to see whether something different and transforming has occurred. The impending challenge that lay before the inhabitants of Earth was what would fill the void that had been created by the two pandemics and the absence of the Consortium.

A template, "The Seven Principles of Social Equality," had already been established and tested by the Renaissance Communities. The question was, would it work equally well for the broad societies around the world, or would it experience a fate similar to that of the Constitution of the United States, which had been created in 1776 and had never fully become a reality for many of the country's inhabitants?

The Seven Principles of Social Equality

1. All humans are equal by virtue of their existence; no human should be exalted as superior to others.

2. All humans have an inherent right to be fed, clothed, and sheltered, with the support of others where necessary.

3. All humans have an inherent right to be educated to learn both physical survival and global adaptation.

4. All humans have an inherent right to freely explore and express their spiritual values through creativity, innovation, and any other form of human understanding, compassion, and love.

5. All humans have an inherent right to explore consciousness for the continual acquisition of wisdom.

6. All humans have an inherent right to religious expressions that provide spiritual growth in concert with the well-being of all humanity.

7. All humans have an inherent personal and collective responsibility to preserve a planetary social, physical, and spiritual environment for their continued existence.

No one was sure of the sustaining influence of the combined efforts of galactic immigration, the Star Network, the Renaissance Communities, the Rebels, the United States president, Bill Bradley, and the remaining Pleiadian team, but particularly the work of the Institute for the Study of Human Consciousness in both validating its scientific basis and implementing practical applications for business and societal functioning. A new era was dawning, strongly influenced by the president. He had privately begun discussions and planning for the foundation of a One World Federation.

Additional looming challenges that the inhabitants of Earth were faced with were the uncontrolled development of technology as an inseparable part of human existence and the simultaneous emergence of an AI android-based world. The most critical question was whether the Pleiadian Council would increase the life-force to its initial intensity or leave it at its present level.

Finally, what would be the impact of the critical emerging element that would determine the future of human existence on Earth? It would depend on the new generation born after 2025. How would they create the future reality of humankind as descendants of a global society with greater wisdom? Organic, inorganic, or both?

ACKNOWLEDGMENTS

First and foremost, I acknowledge my sister, Barbara Thompson Guillory, who passed away in 2015. She was my constant source of encouragement and inspiration throughout my life and is still with me daily.

I acknowledge Ulla, who insisted that I go wherever my thoughts led me and not question or compromise my intuition. She was a constant source of divine inspiration. Ulla and Galina both provided the support for me to stay true to the ideas expressed in this book. Without their support and encouragement, I might have compromised my message to fit the comfort level of much of my audience, thus denying them opportunity to achieve a higher level of thinking and possibility.

Deep appreciation goes to LaRay Gates for typing the original manuscript and making recommendations along the way. I also appreciate Dr. Heather Renee and Dr. Melody Cofield for reading and reviewing the manuscript. I appreciate immensely the conversations I had with my luncheon partner, Kirk Peery. He continually challenged me to think and reflect on every controversial thought I shared with him.

I am most grateful to Jessica Vineyard, who edited the book and made valuable suggestions throughout the second edition revision.

Special thanks to Martha Bullen of Bullen Publishing Services for guiding me through the publication and launch process.

I would also like to acknowledge reference to a phrase (page 270), similar to my own thinking, from the book *Homo Deus* by Yuval Noah Hariri: "Technology is the greatest elixir for mankind's greatest desires; immortality, agelessness, and pleasure."

Most of all, I acknowledge those courageous souls who stood by my freedom to go places many of them found difficult to personally explore and accept.

AUTHOR'S NOTE

Although *The Aftermath* seamlessly wanders back and forth between fiction and reality, the gray area between the two is probably the most interesting. Phenomena such as channeling, astral projection, extraterrestrials taking on human bodies, Greek mythology (possibly based in fact), extrasensory skills, and most of all, the science of consciousness—whether or not we have the courage to scientifically study the latter—cracks open the door to unlimited human exploration and wisdom.

The continued unilateral study of the physical world will primarily lead to more sophisticated technological devices—as that is what our theories and instrumentation limit us to—and give us the illusion of true breakthrough thinking, although many of the inventions are impressive. The true breakthrough area of scientific study is the study of the nonmaterial world—a true quantum jump in human exploration. That is where the next frontier of science is, not more of the same in advanced forms and formats.

I wonder if the nonmaterial world of consciousness, beyond the software of the brain (which I define as the mind), is a state of being that we describe as wisdom: an in-depth understanding, empathy, and compassion of human existence—that is, the wisdom to learn how to live compatibly with all organic and inorganic forms, and even reach for higher levels of spiritual enlightenment. In essence, do we, as a species, have the courage to become "astronauts of inner space" as enthusiastically as we explore outer space?

Other Titles by the Author

Realizations
The Guides
It's All an Illusion
Empowerment for High-Performing Organizations
The Living Organization: Spirituality in the Workplace
Animal Kingdom
Living Without Fear
Diversity: The Unifying Force of the 21st Century
*How to Become a Total Failure: The Ten Rules of Highly
        Unsuccessful People*

The Pleiadian Trilogy:

The Pleiadians
The Hunt for the Billionaire Club
The Consortium
The saga continues!

CENTER FOR
CREATIVITY AND INQUIRY

The Center for Creativity and Inquiry is a nonprofit corporation organized to access and draw upon interdisciplinary resources to identify humankind's social and spiritual needs and to produce creative and innovative responses, as may be appropriate. The Center is currently run by the executive director, Dr. William A. Guillory. Programs of the Center include:

Individual Study Sponsorships (Personal Inquiry)

Small or Group Inquiries on Subjects of Present or Future Interest (Collective Inquiry)

Creativity, Innovation, and Quantum-Thinking Seminars

Publication of the Newsletter "Out of Context"

Leadership Programs for Socially and Economically Excluded and Modest-Income Groups

Invited and Sponsored Speaker Series

Advanced Leadership Seminars

Service—An Advanced Professional and Spiritual Retreat

The programs of the Center seek to understand the relationship between human transformation and service to humankind, to understand how to create human compatibility, and to promote the unlimited development of humankind's intuitive and creative abilities in order to discover solutions to problems that minimize global conflict. The ultimate purpose of the Center is to explore consciousness.

ABOUT THE AUTHOR

William A. Guillory, Ph.D, is an authority on personal and organizational transformation. He has published more than thirteen books on this subject including *Realizations, How to Become a Total Failure, Spirituality in the Workplace, Living Without Fear, and the Guides*. He is also the author of the fiction series *The Pleiadian Trilogy* and its sequel, *The Aftermath*.

Prior to founding the consulting firm Innovations International, Inc. and The Center for Creativity and Inquiry, Dr. Guillory was a physical chemist of international renown. He received his Ph.D. at the University of California, Berkeley and an NSF Postdoctoral Fellowship at the Sorbonne in Paris. He has published more than 100 papers on the application of lasers in chemistry and served as chairman of the department of chemistry at the University of Utah. His distinguished awards and appointments include an Alfred P. Sloan Fellowship, an Alexander von Humboldt Senior Scientist award at the University of Frankfurt, and the Chancellor's Distinguished Lectureship at the University of California Berkeley.

On October 3, 1985, he awakened from a deep sleep and spontaneously began receiving "thought-forms" about the nature of reality. These channeled messages have been communicated by one or more of his fifteen Guides. He has sought to combine his background in science and consciousness exploration to discover how to transform humankind from a survival mentality to human compatibility. Dr. Guillory leads international retreats on personal and spiritual transformation through the Center for Creativity and Inquiry. To learn more about Dr. Guillory and his work, please visit thewayoftheheart.org.

For more information regarding the Center, please contact us at:

The Center for Creativity and Inquiry
1416 East Farm Meadow Lane
Salt Lake City, UT 84117
bill.guillory@innovint.com
1-801-274-2885 (office)
1-801-671-8392 (mobile)